D0246909

NICKOLAI'S QUEST

NICKOLAI'S QUEST

LUCY DANIEL RABY

Illustrated by Ted Dewan

Hodder
Children's
Books

A division of Hachette Children's Books

For Izzy

THE CRYSTAL CHRONICLE

(Transcript of town crier's proclamation on Restoration Day.)

(Loud bell clanging. Crowd falls silent)

'OYEZ! OYEZ! KINGDOM RESTORED! NATIONAL HERO RETURNS!

'Never before has the Elfin Kingdom witnessed such celebrations!'

(Loud cheering)

'For twelve long years our beautiful home lay petrified under the North Pole, a dark and silent labyrinth. And all of us frozen in time like statues! Robbed of our very life force on that fateful Winter Solstice Eve, when the evil sorceress Magda returned from exile in the fiery core of the earth and stole the Northern Lights from the sky!'

(Dramatic pause and loud chorus of boos)

'And along with our life force what did she steal? Our Light Fairies! Those dainty creatures who brought the Very First Elves to life by touching the rocks! And when each and every one of us is born, a fairy flies down from the Lights, to stay with us as our lifelong companions . . . yes, they too were taken by Magda – sucked into the fathomless black hole where her heart should have been!'

(Collective groans of horror and more bell clanging)

'But those dark and terrible days are over now! The witch is dead!'

(Loud cheers)

'Magda has returned to the hellhole from whence she came! And all because of one brave young elfin boy! Yes! He was only a tiny baby, but his plucky young mum, Ella Grishkin, escaped from those dreadful scenes of destruction in Solstice Square! Pursued by Magda's wolves, she ran along the tunnels and found a way up on to the surface. Then she too was turned to stone, but her baby son survived – kept alive by his Light Fairy! He was rescued in the nick of time by Comet, queen of the flying reindeer!'

(Whistles of approval and more cheers)

'For twelve years he lived amongst humans, until one day he came back in search of his original home! And what did he find? A gaudy, artificial city, a doomed and terrible place, where many hapless human families were lured in search of riches! Where their children – the poor little mites – were preyed upon by the demon Magda! Yes! The evil one stole their childhood to restore her own youth and beauty!'

(More horrified gasps)

'But this heroic young elfin lad rescued the children from her clutches and with the help of his loyal friends he finally conquered the evil sorceress – and sent her back down to the Vortex!'

(Deafening chorus of cheers accompanied by more bell clanging)

'And now our national hero has brought us all back to life! He has put the Lights back in the sky and given us back our Light Fairies! The Elfin Kingdom is restored to its former glory! Look at us now! The entire city is in a fever. The streets are full of dancing, cheering elves. Music and laughter echo in every corner of our glorious city! The scene here in Solstice Square is quite amazing! Whole families have camped out overnight so they can watch our hero pass by on his victory parade.'

(Voice rises to a hysterical crescendo)

'And here he comes! At last! Look at his chauffeur-driven sleigh! It's magnificent! Made entirely of greenstone and hung with glittering silver bells! And the crowd is surging forward now to get a better view of him. Goodness me, what a handsome boy he is! Look at those lovely blue eyes and that mop of blond hair! And he's wearing his famous red robe, the one we've all heard about! And there's his pretty young mum sitting next to him! How proud she looks! And he's waving at the crowds now, smiling and beaming. It's going down a storm. They love him!'

(Now screaming above the din)

'This is indeed a glorious moment for the Elfin Kingdom! We owe our lives to this boy! So let's hear it for our saviour!

'Nickolai! Nickolai! Welcome home, Nickolai!'

'So let's hear it for our saviour!'

The Solstice Mission

Nick sat in the green velvet passenger seat next to his mother, feeling rather overwhelmed by it all. He just wasn't used to this kind of attention. And it had all happened so fast. One minute he had been grappling with Magda down in the Vortex, fighting off her claw-like fingers as they tried to wrest control of his Light Fairy, Elvina. The next moment he was soaring upwards as though carried on invisible wings, and found himself face to face with his old friend Rudolph the reindeer. Elvina was nowhere to be seen, but he could feel her presence somewhere inside him.

That had been only last night. And now here he was, being paraded through the Kingdom and worshipped like he was some sort of hero, after a very brief reunion with the mother he had never known. It really was a lot to take in.

The sleigh swept into Solstice Square and he caught his breath. Not so long ago it had been a silent cavern full of strange rock formations — the statues of frozen elves. Now it was a magnificent open space, full of

7

bustling life. All around it stood tall colonnades of sparkling volcanic rock carved into intricate patterns, arching up to the domed roof where blue-green shafts of light beamed down through the layers of ice.

He had never seen so many people crowded into one place; *his* people – alive and well again. Their glowing Light Fairies fluttered around above their heads like a million tiny stars. Everywhere you looked, colourful market stalls sold Solstice goodies, Light Fairy dolls and victory flags bearing Nickolai's likeness. Elfin children sat on their parents' shoulders, jiggling around in a state of near hysteria.

When the crowds glimpsed his approach, a deafening cheer rose up to the roof. A forest of flags waved and countless elfin caps were thrown in the air. A sea of faces stretched yearningly towards him and Crystal Chronicle town criers clamoured on all sides for his attention, clanging their bells and bawling out feverish commentaries on his progress. But the uniformed elves that lined the route kept the crowds in check and the sleigh threaded its way through the throng, gliding along like a bird in flight; like all elfin sleighs, it was powered by the driver twitching his ears and connecting with the earth's magnetic forces.

Nick's head swivelled this way and that as voices echoed in his ears from all around.

'Nickolai! Nickolai!'

'Over here, Nickolai!'

'We love you, Nickolai!'

'Keep waving!' whispered Ella. 'And smiling!'

He smiled and waved at the cheering crowds, in what he hoped was a gracious manner.

'Look, Nickolai! See how famous you are now!' Ella pointed at a large shiny disc embedded in the wall, towering over the whole scene. 'That's the famous Crystal Chronicle itself! It's the source of all information in the Kingdom. And you're on it!'

Nick stared at the disc. Its surface shimmered with patterns that constantly changed like the shifting pieces of a kaleidoscope. As he watched, the patterns rearranged themselves into an image of his own face.

'Welcome home, Nickolai!' wrote the message above it. 'Saviour of the Kingdom.'

The crowd went into a frenzy at this, and their cheers filled his ears. Feeling rather embarrassed, as though his underpants were on show, Nick wondered at the mysterious surface. 'What's that, Mum? What's it made from? How does it know things and keep changing all the time?'

Ella smiled. 'It's a mystery, dear,' she said. 'Don't you worry about it. Just carry on waving. You must keep your public happy.'

Nick wasn't sure quite what this meant, but he continued waving and smiling at the crowds that lined the route. When all this fuss was over he could get on with the job of carrying out that promise he'd made last night. The Solstice Mission. His heart missed a beat as he thought of it.

As the sleigh continued its stately progress through the vast underground sprawl, Nickolai failed to notice the Light Fairy that was following him, flitting along behind his sleigh. She had a reddish tinge and a dull, sickly glow about her, like a dying star, but amongst all the other glowing Light Fairies she faded into insignificance.

The sleigh swept around a corner and Nick sat up and gasped. At the end of a sweeping avenue, flanked with ice statues and glowing with Light Fairies, stood the grandest and most magnificent palace he had ever seen. It glittered invitingly in the distance, made entirely of ice crystal, fronted with ornate twisted pillars and gem-studded buttresses. Ethereal elfin music floated out from its magnificent entrance, and splendidly dressed elfin folk were already sweeping up the ice steps.

'There's the Ursus Palace!' cried Ella, pointing ahead. She could hardly contain her enthusiasm. 'I'm so proud of you, Nickolai! To be guest of honour at a special homecoming ball at the royal palace is the greatest privilege in the Kingdom!'

Nick had to admit he felt excited, despite his nerves. Their sleigh swept to a halt and liveried footmen led them up the steps, through solid-silver doors and into a vaulted entrance hall. They followed ushers through grand passageways until they were shown into the main ballroom of the palace.

The sight that met Nick's eyes dazzled him. The

ballroom was lavishly decorated in shades of silver, white, agate, blue and green, sparkling in the glow of Light Fairies. Swathes of silver and mossy blue draped the walls, and a massive crystal chandelier hung from the ceiling, reflecting rainbow beams around the ballroom. Dancers whirled around the ice floor, their coloured ball gowns swirling to the music of an elfin quartet.

At the centre of the ballroom stood old King Vilmar himself, accompanied by his two crusty manservants. As soon as he saw Nick he held his hands up for silence. The dancers stopped, the music faded and the entire assembly cheered as Nick and his mother came down the stairs. Every face was turned towards him, wreathed in smiles.

The nervousness was making its way up through Nick's chest, but he fought it back down. He wanted to make a good first impression in his new home.

The king hobbled forward to greet them. Vilmar was the oldest elf in the Kingdom, reputed to be a thousand years old and a direct descendant of Solmar, the Very First Elf, founder of the royal line. He was a frail man who reminded Nick of a little bird. Ice-blue eyes gazed out from under wrinkled folds, long white hair and beard flowed over long white robes, and an icicle crown was perched precariously on his head. His Light Fairy Lenka, an aged creature with a wavery glow about her, nestled in his beard like a cat on a rug, whistling quietly as she snoozed.

Vilmar held out his wizened arms and smiled warmly.

'Welcome, Nickolai my boy, and Ella, my dear, how nice to see you.'

Ella swept a deep curtsey. Nick did as his mother had instructed him and bowed.

Vilmar turned to the guests and raised his voice. 'Nickolai the Saviour has come to honour us with his presence!' A tumultuous cheer rang out. 'Tonight we celebrate the glorious Restoration of the Kingdom!' Another cheer. 'Tomorrow, after the festivities, we begin the great work. Every elf in the Kingdom will be helping Nickolai to achieve our common aim – the Solstice Mission!'

The crowd went wild and Nick noticed several tiaras thrown in the air.

'Nickolai has created this Mission to commemorate the rebirth of the Kingdom, and to remind the world that childhood is precious, that no one, including our mortal enemy Magda, should ever be allowed to take it away again!'

Boos and cries of agreement broke out at this.

'So we must ensure Nickolai's promise to the world is kept! His daring plan to deliver gifts to every child in the world on Winter Solstice Eve will come about, and we will help him do it! It will be the greatest achievement of the Elfin Kingdom!' The roars rose to the ceiling. 'But first, let us enjoy our new-found freedom and celebrate!'

The music started up again and the dancers resumed their whirling.

Vilmar took Nick's hand. 'Come and meet the rest of the royal family.' He creaked over with them to a group of crowned heads who stood apart, chatting politely with guests. Ella and Nick were introduced to Vilmar's son, Crown Prince Ivan, a dark and rather weedy-looking man, and Ivan's wife, Olga, who had a bright, social smile pasted on to her face.

'Good evening, Nickolai,' she said gushily. 'Allow me to introduce our darling daughter, Crown Princess Krista.'

A young girl about Nick's age turned around and looked him up and down. Nick gulped. She was quite nice-looking, he supposed, if you liked that sort of thing. In fact she would have been pretty in a cute, chocolate-box sort of way, had it not been for the determined set of her chin. Her blue eyes were so bright they seemed to radiate light in a room already full of it. An extravagant riot of reddish-blond curls fell around her face and tumbled on to her shoulders. A sparkling silver coronet nestled in her curls, where her Light Fairy perched, surveying all she saw. Precious gems glittered at the princess's throat and rings sparkled on her fingers. The whole effect was dazzling and, in Nick's opinion, totally unnecessary.

He didn't like her at all. Not one bit.

'Ah, so here he is, the young prodigy himself!' she trilled. 'At last! I've heard so much about you!'

'Er – good evening, Your – er, Highness …' mumbled Nick.

'Your *Royal* Highness,' she corrected him. She raised one perfect eyebrow. 'Aren't you going to bow to me?'

Nick blushed furiously. He had completely forgotten his manners. He did an awkward sort of lurching dip.

'You need to work on that,' she remarked. 'Here, you may kiss my hand to make up for it.' She held out her hand.

They did have some strange customs here. Bristling with discomfort, Nick bent over and planted a reluctant kiss on Krista's hand. It felt like polished silk and smelled of some flowery fragrance.

'I expect you young people would like to join in the festivities now, wouldn't you?' said Olga, giving him a meaningful look.

He glanced at his mother, who nodded in encouragement. Oh, Ursus! He was obviously expected to dance with the girl!

'Oh. Right. Would you like to dance, Princess Krista?' He offered a tentative arm.

She smiled for the first time and her whole face lit up. 'Frostcakes! I thought you'd never ask. Come on then, Saviour Boy.'

He wasn't sure if he liked her calling him that, but he led her uncertainly into the swirling mass of dancers. How agonizing was this going to be? He put clumsy arms around her shoulders.

'No! Not like that, silly!' she giggled. 'Put your left arm round my waist, and take my hand like this.'

He did as she instructed and they set off into the crush. Nick discovered very quickly that ballroom dancing was not his thing; he stumbled around like a shambling bear, trying not to tread on Krista's dainty slippered feet. He knew his mother was watching anxiously from the sidelines.

'Oh, do look where you're going, you clumsy twerpicle!' hissed Krista as he trod on her toe for the third time.

'Sorry.' Determined not to let his mother down he tried his best to get into the swing of the music, but they kept bumping into other dancers. Even though they smiled indulgently, Nickolai's ears began to twitch. They always did that when he felt embarrassed, or cross, or any other uncomfortable feelings.

'Oh, look at your ears!' giggled Krista. 'Can't you control them? You know it's bad form to let them go like that.'

Nick blushed and struggled to get them under control. To his great relief, they began to calm down. His mother had told him it was not 'done' to wiggle your ears in public, unless you were tapping into the magnetic forces to power your sleigh or some other machinery.

The princess began chattering away, making polite, princessy conversation.

'So, jolly exciting project, eh? The Mission?'

'Yes,' said Nick. This was more like it, his favourite subject. He began to relax. 'The Equinox Plaza toy workshops are already being set up. Loads of toys for the kids. I've got hundreds of designs.'

'How splendiferous!' she exclaimed. 'Well, I shall expect to be the first to see them. And to try them out,' she added, arching one eyebrow imperiously. 'I presume I shall be welcome at the workshop?'

Suddenly Nick didn't feel so relaxed any more. He didn't want some stuck-up princess interfering with his Mission. She started and gave a little gasp, staring closely at his head.

'Flippertyfrostcakes! What's that? In your hair?' she hissed quietly.

Instinctively he felt his curly head. Something flew out, making a nasty high-pitched whining noise, then shot away so fast he didn't see it. It was gone in less than a moment. Nobody else had noticed it.

'Yuk! What was it? Some sort of insect? Not your Light Fairy?'

'No. Elvina sort of went inside me, when I was down in the Vortex with Magda,' explained Nick uncomfortably. 'Kind of for safekeeping, I think. I can feel her in my heart.'

Krista furrowed her pretty brow in puzzlement. 'Oh. How frightfully romantic. Although a tad unusual. So what was that thing then?'

'I don't know,' said Nick helplessly, anxious to change the subject.

'Well, I hope it isn't something you've brought in from up there!' She jerked her head towards the outside world above, which was forbidden to all elves.

Nick coughed in discomfort, wondering uneasily what the strange buzzing thing had been. 'Well, whatever it was, it's gone now.' He felt disconcerted and rather out of place next to the dazzling, confident princess, and was relieved when the dance finally finished and he could lead her off the floor.

Vilmar came forward to meet them, the picture of hospitality. 'Well, here you are!' he beamed. 'You lovely youngsters! Enjoying yourselves?'

'Yes, Grampy, it's supersplendiferous. And Nick's said it's all right for me to go to the workshops, haven't you, Nick?' She cocked her head on one side, looking at him with innocent blue eyes.

'Oh, that's nice, dear. And what fun for you, Nickolai, to have someone your own age to help you.'

Nick nodded dumbly, too shocked to speak.

Krista suddenly shrieked with delight. 'Mariska! I've been looking for you everywhere! Bye, Saviour Boy, see you later!' She swept off in a rustle of gossamer towards a girlfriend who had just appeared in a froth of pink petticoats.

Vilmar watched her go with an indulgent look on his face. 'Ahh, what a girl, that granddaughter of mine!'

Nick gave him a rather rigid smile. 'She is charming, sir. It is an honour to meet her.' This cost him such a lot to say that his teeth were hurting. She was the most arrogant, frivolous, shallow creature he had ever met.

Vilmar leaned towards him and whispered conspiratorially. 'Well, it's nice of you to say so, but I'm afraid she is rather spoiled and headstrong. However, she can learn a lot from you and you from her. I do hope you will be friends.'

Nick managed a weak smile. Not a snowflake's chance in the Vortex of that.

A sinking feeling in the pit of his stomach told him this girl was going to be trouble.

'Misstress? Are you there?'

The sick Light Fairy's voice scraped against the darkness. She hung motionless in the silence, glowing the colour of dried blood, quivering with a strange, static energy. Waiting, waiting. She began zigzagging around impatiently.

Where was her mistress?

Finally it came. A hissing noise like the rustling of a thousand snakes, coming from everywhere and nowhere. Slowly, the hissing gathered into one voice, curling around the blackness. It was deeper now, thick and heavy, as though it had found a body. It seemed as if the earth itself was speaking.

'I am here.'

The Light Fairy felt the force of her mistress's personality seeping back. Her dingy pallor brightened and she began to glow fiercely.

'You are all that is left of me now. Tell me the news,' hissed the voice.

'I have extremely annoying news, misstress. The Elfin Kingdom is resurrected to itsss former glory. Full of it, they are. It's positively ssick-making. After all we've been through. All our grand plansss.'

'And the boy?' rasped the distant, long-forgotten echo of Magda's voice.

The fairy buzzed like an angry wasp. 'The brat isss being feted as their Saviour. Young upstart. We should never have let him ssslip through the net when he was a baby. But it'sss too late now.'

'It is never too late. What about the Mission?'

'It'sss going ahead. They're making a huge fussss about it,' spat the fairy.

'That's good. We can use it to our own ends. But *he* must not be allowed to do it! He must be destroyed! You must create something of such awesome power he cannot survive again! There is much work for you to do.'

The fairy listened, straining into the darkness as the voice whispered on, issuing its deadly instructions. When it had finished she let out a shrill, high-pitched shriek of joy that pierced the darkness.

'Yessss! The boy will die! And you will live again!'

A Spanner in the Works

Nickolai's chauffeur-driven sleigh started to cruise silently along Ice Ridge Avenue. The street stood peaceful with promise in the early gloom. Nick turned to wave at Ella, standing in the doorway of their home – a fragile wisp of an elf, who seemed more like a sister than a mother – and sighed at the strangeness of it all. They were together again, but with a huge chunk missing from their lives. Because time had stood still for her while he was growing up, there was only a five-year age gap between them. It was weird. His mind seized up when he thought about it.

Several months had passed since his homecoming ball, but Nick still hadn't got used to his new life. OK, so he was a national hero, a legend in his own lifetime, feted and adored wherever he went. But he never had a moment to himself and he couldn't come and go as he pleased. He was constantly accompanied by two burly bodyguards. The lack of privacy was suffocating, and the worst thing was he wasn't allowed to drive a sleigh – the one thing he loved doing most in the world. He was underage, apparently. It was illegal for any elf under sixteen.

Nick's ears began to twitch at the unfairness of it. He was being treated like a captive in his own home. No freedom at all, no friends – except for that beastly Krista girl. And he had as little to do with *her* as possible.

They were coming into a busier part of town now. Nick braced himself and pulled his robe around him. The famous red velvet robe that the Crystal Chronicle town criers loved going on about.

'OYEZ! OYEZ! NICKOLAI'S MAGIC CLOAK! HEAR ALL ABOUT IT!' they would bellow, clanging their bells around the streets. 'The tot's mother wrapped it around the tiny helpless infant just before he was rescued! It stayed with him all through his turbulent childhood! It's been down into the Vortex and back with our boy! And now it's invested with magical properties! King Vilmar has given special orders for a new one to be made for the next Solstice Sleigh Race Champion, because our Elfin Hero refuses to be parted from it! We say it is right that such concessions are made to the Boy Who Saved the Kingdom! Oyez!'

And so on and so forth. It was quite flattering, but Nick felt embarrassed by people ringing bells and doing all this proclaiming about him every five minutes.

His ears pricked up as a babble of youthful voices floated towards him down Solmar Way. With a soft jingling of bells the school sleigh swished past, bristling with elfin children of all ages. They caught sight of him and burst into an excited clamour, waving and cheering. He waved back and watched wistfully as they passed out of sight, their voices evaporating like mist. How he wished he could go with them. That was another thing he had missed out on – Elfin school.

They were approaching the centre of the city now, and the usual crowds were waiting. They would gather every morning to watch him pass on his way to the Equinox Plaza workshops. At his approach a loud cheer went up. The elves surged forward and trailed in his wake, their Light Fairies fluttering round his head like a halo.

Before long he was surrounded by the familiar horde of news-hungry Crystal Chronicle town criers. They'd appear out of nowhere, like a pack of stray dogs, snapping at his heels and firing questions at him before rushing off round the tunnels, clanging those infernal bells and bawling out garbled versions of what he'd told them.

'How are the preparations for the Solstice Mission going, Nickolai?' barked one, running alongside the sleigh.

'Have the route plans been worked out yet?' called another.

'What about the flying sleigh? And the flying reindeer?'

'And the gifts for all the world's children? Will there be enough?'

Nick planted a practised smile on his face.

'Everything's in hand, thank you,' he said politely. Feeling that he had dealt with this latest onslaught rather well, he allowed himself to relax a little, until a shrill voice pierced his brain.

'But how are you going to get to every child's house in one night, Nickolai? It seems an impossible Mission. Have you worked out how you're going to do it yet?'

He found himself staring into the ferrety face of a young female town crier and felt a plunging sensation in his stomach. This was the one question he had been dreading, because he didn't know the answer. It had been plaguing him for months, keeping him awake at night. But no one on the Solstice Council seemed to be taking it seriously.

He swallowed and smiled weakly at her. 'It's all under control. The Solstice Council is dealing with it.'

The crier didn't look at all convinced.

Nickolai flinched as another barrage of questions rat–a–tat-tatted around him. The sleigh pulled away smartly, shaking the criers off. Nick tried to suppress the panic as it ballooned up into his chest. Well, he had to face it sooner or later. How *was* he going to get to every child's house in one night? It sounded impossible. It defied the laws of logic and all the known rules of the universe.

But he had to find a way. Because he'd made a promise to the world's children. If he didn't keep it he'd be letting them down. His lungs almost forgot to breathe as the tide of panic engulfed him. The Spring

Equinox had already come and gone, and time was ticking by.

And he still hadn't a clue how he was going to do it.

Far below him, unseen life forms lurked in uncharted territories. Sandwiched between the icy upper regions of the Kingdom and the fiery core of the earth, the NetherWorld heaved and twisted, constantly changing into hideous new shapes. The whole fabric of the place was soggy and very unstable. Molten materials bubbled and belched. Lakes of putrid slime festered in hidden places. Weirdly shaped fungi grew out of the walls. A few primitive organisms had managed to survive down here, living a twilight existence. They squirmed in the darkness, oozing through dripping underground forests and stinking rivers.

It was a revolting landscape to work in, but it was the only place where she would find what she was looking for. The Light Fairy streaked along in the murk with the high-pitched whine of a malevolent mosquito, no longer a lost soul. She burned with a new and savage purpose, shining her red beam across the craggy surfaces, searching for signs of life.

There must be something here that suited her purpose – the place was an entire catalogue of life on earth. The fossilized remains of many prehistoric species lurked in the layers, thrown together in a jumbled assortment. On and on she flew, scanning the walls, occasionally resurrecting a pathetic half-formed rodent, or a crude apology for a lizard. Hopeless. She buzzed in irritation and flew on.

As she passed a particularly monstrous outcrop, something pulled her back. She looped around in the gloom and hovered over it. Yes. Something dark and primitive lay below. Something of such ferocity it must have struck terror into all other creatures during its time on earth. Here was material worth working on. A little bit of this, a little bit of that, and she could create something truly terrifying, ruthless and invincible. Something that would guarantee that her mistress's enemy was taken out for ever.

The Equinox Plaza was a system of huge, arched interconnecting caverns, including the Arkfel Caves, where the reindeer were to be housed the night before Solstice Eve. The floors were of gleaming marble and the walls glowed brightly with extra phosphor lamps. Everywhere you looked, machines hummed and whirred; ingenious contraptions with wheels and pulleys and levers and conveyor belts stretched all over the complex.

Hundreds of green-clad elves toiled all day long, their pointed ears twitching as they connected with the magnetic forces to channel the energy into the machines. Their Light Fairies fluttered around purposefully, hovering over the toys to inject them with life.

The toys themselves were beyond any child's wildest

imagining. There were Light Fairy dolls that danced and sang, baby elfin dolls that cried real crystal tears, dolls that transformed from stalactites and stalagmites into elves and back again, even a Queen Magda doll that went from witch to beautiful queen, depending on which way up you held her. There were tumbling clowns and jesters, dancing bears and wolf orchestras, miniature reindeer carousels, furry polar bears, elfin dolls' houses with tiny moving figures, a grow-your-own-pine-forest kit, a design-your-own-planet kit, scale models of the Elfin Kingdom and the Golden City of Doransk, miniature galaxies of spinning planets, and ice floes that cruised through the air, populated by Arctic animals.

The list went on and on. And Nickolai had dreamed them all up. Pausing for a moment on the steps of the vast workspace, he let his gaze sweep across it. The place never failed to make him catch his breath.

There was a burst of manic energy to his left and a tall, rangy elf with a shock of red hair and pale-blue eyes strode down the aisle towards him. His cap was askew and his apron was tied on inside out. His Light Fairy, Lorca, orbited his head in an electric blur.

'Nickolai!' Anatole yelled excitedly, his ears twitching like an eager dog's. 'Great news! We've just managed to get them to regenerate! Come and have a look!'

'Brilliant!' Nick cried back. Anatole was the workshop's chief designer and manager and the nearest thing he had to a friend. Feeling considerably brighter, he followed Anatole down the aisles. Rows of elves turned to greet Nick as he passed.

'Morning, Nick!'

'How's it going, mate?'

'What's the latest wheeze then?'

None of your stupid fawning adulation. This was where he belonged: in a busy place where everyone worked together, putting ideas into action.

A crowd of elves clustered round a bench at the end of the aisle, roaring with laughter. Bangs, clattering noises and strangled gasps issued from their midst. At Nick's approach, the wall of green backs parted to reveal a bizarre scene unfolding on the bench. A miniature army of bronze goblin figures marched in jerky formation, their feet thumping tinnily. Suddenly they began lurching around like demented pinballs, collided, and fell apart with metallic bangs and rude phuttering noises. After a few seconds the scattered pieces jerked back into life, reassembled themselves and staggered back into action.

'What d'you think then, Boy Wonder?' said Anatole, grinning from ear to ear. 'Pretty good game, eh?'

Nick could hardly contain his excitement. 'I think it's fantastic! The kids'll love it! We could have opposing sides and—' He was just warming to his theme when there was a flurry of arrival at the end of the hall.

'Oh dear . . .' muttered Anatole. 'It's our royal visitor again.'

Nick's heart sank. He turned to see Princess Krista

27

standing on the steps, surveying the factory floor. Like a breeze rippling through a green meadow, the workshop elves bowed in her direction.

She nodded graciously. 'Take this, Agnethe,' she said, slapping a diamante handbag at the maidservant on her right. 'And this, Helga,' she continued, sweeping off her cloak and thrusting it at the maid on her other side. Today she was wearing a confection of lavender gossamer that was no doubt the height of fashion for girls of her age. She swanned down the steps towards him, bestowing princessy smiles on the elves as she passed. A disjointed jingle pattered across the floor as they doffed their caps.

'So how's it going, Saviour Boy?' she said breezily, as she swept to a magnificent halt in front of him.

Nick had decided he really didn't like her calling him that. He gritted his teeth. 'Good morning, Your Highness.'

'You mean Your *Royal* Highness . . .'

'Whatever . . .' Nick muttered under his breath.

Krista's blue eyes widened with shock. 'Don't you get clever with me,' she snapped.

'So what brings you here today, Your *Royal* Highness?' Nick dredged the words out from somewhere inside his chest.

'Why, daily inspection, of course,' she said with an airy wave. 'I hope you've got some new ideas to show me.'

'There's a new game here, Highness,' Anatole cut in, waving an angular arm towards the workbench. 'One of Nickolai's best. A real riot.' Flicking a finger, he reactivated the game. The bronze goblins jerked into life, resuming their haphazard routine.

Krista watched the display with an expression of horrified disdain. 'Exploding goblins? Yukitty yuk! I think it's in very poor taste.'

'But the kids'll love it!' Nick burst out.

'No no no no *no* . . . entirely the wrong kind of image for the Elfin Kingdom. I think you should take that one out . . .' she said dismissively.

Nick's stomach knotted into a fist. Before he could stop it, a prickle of rage ran all the way up his spine and erupted out of his mouth. 'Excuse *me*! But this is *my* workshop and *I* decide what toys we make!'

Her blue eyes met his. She didn't blink. 'Oh, I think you'll find it all belongs to the Kingdom,' she replied with a sweet smile. 'We're all supposed to be in it together. And Grampy *has* said it's OK for me to get involved . . .'

'What would *you* know about toy-making?' Nick couldn't stop himself.

There was a gasp of shock from the elves behind him. Krista gave him a mocking stare. 'I'm the princess! I've got the largest collection of toys in the Kingdom! Right from when I was a baby! And anyway I've got really good taste in everything. Whatever I like, anyone else will like. Now, this one is more like it . . .' She had moved to the next bench, where a collection of dancing Light Fairy dolls

29

performed an elaborate minuet. 'Oh, yes! Very stylish.'

Bristling with suppressed rage, Nick followed her as she swept on down the aisle. 'Not sure about that one . . . dancing bears . . . yes, why not? Scrabbling beetles, hmmm . . . quite fun, I suppose . . . I like this toy circus . . . where *do* you get all these ideas from, Nickolai?'

'Where d'you think?' he shot out through clenched jaws. 'The surface! And guess what, I know all about it and what kids up there will like, 'cos I've been there and you haven't! So if you don't mind just leaving us to it . . .'

Krista glared at him haughtily, and for a moment he thought he saw a hurt look flitting across her face. Then her eyes hardened. 'I strongly advise you to treat me with more respect, Nickolai!' she said sharply.

Machines faltered and elves slowed their pace. An uneasy hush fell over the place. Anatole twittered nervously.

'I am the Crown Princess, after all. I'm only trying to help. You should be grateful! Just 'cos you saved the Kingdom doesn't give you the right to be so high and mighty! You're not that clever. You can't do the Solstice Mission all on your own.' Krista turned to go, then turned back. 'And anyway,' she added as a final taunt, 'I hear that you haven't even worked out how you're going to visit every child's house in one night . . . it's all over town. So don't you lecture me, Mister Saviour Boy!'

She spun round and nearly trod on her maidservant Agnethe, who was hovering anxiously behind her like a second skin. 'Come along, Aggy! I've got better things to do than squabble with this upstart! And I want a game of ice scribble before lunch.' She flounced off in a rustle of gossamer, with Helga and Agnethe scurrying in her wake. 'I shall be back tomorrow!' she flung over her shoulder. 'When I shall expect altogether more appropriate treatment!'

There was an appalled silence. The workshop elves had given up all pretence of work and stared at Nickolai open-mouthed. He stood rooted to the ground, rigid with rage. How dare she speak to him like that? And in front of everyone, too! His insides writhed in annoyance: she had goaded him with the very problem that was torturing him.

He made a superhuman effort, but the anger was building up inside him, ready to surge out in a black wave.

'Nickolai, please calm down!' cried Anatole, waving his arms about. 'You know what happens!'

Nick had learned, to his dismay, that his ears were a liability. But the princess had pushed him too far. They began to twitch, and there was a sudden commotion on the factory floor as the machines began to go crazy. Conveyor belts jerked and shuddered, making horrible grinding, crunching noises. Toys began to hop around in a frenzy, as if they were dancing on hot coals. Some of them fell off the machines and tumbled around, crashing into each other.

'Please try to stop!' pleaded Anatole, wringing his hands. His face had gone ashen white as he gazed round at the chaos. 'You know how it affects the machines when you get angry!'

Nick finally got his ears under control, but it was too late. He gazed at the mayhem he had caused, feeling mortified. How could he have put his own Mission in jeopardy through his lack of self-control?

Anatole and the other elves got back to work, trying to repair the damage. Through his distress, Nick noticed something strange about the dancing Light Fairy dolls, which had tumbled down like ninepins. One was still upright and had a strange reddish glow. Suddenly the glow peeled away from the doll, leaving it to tumble over, and whizzed off at lightning speed.

Nickolai felt a sudden desperate urge to run. He glanced round to see if the Light Fairy belonged to anyone. But there was no elf nearby. She must be a stray. Apparently, the stray Light Fairies were lost souls, who wandered round the Kingdom instead of flying back to the Lights after their owners had died. If they could be caught they were put into the Ice Chamber, where they were frozen in time for ever. Nick didn't want this to happen to her. And he missed his own Light Fairy, Elvina. He could do with a friend.

His eyes followed the glowing red shape as it swooped under the workbench. He felt curious about her, and now was the perfect chance to escape. No one would notice if he slipped off. It was a cowardly thing to do, leaving everyone with this mess, but he had to get away.

Nick dropped down and rolled under the workbench. Ahead of him, the red glow flitted around in circles, then shot off. Nick scrabbled along under the benches and saw her hovering by the side door, which stood ajar. She definitely wanted him to follow her! He broke out across the open space and darted after her into Equinox Alley. His eyes raked the busy thoroughfare. She was minnowing through the mass of bodies, leaving a faint trail of red light.

Taking off his red robe so no one would recognize him, Nick barrelled through the crowds and followed her into a narrow passage. The red glow danced along in the air, then melted into the bright scene beyond. He dashed down the tunnel, emerged into the Hyperion Market and glanced around wildly. In the riot of colour and movement she was hard to find. Then he saw a red pinpoint of light, loitering at the entrance of another dark passage.

'There he is!' came a cry from his left.

Oh, no. He'd been spotted. Further down the market a pack of Crystal Chronicle town criers pushed towards him, bells at the ready. At the front was the ferrety one, her eyes blazing with the scent of the hunt.

'Oyez! Oyez! Nickolai causes chaos in Equinox Plaza!' she yelled.

'Saviour breakout!' bawled another one.

'Spat with Royal Princess!'

How fickle these town criers were! They could turn on you in a moment. As they shouldered through the crowds towards him Nick dropped out of sight, tunnelled through the forest of legs and somersaulted into the alleyway. Far ahead of him the faint red glow flickered in the gloom. She was waiting for him! He scrambled up and raced along, feet pounding on the hard ice floor, until he came to a junction. Again she had vanished. He stood breathless, glancing round wildly, then took a chance on the right-hand fork, dashing down more twists and turns, until he found himself in a quieter part of town. He must have reached the outer limits of the Kingdom. The tunnels were dark and empty: no houses or shops, no phosphor lamps glowing inside the ice walls.

The fairy was nowhere to be seen. What now? Nickolai stumbled on, not quite knowing what to do next.

He was too exhausted and bewildered to notice the rumbling noise, or the tremor in the rock floor ahead of him. Shards of hardened ice were spitting out of the ground. He was almost upon it when the object sliced up through the rock beneath his feet and nearly impaled him.

It missed him by a hair's-breadth. Curving up towards a dagger-sharp point at the top, the towering claw gleamed whitely in the gloom. Nick gasped in shock and leaped backwards. A deep growling noise from below made the ground shake. Icicles of fear ran up and down his spine. He began to back away on unsteady feet. Maybe it was just a new rock formation, or a shard of ice that had pushed its way up through the layers. But then came another roar, deafening this time, filling the tunnel and crushing his eardrums.

Great Ursus! What on earth was down there? His knees buckled. Shaking all over he turned and ran back the way he'd come, his breath coming in ragged gasps. He gulped as he heard a crunching noise behind him. Glancing over his shoulder he couldn't believe his eyes.

The huge white claw was chasing him, slicing through the surface like a shark's fin through water, scoring a deep gash in the ground as it savaged its way towards him.

The Claw

There was nothing to do but keep running. The claw was bearing down on Nickolai fast. He dashed on blindly, lungs tearing themselves apart, legs working like pistons, as though they weren't even part of him any more. Another deep roar boomed up from just below his feet and a horrible tearing sound filled his ears, closing in from behind . . .

Suddenly, light. People. Civilization. He became aware of a dim blue glow: phosphor lamps. The corners of his eyes told him he was passing numerous alcoves laden with piles of something glistening. He must have stumbled into the Moonstone mining complex. To his right, a narrow tunnel stretched away into darkness. It was full of metal sledges, gleaming dully in the gloom. They were connected in a long line and piled high with phosphor coal and precious stones, ready to be hauled away. In the far distance he heard metallic clinking noises, the sound of picks and shovels and men at work.

The claw nudged at his heels, ready to tear him apart.

Only one way to go.

Behind him, the claw crashed into the back sledge . . .

Veering sharply into the tunnel, he took a flying leap, scrambled on to the back of the rearmost sledge and began running along the line from one to the other, feet slipping in the piles of stones. Behind him, the claw crashed into the back sledge and the entire line buckled and heaved. Nick's heart convulsed with terror. He put on an extra spurt and vaulted along like a demon in a hurdle race, legs windmilling, feet clattering on the shingle, sending out sprays that spattered against the walls, until he finally reached the sledge at the front of the line. It stood empty, waiting for a driver to haul the load away.

Nick perched breathlessly for a moment, listening. Nothing. His heart leaped with hope. Maybe the thing couldn't follow him! Maybe it couldn't get past the metal sledges! Then his heart sank again, the flicker of hope sputtering out. Metallic crunching noises were echoing down the tunnel behind him. The gigantic claw must be hacking its way around the sledges. What now? Nick glanced about in desperation. A wild thought came to him. These sledges were made of metal, tougher than rock or ice, harder to cut through. Maybe they could be used to block the moving claw's path, slow its progress. And there was only one way he could do that.

It was strictly forbidden, of course. Even to him. The old king had told him personally, in no uncertain terms.

Another sickening jolt snapped him forward, plucking at his spine like a bow at a string. He had no choice. Break the law, or die.

Without further hesitation, he gathered up the reins of the front sledge in shaking hands. He closed his mind against the terrible din behind him and tried to concentrate. Would he be able to do it again? He reached out towards the power of the earth's magnetic forces and slowly began to feel them rising up and swirling around him. He relaxed and let the power surge into him, filling him with a unearthly sensation. Oh, how he'd missed it! There was no other feeling like it. It was like being at the centre of the universe, completely in control, yet at the same time completely at the mercy of something vast beyond comprehension.

Nick began to twitch his ears, tapping into the power that flowed through him, gathering up the energy and channelling it down into the sledge. A tingling sensation ran up and down his arms and the bells gave a soft jingle. But the reins remained still.

The noises behind him were getting closer now, and the sledge underneath him lurched horribly. He groaned in despair. Had he lost his touch?

He closed his eyes and tried again. The bells jingled louder this time, and the reins trembled as the magnetic energy shivered through them. There was a sudden release, like a cork blowing off a bottle, and the sledge jolted. Pouring every last bit of his willpower into the reins Nick urged the sledge on, trying to pull away. It shot forward, then jerked violently as it was tugged back by the coupling. Quick as a flash, Nick rotated his ears backwards, reversed the sledge and rammed it into the ones behind at top speed. With a deafening crash, the line of sledges backed up, piling into one another like a concertina, spilling their contents and blocking the tunnel completely.

Nick glanced over his shoulder. No sign of the claw, just a tunnel full of twisted metal. The ripping noises had stopped. There was a loud silence, followed by a muffled roar of rage. It had worked! He'd momentarily slowed the thing down, given himself some time.

Shaking the reins and twitching his ears furiously, Nick put the lead sledge into forward thrust. It broke free from the coupling with a shudder and zoomed off at top speed, skimming the ground. His heart nearly burst with relief. He'd done it! A familiar thrill ran through him as he raced along at breakneck speed, swerving recklessly round the twists and bends, pulling the energy down into the reins, going faster and faster until . . .

. . . he slowed down as he saw what lay ahead.

The tunnel gave out abruptly into a huge cavern, flooded with yellow light. It must be the main entrance to the mines. A crowd of miner elves stood at the end, waiting for him. They didn't look unfriendly, but numerous pairs of large, luminous, extra-sensitive eyes were staring down the tunnel with intense concentration. Something told Nick that they knew it was him coming towards them, in one of their hijacked sledges.

He slowed to a halt and prepared to dismount. His joyride was over.

The Solstice Cup

Zak made his way along the rutted track that led to Hannah and Joe's cottage. He'd grown very fond of Nick's old foster parents during the winter he'd spent in the town where his friend had grown up, and he wanted to say goodbye to them.

As he trudged along, the jagged tree-line in the distance caught his eye. Dark green against dazzling blue and still topped with snow, the forest sparkled in the sunshine, bringing back memories of that wild night last Winter Solstice Eve, when he and Nickolai and their friends had dashed through its moving paths towards the reindeer's cave, seeking their help. He wondered wistfully if he would ever go on another adventure like that again . . .

He neared the cottage and saw Joe's old red-painted delivery cart outside. It was harnessed to the ancient cart horse, which stood waiting patiently, snorting and stamping its massive hooves in the mud. Hannah and Joe were bustling in and out of the cottage, loading up the cart with sacks of provisions. They

41

turned their grey heads as he approached.

'Zak!' exclaimed Hannah as he drew nearer. 'You off on your travels too?'

'Yes. I'm going to try and find my family,' said Zak, drawing level with them. 'They usually head north at this time of year to follow the herds.'

He noticed that Hannah was beaming with excitement and Joe's gaunt face wore a look of anticipation. Hannah was shoehorning a sack of woollen garments into the already bulging cart. This was no ordinary trip into town for market day.

'Woolly stockings,' she announced, 'for all the children to hang out on Midwinter's Eve for Nickolai. My idea!' she said proudly, tapping her ample chest. 'I'm selling them as I go. And Joe here,' she indicated Joe, who grinned bashfully at Zak, 'is the most important postman in the world now! He's collecting all the letters from the children, telling Nickolai what they want. Then he'll deliver them to the reindeer in the forest when we get back, to take up to the Pole. We're heading south now, touring the whole of the Arctic Circle. It'll take us all summer!' She nudged Joe with her elbow. 'Won't it, Joe?'

Joe jumped to attention. 'Oh, yes, dear. It will.'

'Sedna's toenails! You've got your work cut out for you then,' said Zak.

'Yes! But we've really got the taste for travel now, haven't we, Joe?'

Joe nodded. 'Oh, ay. It'll be grand. I like a change of scenery.'

'Well, I'm off in the other direction,' said Zak. 'So I'll say goodbye, and may Sedna be with you.'

'Whoever he is . . .' muttered Hannah.

'*She*,' Zak reminded her. 'The Inuit Goddess of all things.'

'Of course she is, love.' Hannah enveloped Zak in a motherly hug. She went to kiss him, but Zak insisted on rubbing noses with her and Joe, which they had always found disconcerting. 'You take care, love, and have a safe journey. I hope you find your folks. And if you happen to see Nickolai give him our love, won't you?'

Zak grinned, his brown face creasing up so that his eyes disappeared. 'Less chance of that than a flying fishbone! See you!'

He turned and continued down the track towards the scrubby open tundra, wondering what his old friend was up to now. He did miss him. As he scanned the horizon, something flickered at the corner of his eye. He glanced round, and for a fleeting second he thought he saw a flying shape above the distant treetops. But then he blinked and it was gone.

The Kingdom was in uproar. The tunnels echoed with the clamour of the town criers' bells and their self-important proclamations.

'Nickolai in more trouble!'

'Saviour leaves trail of destruction in reckless joyride!'

'Mayhem in Moonstone mines!'

Their cries reached as far as number 27 Ice Ridge Avenue, where a stony silence hung over the living room. Nick sat uncomfortably on the chair by the fire, fidgeting under his mother's gaze. He had been hustled home through the back streets in an anonymous delivery sledge, to find a rabble of Crystal Chronicle town criers already camped outside his house. It had been quite a kerfuffle getting him in, and his bodyguards had been stern. For once, he was glad to have them with him.

Now his mother stood in front of him, waiting for an explanation. Stray wisps of fair hair fell across her eyes, which looked unusually pale and large.

'So. You expect me to believe this ridiculous story, do you?'

'Yes, Mum! I told you, there *was* something chasing me!' he pleaded, desperation rising in his chest. Why didn't she believe him? It was like being in a nightmare. He was beginning to doubt his own sanity.

'How could you run away like that, leaving everyone to clear up the mess? So irresponsible! Anyone'd think you didn't want the Mission to go ahead! But worst of all, you broke the law! Ursus knows what repercussions this is going to have! You're in very serious trouble now, Nickolai!'

She exhaled angrily and began pacing the room. 'Do

44

you have any idea how awful it's been? Not knowing where you were, wondering if you were dead or alive, trying to fend off that mob out there?' She flung an arm at the front of the house, where loud cries of protestation came from the town criers as they were herded away by the bodyguards. She stopped pacing and whirled on him. 'And what were you doing down in the mines anyway?'

Nick groaned. She didn't understand. Nobody knew the suffocation he was feeling. 'I just had to get away! And that Princess Krista was getting right up my nose.'

'Why, what did she say? She seems a charming girl to me.'

Nick gave a contemptuous snort. 'What? She's a right stuck-up madam. She keeps telling us what toys to make. She should keep her nose out! I don't care *who* she is!'

Ella sighed and let her shoulders slump. 'Look, you have to respect the royal family, Nickolai. They run the Kingdom. Nothing can happen without them.'

Nick felt his frustration mounting. Why did everything have to rely on others? 'But she was really rude. She made out I was a failure and wouldn't be able to deliver gifts to every child's home in one night . . . says it's impossible!'

Ella made a face. 'Well, yes, it is a tricky problem, but I'm sure it will be sorted out. You should leave that sort of thing to the Elders . . .'

'But they've got no more idea than I have!' cried Nick explosively. 'And they won't listen to me!'

He subsided into a gloomy heap and stared moodily into the fire. On reflection, he'd decided not to tell his mother about the stray Light Fairy. She would only lecture him about how he should have reported her to the authorities. She had no idea how it felt, not having a Light Fairy of your own like everyone else. He hated being different and he missed Elvina more than ever.

Ella folded her arms and looked at him. 'Well, maybe you should try a more grown-up, diplomatic approach. You can't expect people to listen to you if you keep losing your temper.'

Nick fell silent, and his lower lip began to jut out stubbornly. He looked away, cut to the quick that his own mother had doubted his word. His eyes wandered over to the mantelpiece, where the Solstice Cup stood, sparkling in the flickering firelight. He watched the moving patterns playing across its surface, narrowed his eyes and just made out the inscription on it:

The Winter Solstice Cup
Presented to the winners of the
Winter Solstice Sleigh Race
Ella Grishkin and her son, Nickolai.
Year of Cygnus

He'd won this trophy with his mother when he was a baby. Apparently it knew who'd won the last race, wiped off the old names and wrote the names of the new winners on its surface.

A sudden insight struck him like a thunderbolt. He sat up straight.

'Hey! I've just had a thought!' He bounded over to the mantelpiece, snatched up the cup and turned to his mother. 'It was right under my nose all the time! Isn't this cup made of the same stuff as that Crystal Chronicle disc in Solstice Square, the one that keeps changing and rewriting things?'

Ella shrugged. 'Yes . . . but why is that important?'

Nick's mind groped around, trying to make sense of the idea that had just taken root. 'Well . . . if it can rewrite things, recording events as they change, then maybe it can actually change events themselves . . .'

'I don't follow you, Nickolai . . . and anyway—'

But he was striding around the room excitedly, thinking aloud. '*Can* it change events, do you think? Or change *when* they happened? Maybe even – rewrite time itself? Like, sort of say that something happened before it actually happened? Or afterwards? Maybe freeze time altogether? Make it stand still?'

'I don't know what you mean,' stammered Ella, looking completely confused.

But Nick was still muttering feverishly to himself as his mind chased a new and exciting possibility. 'Maybe . . . maybe if I had some of that stuff with me, it could *say* that I arrived at a child's house and left it before I actually did! So I would effectively buy myself some time! In other words, make time stand still by putting the clock back over and over again!'

Ella was looking totally bewildered now. 'Nickolai! What on *earth* are you going on about?'

Nick turned to her, his eyes blazing with a new passion. 'The time problem, of course! This whole thing about how to get to every child's house in one night! I think I might have the answer! What *is* that substance? How does it work?'

'Well – er, it's the Crystal Chronicle, of course.'

'Yes, but *can* it do stuff like that? Sort of, tinker with time?'

Ella looked evasive. 'Well, yes, I suppose it can – it's an extremely powerful and magical substance . . .'

'And where can I get hold of it?' he persisted like a dog at a bone.

'Well . . . there is an original source of it somewhere, but it's a state secret . . .'

'*Mum!*'

Ella shook her head and brushed the subject away. 'Anyway – you shouldn't be worrying about things like that. You should be worrying about the trouble you're in and how you're going to make amends. And please don't put me through this again. I don't want to lose you a second time. I don't think I could bear it.'

Her eyes went a funny shape and her lower lip began to wobble. Nick felt a sudden rush of remorse. 'Look, I'm sorry, Mum. But I'm so worried that I won't be able to keep my promise . . . and time is running out.'

They were interrupted by a knock at the door. Ella jumped and her hand flew to her mouth. 'See? I knew it! You've been summoned to the palace. To explain your behaviour.'

'Wake up, Grimgorr. You lazy beassst.'

The red Light Fairy strafed one of the monster's massive ears, trying to sting him into life. It twitched, causing a small gust of wind to ripple across the scummy surface of the water nearby. The beast's great whiskers began to vibrate and the steel-tipped ends flapped sluggishly on the rock. One baleful red eye opened and scanned the cave.

The Light Fairy regarded him with contempt. 'You have failed,' she buzzed in annoyance. 'You let him get away, you useless creature.'

His throat made a low guttural sound. He stretched nonchalantly and yawned. His open mouth looked like the entrance to another cave, lined with sharp white pillars.

The fairy hissed with impatience. 'Pay attention, you great scurvy beassst! You nearly had him then! Fancy letting a few bits of metal get in the way. It'sss pathetic!' she spat. 'My misstress would not be pleased at all. She'd turn in her grave, if she had one.'

Grimgorr grunted, curled his lip and threw her a contemptuous glance. 'What do I care for her? And it is not my fault,' he snarled. 'I am as you made me!' He unsheathed his claws and sharpened them on the floor of the cave. A selection of wormlike creatures wriggled away through the slime in the trenches he'd scored. 'Raargh! Come back, you horrible little things!'

'Not impressed,' snapped the Light Fairy. She flew around his massive bulk, eyeing him speculatively. 'Yesss, you do need more work. I will have to add further modifications. Special reinforcementsss. Superior powersss. Better surveillance and tracking, greater abilities to penetrate solid materialsss.'

She was already flitting over the surface of the walls, shining her piercing red beam. 'Hmmmm . . . let'sss see . . . pterodactyl, sssmilodon, gigantosaurus . . . yesss! . . . tyrannosaurus . . . carnivirotops . . . even better . . . megalithodon . . . by the time I've finished with you, my creature, you'll contain all the worssst features from every predator who's ever stalked the sssurface above! Multiplied a thousand timesss!'

The monster hauled himself up and began pacing around after her, his long tail swishing against the rocks, leaving deep dents. 'Rarrrr! I'm hungry!' he growled. His hot breath fanned the cave and his eyes glowed in disgust as he glanced at the wormy creatures that crawled around nearby. 'I will not eat these!' he spat. 'You get me better things to eat or I'll eat you!'

His jaws snapped at her, but she ducked out of the way, sniggering nastily as they clanged together like two halves of a giant machine.

'Ha ha! You can't!' she shrieked. 'Fool! I am pure ssspirit essence!'

'Then get me better food!' he roared, his eyes glowing dangerously. 'Or I will not perform!' He slammed his paw furiously on the ground and the whole cave shuddered.

'Patience!' she purred. 'And get thisss, Fangface. Above us lies the Elfin Kingdom. And it's full of – guess what – sweet little elvesss! The boy we're after is one of them – but there are more like him!'

'Elves . . .' grunted the monster. 'What are they?'

'Oh, they're deliciousss. Little two-legged things with pointy earsss. Quite pretty to look at, if you like that sort of thing. They make me sssick, personally. But you will like them. Sweet and juicy. If you fulfil your task, you will live for ever and you will be able to feassst on them for all eternity. That will be your reward!'

Grimgorr leered horribly and began licking his lips. Gobbets of spittle rained round the room, drenching the rocks. 'Yes! I like the sound of that!'

He lifted his enormous black head and let out a deafening roar. It shook the NetherWorld to the core, and sent a million squirmy things slithering off in all directions.

The Wrath of Elders

A leaden feeling descended into the pit of Nick's stomach as he was shown into King Vilmar's stateroom. It was a grand and somewhat intimidating chamber where all the Solstice Council meetings were held, lined with carvings of former Elders. At the end of the room stood a long ice table, lit from within by an eerie blue glow. Suspended above it was an ice globe showing all the continents of the world above. It was the pride and joy of Doblov, chief navigator of the Kingdom, who was using it to design Nickolai's Mission route.

Behind the table sat a row of stern and ancient elves, King Vilmar at the centre. Nick approached the table, trying to conceal his nerves. There was an icy chill in the room. Light Fairies hung in the air above their owners' heads, stilled by the tense atmosphere.

Vilmar's eyes, usually so kindly, glinted fiercely now. 'So, Nickolai. What have you got to say for yourself?'

'I – I er . . .' Nick's brain and his mouth didn't seem to want to connect.

Vilmar's icy gaze bored into him. 'Not only have you caused untold damage in the Equinox Plaza workshops, setting the Solstice Mission back by several weeks . . .' a chorus of geriatric gasps went up at this '. . . and further chaos in the Moonstone mines,' continued Vilmar in a quavering voice, 'but you have also broken the law!'

Nick gulped, not knowing what to say. 'I'm sorry, sir,' he babbled. 'I didn't mean to cause all that damage! It was an accident! And I only hijacked the miners' sledge because I had to! I got lost, and then I was being chased by this huge monster claw thing and the only way I could get away from it was to—'

'Enough!' roared Vilmar, in a surprisingly loud voice for such a frail man. 'Do not make your position any worse by fabricating such ridiculous stories!'

Nick gave in to furious frustration. It prickled his hands and feet. Why did nobody believe him? 'But I'm telling the truth!' he blurted. 'You've got to believe me!'

The Elders shook their old heads and began whispering in dry, crackly voices.

Vilmar sighed. 'Boy, you have been through many ordeals in your short life and it is understandable that you may fall prey to fearful fancies in the darker regions of the Kingdom. But even if there was something down there, your life wouldn't have been in danger if you hadn't run off in the first place! Which is precisely why you are forbidden to venture anywhere unattended. You are very precious to us all.'

There were general nods and murmurs of assent. The Elders regarded him with something of the usual warmth in their rheumy old eyes.

Nick was chastened. 'I'm sorry for all the trouble I've caused, sir,' he said humbly. 'I didn't mean to. And I don't want to seem ungrateful for what everyone's doing. But – I feel like a prisoner in my own home. I miss my freedom. I was used to it!'

'I'm afraid things have changed now, Nickolai,' said Vilmar in grave tones. 'You have the mantle of responsibility on your young shoulders. You are very important!'

'But if I'm supposed to be so responsible, why does everyone keep treating me like a child? Why won't you believe me about that claw thing down there? And why am I not allowed to drive a sleigh?' Nick couldn't stop himself railing against this unfair restriction.

'Because it is illegal!' boomed Gogol, a plump Elder with bulging eyes and quivering jowls. 'You are underage!'

Nick felt a surge of righteous indignation. 'But surely I'm different!' he cried. 'I've driven a sleigh before! Up on the surface! Across the sea and right down to the reindeer's forest! While you were all frozen in time down here, I learned how to do it all on my own. That's how I managed to save the Kingdom! If it wasn't for me, none of you would be here!'

The look on their faces told him he had gone too

far. There was a shocked silence and everyone shifted uncomfortably in their seats.

Vilmar blinked and straightened up. 'Are you going to keep holding that over our heads for the rest of eternity? Using moral blackmail to get your own way at every turn?' His eyes glinted.

'No, sir. Sorry, sir,' mumbled Nick, looking down at the floor. It *was* a bit unfair to remind them. It wasn't their fault.

'You must accept the restrictions placed on you,' continued Vilmar in his cracked old voice. 'They are there for a good reason. It is all for the good of the Solstice Mission. To keep you safe so that you can carry it out.'

Nick struggled to keep his patience. 'That's exactly what I'm trying to do, but no one's listening to me,' he said levelly. 'And you still haven't told me how we're going to solve the most important problem of all – how I'm going to visit every single child's house in the world in one night!'

The Elders looked uncomfortable. They were obviously still stumped on this one. Nick felt that at last he was getting through to them. He pressed his advantage. 'But guess what – I've got an idea how we can solve the problem!'

The Elders stared at him in astonishment. Gogol's crystal eyeglass popped out.

'Would you care to elaborate on that, young man?' enquired Doblov, waving a spidery arm at the globe. 'I have spent many months working out your route plan, and your sleigh will be endowed with the speed of Light.'

Nick seized his chance. 'Yes, but it's still not enough, sir,' he explained politely. 'It needs some sort of time-warp device. Something that stops the clock while I'm carrying out my Mission. Then I can make the night last as long as I need to give myself enough time to do it all!' He began to gabble animatedly. 'And I reckon the key to the whole thing is that . . . *stuff* . . . that the Solstice Cup and the Crystal Chronicle disc come from!'

'How can that be?' murmured Doblov. The other Elders gazed at each other quizzically.

'Well,' explained Nick patiently, 'if it can record events as they change, then maybe it can change the record of *when* they happened . . .' and he explained the theory that he had expounded to his mother and had mulled over during his journey here. 'And so,' he concluded, 'since the Crystal Chronicle stuff is such a magical and powerful substance, powerful enough to change the record of events, times and dates, I can tell it to make time stand still when I set off on my Mission on Solstice Eve. Sort of, stop the clock! So I'll have plenty of time to carry it out! It might take days, or even months, but it won't matter, because time will stand still for everyone else, and when it starts again, no one will know the difference! It will still be Solstice Eve, the very same moment I left!'

He finished with a triumphant flourish and looked

around. 'It'll be just like when Magda came back, took the Lights and froze you all, while I survived and grew up somewhere else. And then when I – when you all came back to life again, you carried on as though nothing had happened!'

There was a stunned silence. Twelve withered old faces stared at him in astonishment. They looked like he'd said something blasphemous and heretical, that went against all their beliefs and superstitions. But they were looking at him with new respect now, and a hint of awe. He must have stumbled on a pretty ingenious theory.

When Vilmar spoke at last, his voice was trembling with rage. 'That is the most audacious and dangerous plan I have ever heard of. It is like trying to exercise the powers of the great Creator herself!'

'But I am sort of slightly superhuman now!' protested Nick. 'I've been into the Vortex and back!'

There was an outraged gasp.

'You are not as invincible as you think you are!' boomed Vilmar. 'There are still others with greater powers! Do not let your new status go to your head!'

'But tell me – can the Crystal Chronicle do what I just said it could?' persisted Nick, refusing to be thrown off the scent. 'Is it not an unimaginably powerful and magical substance?'

The Elders glanced at each other warily. Vilmar looked evasive. 'Yes, it has powers that even we cannot comprehend,' he admitted finally.

'Then for Ursus' sake, tell me where I can find it!' cried Nick hotly. 'Surely there must be some original source somewhere? Why are you holding back on me?'

An icy stillness fell over the stateroom. He had obviously hit on a taboo subject, spoken the unspeakable.

'You are talking of the most sacred object in the Kingdom,' whispered Vilmar in a reverent voice. 'No elf should ever meddle with that kind of power. The original crystal lies in the Cave of the Crystal Chronicle, under the True North Pole, which as you should know by now is impossible to locate, since the earth moves constantly on its axis. No one has ever found it.'

Nick rallied. 'Well, I think I can!' he declared.

'No! Out of the question,' roared Vilmar. 'The cave is situated far beneath the Kingdom, down in,' he paused for dramatic effect, 'the Nether-World!' A hushed gasp. 'It is a dark and terrible place, governed by awesome forces, inhabited by many strange creatures of unknown origin. It is strictly out of bounds! And anyone who ventures there risks the safety of the Kingdom.'

'But why?' Nick was getting fed up with all this mystery.

'Because,' Vilmar glanced round meaningfully, 'the NetherWorld lies close to the Vortex, where our oldest foe may still be lurking in some form, with all her goblins and demons.' There was a sharp intake of breath and a shudder ran down the table. The word 'Magda' hung in the air like a sword. Lenka woke up momentarily and squeaked in alarm.

'I would have thought you would be the last person to want to encounter *her* again, Nickolai.'

This simply didn't make sense to Nick. 'But I conquered her! I sent her back down there. She's dead and gone, surely?'

Vilmar sighed with weary patience. 'A sorceress of her magnitude may have powers of regeneration beyond our imagining,' he replied heavily. 'Moreover, many spirits linger down in the NetherWorld. Some are demons – Light Fairies who have escaped from evil elves banished to the Vortex. Some are simple strays who never found their way back to the Lights when their owners died. As a precaution, if we find them we incarcerate them in the Ice Chamber, to be frozen for ever in suspended animation. By venturing into those darker regions, you render the Kingdom more vulnerable to these dangerous forces.'

'Well, I'm prepared to risk it!' said Nick. 'If the original crystal can solve the problem, I *have* to go and find it. I can't let the children of the world down, sir, I've made a promise! And we're running out of time!'

Vilmar's face turned thunderous. His eyes glittered with anger and his beard began to tremble. Lenka fluttered out and flew up creakily to perch on top of his crown. 'You will do no such thing, Nickolai! We will shortly be borrowing the Solstice Cup from your home. My team of top scientists will be working to distil its essence and find the solution we are looking for.'

'But it won't work!' shouted Nick. 'It won't be powerful enough!' He felt his ears beginning to twitch again.

'Silence!' roared Vilmar. 'You must learn to trust your Elders and accept our authority. You are still a child and have not yet learned to master the great forces working within you. And if you're thinking of running away again, I have put a special magnetic lock on all the rocks in the Kingdom and the Nether World, so that even you cannot move them! So I suggest you continue your work at the Plaza and let us get on with our job.'

Nick sank into a well of despair. He saw his only chance of keeping his promise dwindling away. Why were they shutting him out like this? His ears began twitching wildly. Elderly Light Fairies began wavering in agitation, making weak buzzing noises. Hairline cracks began to appear in the ice table. The globe started spinning and pulsating dangerously.

Doblov stood up and waved his arms about. 'Please, Nickolai. Don't ruin weeks of work!'

Vilmar struggled to his feet and stood swaying over the table, holding on to it for support. His frail body was trembling. 'Get a grip on yourself, boy!' he cried sternly. 'If you do not prove yourself more adult, responsible and capable of managing your emotions, you will not be carrying out the first Solstice Mission. Someone else will have to go in your place, until you are fit to undertake the task!'

Tantrums and Tiaras

'Please, Master Nickolai, do try and calm down!' puffed Boris, Nick's number one bodyguard. He and the other bodyguard, Olaf, were lumbering behind Nick as he stormed along the glittering corridors of the palace, nervously eyeing the effect that his agitation was having on their surroundings. It was indeed an unnerving sight: ice statues trembled perilously on their stands, and tiny cracks were appearing on the portraits of elfin kings and queens, marring the regal smiles of Astrid the Seventh and Timov the Tenth.

As Nick turned the corner into yet another grandiose passageway he came face to face with the last person he wanted to see. She was sashaying along, resplendent in pale-blue taffeta and lace, accompanied by her maidservants who scurried along in her wake like two apologetic shadows. Her Light Fairy, who had the rather pretentious name of Petronella, perched on her tiara. Krista was carrying something white and fluffy which was emitting little squeaks and mews.

'Well, look who it is!' exclaimed Krista, sweeping to

a halt and feigning elaborate surprise. Nick was sure she had been hanging around, waiting for him. 'Our very own Saviour Boy! How's it going?' She looked at him. 'Oh, dear! A bit miffed, by the looks of things. What's up, SB? Bad interview?'

Nick gritted his teeth and bowed. 'Er – good afternoon Your – er, Royal Highness.'

'Oh, please, Krista from now on. I was only teasing you the other day, you twerpicle!' Her laughter tinkled around the ice walls. Nick wondered if she was going to mention their little episode in the workshop. But she didn't.

'Say hello to Snowflake. He's my new pet.'

Krista nodded at the furry bundle in her arms. Nick recognized it as a Mingle, the only other life form that had evolved down here in the caverns, apart from the elves. Yet another amazing phenomenon that confounded him about this place. They were hybrids which had somehow bred from snow crystals and the fur particles of Arctic rodents, brought alive by the Light Fairies. This one was a particularly fluffy specimen, with snowy fur, long sparkly whiskers and tufty little ears. Mingles were considered very cute. Many variations had been bred, and they had become popular pets in the Kingdom, especially amongst young elfin girls.

'Er, hello, Snowflake,' said Nick awkwardly.

Two beady little eyes regarded him with suspicion.

'Say hello properly, give him a nice pat,' said Krista fondly.

Nick reached out a tentative hand and patted the furball. It squeaked and twitched its whiskers in a most alarming way. He withdrew his hand instantly.

'See? He wants to be friends . . . don't you, Snowflake . . . yes, he's a lovely boy, isn't he?' she crooned, stroking the soft white fur.

'Who, me?' asked Nick in bewilderment.

Snowflake let out a stream of chittering noises and Nick heard suppressed titters from behind him.

'No, not you, twerpicle, Snowflake!' said Krista, giggling. 'Isn't he cute?'

'Yes. He is charming,' said Nick in a voice that sounded as though it had been forced through a sieve. He didn't like the look of Snowflake one bit. The creature was probably as spoiled and petulant as its owner, and it must have teeth.

Krista cocked her head on one side and flashed him a dangerous smile. 'Well, I heard about your . . . *antics*! Quite a lot of damage, eh? Frostcakes! Couldn't have done better myself, even in my best tantrums! I'm impressed.' Nick felt sure she was mocking him. She leaned forward and patted him reassuringly on the shoulder. 'But don't worry. Grampy will forgive you. We're terribly nice people, us elves. We *so* understand what you've been through. And of course we're sooooo grateful to you for restoring the Kingdom.'

Nick grunted. 'Yes, well, I have been causing a bit of a kerfuffle lately,' he admitted. 'Didn't mean to. Haven't quite got the hang of this place yet.'

'No, you haven't really, have you? And what's all this about a giant claw chasing you?'

Nick suppressed a shudder as he remembered the horror of the experience. Then he shrugged carelessly. 'Oh, well, I don't expect you to believe that. No one else does.'

'Not surprising. You must have a *fabulicious* imagination. Are you sure it wasn't a shadow or something? It's very dark in those mines, you know.'

'I *did* see something!' said Nick, trying very hard to appear unruffled.

'OK, OK. Let's just say you saw it then! Oh, look, there you go with your ears again. You seem frightfully het up, SB. What's up?'

'*What's up?*' Nick said in disbelief. 'What d'you think is up? No one's listening to me and I'm running out of time and they won't let me do what I have to do to fulfil my Mission!'

'*Our* Mission, SB,' Krista reminded him.

'Whatever,' said Nick irritably. 'I'm beginning to think it's never going to happen!'

'Oh, dear. Not getting our own way? What a shame. Trouble is, you have to be a royal before you can throw your weight about round here. But of course you wouldn't know that, being a new boy.'

He immediately regretted letting his guard down. She was just too cocky for words. And why did she keep needling him? He made a superhuman effort to contain his annoyance, determined not to look stupid in front of her, but there was a quiet splintering noise from a nearby copperstone vase and a huge crack ran from top to bottom.

Krista glanced at it carelessly. 'Oooopsi! Never mind, didn't like that vase anyway. But you know, you ought to watch yourself, SB. Old Grampy won't be very pleased if you keep wrecking the place. Why don't you just lighten up and enjoy this splendiferous place? The Elfin Kingdom's the best place to live in the world! So much to see, so much to do. I can show you round. In style.'

'Thanks, but I haven't got much time for sightseeing,' sniffed Nick. 'It'll have to wait till after the Mission.'

'OK, SB, but do try and calm down and wait and see what happens next . . .'

'I – am – perfectly – calm – thank you, Your Highness,' replied Nick in a strangled voice. 'And why do you keep calling me SB?'

'Because it suits you. It's a friendly nickname.' Krista smiled sweetly and fluttered her eyelashes. 'You know, you really ought to let me help you. I am the Crown Princess after all. We could be a good team. Unless you think I'm not up to it because I'm only,' she spoke the word with exaggerated sarcasm, 'a *girl*.'

Nick couldn't think of anyone less useful on the Mission. She'd be about as much good as a rubber pickaxe.

Shrugging dismissively Krista waved a languid arm

at her two maidservants. 'Please yourself, then. See if I care. Helga, Aggy, come on, I'm starving. I want crystal honey sandwiches for tea. And lots of yummylicious starlight syllabub for afters. See you around, SB.'

She swept away in a rustle of satin and lace. Nick watched her go, turned on his heel and marched off, filled with conflicting feelings. The girl really did have some nerve. Talk about pulling rank. And why was she so nosy and interfering? Couldn't she just mind her own business and get on with princessy things, like dressing up and playing with her pets and trying on tiaras?

He ground to a halt as a horrible thought struck him. What if . . . no . . . surely not. She seemed very keen to get involved with the Mission. And Vilmar had threatened to replace him, but that was only a warning. And it would be with an adult. Except, Vilmar doted on her, he'd probably let her have anything she wanted. Maybe that was her game! Maybe that was why she kept winding him up all the time – to get him into trouble, so she could muscle in on his act! The thought of anyone else – especially a *girl* – replacing him on the Mission made his blood run cold.

But it looked as though no one would be going at all if things carried on the way they were. Oh, blast and Vortex!

'Nickolai, sir, the sleigh awaits us!'

He set off again, his head whirling with very unsettling thoughts.

'Oh, yes! I like the smell of him even better now! Very tasty!' growled an unseen voice far below Nickolai. Its owner prowled along, many fathoms underneath, tracking his path with chilling precision. His huge pointed ears flicked the ceiling and his whiskers brushed the walls as they twitched this way and that, picking up Nickolai's scent through the layers of ice and rock.

'Yesss, well, anger does always make for a nice flavour,' sniggered the red Light Fairy. 'You should be able to track him more easily now, with your new powersss. Which I have given you. Which I don't remember you thanking me for.'

'Shut up, you nasty little buzzing thing!' roared the monster, momentarily blowing the fairy off course. 'I didn't *ask* to be born! And now I'm here it's your job to feed me properly!'

'Well, you'll jussst have to be patient!' spat the Light Fairy. 'You can't get at him properly from here. You could blast your way up there, but we don't want to alert anyone. That Vilmar is a wily old so and so.'

'I want Elf Boy now!' snarled the creature, baring his giant fangs. 'Bring him to me!'

'OK, OK, keep your fur on, Fangface . . .' buzzed the Light Fairy. 'I'll have to think of sssomething . . .'

The air around them thickened suddenly. The fairy froze in mid-flight and the monster stopped pacing and crouched motionless, all his senses alert.

'Who is there?' he growled. His ears and whiskers began vibrating violently and his tail scraped against the walls as he lashed it to and fro. The unseen presence made even him uneasy.

'It's my mistress, you fool!' rasped the Light Fairy. 'I sssaid she would be angry! Now look what you've done!'

Her fierce red beam quailed as the rustling grew louder and louder, till it became a deafening roar. Then came the voice. Deep and solid, it seemed to echo from the walls themselves.

The beast let out a roar of pain as the sound penetrated his skull and boiled through his brain like a red-hot poker. It seemed to come from everywhere, inside and out.

'You have failed me!'

'Sorry, misstress!' wailed the Light Fairy in a high-pitched whine. 'I have tried my bessst!'

'It is not good enough!' boomed the voice of Magda. 'You must try again to lure him down here. You must show him that you will take him to the cave. He wants to find it. And keep the beast hungry. The boy must be destroyed!'

As quickly as it had rushed upon them, the voice receded and faded away. The beast shook his ears and snarled in annoyance.

'Well,' said the Light Fairy, 'as you see, you will have the elf boy sssoon. Hey, what d'you think you're doing?'

The monster had galvanized into life. He crouched low in the tunnel like a great praying mantis, his eyes alight. His huge tarry wings unfolded and refolded again as all his senses stirred in excitement. 'Mmmmmmm . . . something smells good . . .'

The fairy let out a shriek of annoyance. 'No! Didn't you hear? You're to wait! After the boy is dessstroyed you will be able to eat all that you can! Come back, Grimgorr!'

But the monster swung his great head around and growled at her. 'I am not waiting any longer! You cannot deny me any more!' And without another word his massive bulk bounded off down the tunnel, towards the tantalizing scent of life.

As Nick left the palace, a pack of Crystal Chronicle town criers surged forward in a threatening tide. The ferrety-faced woman was right at the front, jostling for space and calling out his name. Nick's bodyguards shielded him, bundling him through the crowd into the royal conveyance. It shot off through the mob like an arrow, town criers dragging in its wake, some of them even trying to jump on to the sleigh.

As they passed through Solstice Square Nick noticed that the shafts of daylight filtering down through the thinner ice of the dome above their heads were much brighter now. Outside on the surface the sun must be climbing high in the sky, reaching its zenith, when it shone round the clock. Then it would be downhill fast to the Autumn Equinox and the endless dark days of the Arctic winter. When he was due to deliver his promise. Another little pinprick to his conscience . . . another little reminder that time was ticking by . . . and all those children who would be waiting for him to come on Solstice Eve . . .

He was jerked out of his musings by a sight that was becoming painfully familiar. There was his face, up on the Crystal Chronicle; but now it was depicting him with a variety of surly expressions. He forced himself to smile. His cheeks began to feel tight and he realized he was grinning idiotically at the crowds. The elfin people he passed did not cheer, wave or smile; instead, they gathered in small groups, whispering and staring.

Town criers' bells echoed in the tunnels all around them, ringing out negative messages.

'Oyez! Nickolai falls out of favour with Solstice Council!'

'Saviour setback! Will Mission go ahead?'

'Danger to the Kingdom! Should someone else go in his place?'

'Let the people decide!'

Great Ursus! News travelled fast! Especially bad news. It seemed that an invisible cloud hung over the Kingdom, as though the atmosphere had suddenly turned sour. Nick's insides crumpled and he suddenly felt bewildered and disorientated. What was happening? This was his beautiful home, the Kingdom

70

he had fought so hard to save. An idyllic paradise, a utopia where all was sweetness and light. But something had gone wrong. This wasn't how it was meant to be. It reminded Nick horribly of when he was labelled the Evil Elf Boy by Magda, in the bad old days of the Golden City.

Down in a far-flung corner of the NetherWorld two figures stood in the gloom, weaving about helplessly. One of them was waving his arms around, but the other didn't have arms, so she waved her head about instead. They were trying to control a swarm of dingy, glowing creatures who were buzzing around in the air like a crowd of demented hornets. They had a dull look about them, like stars about to go out, and their colours ranged from sludge green to murky purples and browns. They darted here and there, giggling in shrill, high-pitched voices, competing with each other to animate the rocks into grotesque forms. Every time they touched a surface, the craggy rock face would heave and contort into yet another ugly configuration: misshapen faces with bulbous eyes and elongated noses bulged out of the rocks, then retreated again.

Around them, a litter of small four-legged creatures scampered about, yelping and grunting at the faces that loomed out and shrank back again like a hideous magic mirror show. And all the while the darkness oozed around them.

'Stop that! Stop it at once! Leave them alone,

children!' cried the female creature in a shrill and commanding voice. 'Fangle, do something, you great lump!'

'I'm trying, lady!'

But the swarm of creatures took no notice and continued buzzing about riotously.

The two figures sighed and gave up for a moment, taking a breather. Fangle, the more human-looking of the two, leaned his enormous bulk against the wall for support. He was tall and two-legged, and vaguely resembled an elf, but his features were lumpen and craggy like kneaded dough. He had a squashy nose, a domed head and, instead of dainty pointed ears, his were large and wavy. Flamboyantly curved tusks grew out of his mouth, and when he spoke a lot of spitting seemed to be involved.

'Shomething's unshettled my Peshkiesh,' he said, spraying the nearby wall. 'They're very shensitive.'

'Tut tut! Excuses, excuses!' said the other figure, who was not human at all. Moomsa was a large and ungainly four-legged creature who looked very much like a dinosaur, with a tiny head on the end of a long neck, a frilly crest down her back and a long tail that dragged in the slime. 'Have you no control over your charges? Make them behave! They're leading my little ones astray!'

'Fungushrot! Your lot aren't any better than mine! They're jusht as naughty!' He nodded at her babies, who were running riot like delinquent puppies, grunting with delight. 'They don't need much encouraging!'

The dinosaur lady waved the tufts on her head. 'Now look here, you lump of dough, I'll have you know I'm a good mother! Watch this! Come here, children!' she called sharply. At first they didn't respond. 'Now!' she cried in a shrill voice. The baby dinosaurs ceased their gambolling, hesitated, then ran towards her in a straggling mass.

'See? That's what superior genetics does for you,' said Moomsa. Her miscreant infants clambered on to her back and settled down between the folds in her crest, squabbling amongst themselves.

'Fuh!' snorted Fangle. 'Don't flatter yourself, Moomsa. At least I can stand upright!'

She was about to issue a smart reply when they both stopped and stared. A fierce red glow streaked towards them, making a high-pitched whining noise like a predatory insect. It zigzagged nastily above their heads and did a sharp turn back down the tunnel.

'Who is that?' asked Moomsa. 'Not one of yours, is she?'

'Shertainly not! I don't like the cut of her wing,' muttered Fangle. 'Looks like a bad 'un to me.'

Moomsa swung her long neck round to stare at him. 'Oh, lordylumps! It's one of *them*! We don't want *her* sort round here.'

They stared at each other in the darkness. Suddenly the whole fabric of the place seemed to rip asunder. A resounding roar echoed around them, and the tunnel walls shuddered and heaved. Something thundered towards them. Something huge.

'Oh, lordy lordy chitterbangs. This doesn't sound good. Let's get out of here!'

Moomsa wheeled around and began lumbering away. She could go surprisingly fast for her size.

'Hey, wait for me, dinolady!' spluttered Fangle.

They set off in headlong flight, passing through yawning chasms, rivers of sludge and pools of slime, pursued by the sound of thundering paws and blasts of searing breath. The dinobabies clung on to their mother's back for dear life, squealing with terror, and the Peskies shot through the air behind them in an arrow of dim light.

Moomsa seemed to know where she was heading, and they finally reached the banks of a sluggish river. As they stopped for breath a plume of fire rippled towards them, scorching Fangle's beard.

'Whoof! What ish that thing?'

'Lordy knows!' said Moomsa. 'But it's big, whatever it is.'

'It'sh not a dragon, ish it?' said Fangle breathlessly.

'Of course not, silly lump! They don't exist! Come on, follow me. I know a cave under the water! He won't be able to find us there!'

She flopped into the river and began to swim clumsily through the slime. Her offspring clung on like limpets, caterwauling. The Peskies dived into Fangle's left ear and disappeared with a squeak as he plunged in and began to flail around.

'I've just remembered. I can't swim!'

' 'Bout time you learned, then.'

As soon as he got home from the palace Nick marched straight through the living room, past a white-faced Ella, and shut himself in his room. He threw off his cloak, dropped it on the floor, flumped moodily on his bed and stared around himself.

When Nick had returned, his room had still had baby things in it – fluffy toys and romper suits with pictures of sleighs on them. But his mother had packed them away, and now the walls were plastered with pictures of different sleighs and crammed with sketches and models of his toy ideas. He looked at them, heaped in a mess on the floor. What use were they if he wasn't able to carry out his Mission?

He had begun to doze off when he heard a faint tapping noise at the window. He looked up and saw a pink glowing shape, buzzing to get in. It was her again – the Light Fairy he'd seen at the workshop! Leaping up, he strode over and flung the window open. She flitted into the room, squeaking and diving around in circles.

'Hello, little thing!' said Nick in delight. 'Where did you get to?'

He knew she must be a stray, but she couldn't be one of the demon types – she looked too cute. She was more of a pinkish colour now, up here in the light. She settled on his shoulder and fluffed out her wings, brushing them against him as she preened herself. He had to keep her! It would be so nice to have his own Light Fairy again, a friend and a companion amidst all this loneliness and confusion. He knew Elvina was still inside him, but it wasn't the same.

The fairy made a few more circles in the air, then shot over to the map of the Elfin Kingdom hanging on his wall. She began darting at it meaningfully, as though she was trying to tell him something. He sat up and stared, his heartbeat quickening. Elvina had done this! She used to buzz around, making noises and shapes in the air. For the first twelve years of his life she'd been his guide and companion, showing and telling him things. Elves and their Light Fairies couldn't speak to each other, but they had other ways of communicating. He couldn't have done what he'd done without her.

His heart leaped. Why hadn't it occurred to him before? Maybe this Light Fairy was a messenger, sent to help him, perhaps lead him to this Cave of the Crystal Chronicle! Why else would she be visiting him? And why was she making such a point of darting at the map? She must be indicating something on it! The more he thought about it, the surer he felt. She was zigzagging between him and the map now, making quick detours over to the window. Yes, she definitely wanted to lead him to the cave! If he hadn't lost track of her, and got lost in the mines, and then run into that claw thing, she might have led him there before!

The fairy squeaked and flew purposefully out of the window. He rushed over and looked out; she was flitting away down the street. He felt compelled to follow her – he couldn't miss a chance like this. She hovered for a moment, beckoning him. There was no one about. He began to climb out of the window when a beefy arm suddenly shot out, barring his way. It was his bodyguard, Boris.

'Now where d'you think you're going, young sir?'

'I want to go for a walk!' gasped Nick.

'Not possible, I'm afraid,' said Boris. 'You must be escorted at all times.'

Nick glared at Boris. 'Oh, come on! Just let me go for a little walk on my own!'

'I'm sorry, Nick,' said Ella's voice behind him. 'You know that's out of the question. You're precious, to all of us.'

Nick rushed over to his bed and flung himself on it, banging his fists on the pillows in helpless frustration. He turned on his mother. 'This is ridiculous! I'm beginning to wonder if I should have come back at all!'

Earthly Treasures

Zak had been travelling for some months, hunting and fishing along the way to survive, heading north across the endless miles of rolling tundra on the southern edge of the calving grounds. The sun was higher now, blazing in a brilliant-blue sky, looping around in a strange elliptical arc. It warmed his bones during the day, and for a few short hours it would sink in a glowing streak of orange, violet and cobalt blue on the horizon, before popping back up again in nearly the same place.

The snows had melted and the landscape had come alive, revealing more of its secrets. Icy streams rushed through the boggy ground. Spots of brilliant red and orange appeared amongst the monotonous browns. The vibrant greens of lichens, mosses and ferns, frozen during the winter, began to emerge. The wind-washed air rippled the dwarf birch and willows that grew in sheltered places. But Zak could sense the veins of ice that criss-crossed the permanently frozen layer of ground underneath him.

After a while the tundra began to give way to expanses of weathered rock and gravel, before opening out to reveal the first Arctic mountain ranges standing remotely on the horizon. Beyond their snow-capped peaks lay the ice-bound wastes of the Pole. He had met many Inuit along the way – but only a few from his own tribe. None of them had come across his family. He had begun to despair of finding them.

That day, the shadows were growing long and the sun was heading for the horizon. He had to find somewhere for the night. His eyes scanned for signs of a sheltered place where he could light a fire, camp for the night and cook his catch. In the glow of the sunset something caught his eye. Two long curved spikes sticking up above the ground. What were they?

Zak hesitated, wondering if this was a trap. But no animal would do this, and none of the Arctic people were given to ambushes. As he drew closer, he realized that they were tusks, embedded in the ground, as tall as young trees. Around them was the outline of a crevice that had once been a creek, meandering towards the mountains. It had long since been silted up with mud and covered in ice and rock.

He gazed at the tusks in awe and touched one gingerly. It was still preserved, its grainy markings and colourings intact. The rest of the creature must lie underground, buried in the hardened ice, where it had fallen into the creek. Zak felt the hairs on the back of his neck tingle. He had seen many species of animals

Zak felt the hairs on the back of his neck tingle.

on his travels in the Arctic, hunted them and worshipped them at the same time.

But he couldn't imagine what this one was. The beast must have been enormous.

For Nick the next few days continued on an edge of unease. He went into the workshop every day and got on with his work, designing more toys in his little office. Everyone was polite, but the atmosphere was strained. Krista visited every day and continued to poke her nose into everything. He gritted his teeth and tried to be civil to her, but it was not easy. She, on the other hand, carried on as though they had never had a cross word. In fact she seemed to be making an effort to be nice, which puzzled him.

'Oh, yes, this one is brilliant, SB. You really are a genius toy designer, aren't you?' she would say. Or, 'Those kids up on the surface are so lucky!' And a variety of other conciliatory remarks which he was sure were designed to distract him from the main problem: how to get the gifts to the children. It was as though she was saying, 'You concentrate on your job here in the workshop, and let everyone else worry about the other details.' And his suspicions were still growing that she might want to take over his job.

The Solstice Council sessions continued too, and Nick sat through interminable meetings about route plans and the physics of the bottomless sack that Vilmar and his scientists had created to hold all the gifts. He dared not mention the Cave of the Crystal Chronicle again.

One night soon after, there was an approaching jingle and the swish of an important-sounding sleigh gliding to a halt outside the door of 27 Ice Ridge Avenue. Ella rushed to the window. She jumped as though stung by an insect and patted her hair.

'Great Ursus, it's the King!'

There was a knock at the door. Ella smoothed down her clothes and hurried to fling it open ceremoniously. Vilmar was struggling out of his royal conveyance, helped by his two manservants. Ella curtseyed as he hobbled into the room, and Nick bowed his head briefly.

'Good evening, Your Majesty,' stammered Ella. 'We weren't expecting you.'

Vilmar waved her apologies away with a shrivelled hand. 'No matter, my dear. No need for any fuss or ceremony. I've come to see your son.'

Ella disappeared without a word and left them alone in the room. Nick fidgeted under Vilmar's gaze, ice-blue and sharp as ever. What was he going to do now? Banish him?

'Your Majesty, I . . .' he began.

'No need to explain. I know exactly how you feel. Believe it or not, I was young and headstrong once too.'

Nick looked at his wizened face and found this hard to believe. He was still waiting for a reprimand.

'And it may surprise you to know that your grandfather, Frederick Grishkin, and I were friends once, when we were your age. Inseparable. Terrible tearaways, we were. Always in trouble. Got up to all sorts of pranks and escapades.'

Nick's mouth fell open. What? His grandfather and Vilmar, friends when they were his age? Why had no one told him?

'He went on to become a great pioneer in sleigh racing, of course, discovered how to tap into the forces.' Nick flushed with pride at the thought that he had the sleigh-driving talent bred into him. 'And I went on to become king. But no one knows of our early friendship. Our junior escapades were hushed up.'

'What, erased? By the Crystal Chronicle?' said Nick in astonishment.

'In a manner of speaking, yes. It wasn't reported and all records of it were wiped from memory, as though it had never happened.'

'So the original crystal does have that kind of power then?' said Nick hopefully, trying to find a way to reopen the subject. 'To, sort of, rewrite events?'

But the old king's face had taken on that wary and evasive look again.

'Yes, yes, yes.' He waved his hand impatiently. 'But don't tell anyone I told you about my wild youth. It's our little secret. I just thought it would interest you to know that I was young once too.'

He winked conspiratorially, and Nick felt as though

he had just lifted up the corner of a carpet and seen a whole new pattern underneath. There seemed to be a new warmth between them.

But Vilmar's face was darkening. 'Now, I have to tell you that you have set the Solstice Mission back several weeks with the disruption you have caused recently.'

'I'm sorry, Your Majesty. I'm the last person who wants to ruin the Mission. It's just that no one seems to understand!'

The old king smiled. 'Please just trust me, Nickolai. Everything will unfold as it should.'

'But how do you know?' demanded Nick hotly.

Vilmar fixed Nick with a stern look that silenced him. 'Do not question me any further.'

He doddered over and sat down creakily on the armchair by the fire. The crystal clock on the mantelpiece began to chime out the hour. The miniature elfin figures danced round the ice bell on the mantelpiece, their laughter echoing in the room as they struck their tiny silver hammers on it repeatedly, reminding Nick once more of the passing seasons. Then the room was silent again, except for the sound of Lenka snoring quietly in Vilmar's beard. Nick waited nervously for what Vilmar was going to say next, wondering why he'd come.

'Nickolai, you must learn to work with others,' said the king at last. 'No one achieves anything on their own. All great enterprises are the result of teamwork. And you must take steps to curb your anger – it is jeopardizing the Mission. So I have brought this for you. It is very rare and precious.'

Vilmar reached inside the folds of his robes and pulled out a shining pendant hanging on a chain. Nick's heart leaped. Maybe . . . at last! Vilmar was finally giving him the thing he wanted!

With trembling hands, Nick took the pendant and examined it. It was about the size of his little finger, a smooth piece of stone carved from a milky gem, shot through with iridescent colours. As it swung to and fro in the firelight, it radiated an unearthly glow. He caught his breath.

'So is this it? The original Crystal Chronicle?' he said, his voice trembling with excitement, hardly daring to hope that at last he might be holding the sacred object in his hand.

Vilmar shook his head.

Nick's heart plummeted south again. 'What is it then?' he asked dully.

'It is a Soulstone. Wear it round your neck, and every time you feel your temper rising, or any kind of agitation or disquiet, hold it in your hand. It will calm you.'

Nick struggled to hide his disappointment. 'Is this more powerful than the Crystal Chronicle?'

Vilmar sighed as if he had been expecting this question. 'Yes and no. Only the tiniest vein of Soulstone runs through the Moonstone mines. It was formed on the Night of the Creation. It's the purest stone on the planet, because it cannot be used for selfish ends. Its powers are spiritual, rather than physical. It enables whoever comes into contact with it to understand and communicate with others, to be at peace with themselves and everyone around them. Some say it contains the essence of peace on earth.'

Nick thought this all sounded a bit soppy. And what was the use of a powerful stone if it didn't help him with what he had to do? But he smiled gratefully and hung the pendant round his neck, feeling its cool surface on his skin. 'Thank you very much, Your Majesty. It's beautiful.'

'Never mind what it looks like, concentrate on its inner qualities. Now, if you make an effort to cooperate you are more likely to get your own way. Remember, everyone is on your side. The Solstice Mission stands for everything we believe in.'

Vilmar struggled out of the armchair and prepared to go. 'And do try and get on with Krista. My granddaughter wants to be part of it all. Imagine how she must feel. The heir to the Kingdom, usurped by a newcomer who has not even grown up here. She's used to getting all the attention. Put yourself in her shoes.'

'They wouldn't fit me, sir.'

Vilmar smiled. 'Anyway, I have arranged for you to have sleigh-driving lessons together, to give you the opportunity to get to know each other a little better.'

Nick groaned inwardly. This was the last thing he

wanted. And it was a move that aroused further horrible suspicions in him. He wondered if he should mention his fears about Krista taking his place on the Mission, but decided against it. He nodded silently and forced a smile. 'All right, sir. Thank you, sir.'

'And I want no more talk about trying to find the Cave of the Crystal Chronicle, understand?'

Temptation

'No, not like that, SB! Like this!' Krista grabbed the reins of the dual-control practice sleigh and rotated her ears more elegantly than Nick could ever have managed. With great aplomb she navigated the sleigh round a complicated series of stalagmites, cornered several sharp bends, did a neat turn and drew the sleigh to a gentle halt.

'See?' She indicated her appearance, which still looked as smooth and unruffled as a summer lake. 'Not a hair out of place.' She threw him a radiant smile.

'Well, I don't like to brag or anything, but I've travelled at supersonic speeds, burst through rocks and solid metals, journeyed across ice floes and mountains and crossed the great frozen sea – and nobody gave an icicle's drip what I looked like then!'

'Oh, you old show-off!' said Krista playfully, flipping his arm. 'It's not all about speed you know. It's about style too.'

'Depends on how much of a hurry you're in,' grunted Nick. 'Like, if you're on a Mission trying to save the Kingdom, or deliver gifts to all the world's children.'

Krista rolled her eyes. 'OK, OK.'

Nick thought he saw that hurt look again, and suddenly remembered what Vilmar had said about her feeling usurped. He felt contrite. 'Er, sorry, Princess, didn't mean to be rude,' he mumbled.

He had made quite an effort to be polite all morning, but she still managed to get up his nose, even if she didn't mean to. She constantly reminded him how she had been driving a sleigh since she was three years old. And she was wearing such a silly get-up for sleigh driving: a pale-green satin gown trimmed with lace and a green velvet cloak over the top, all embroidered with gold thread; plus yet another totally unnecessary handbag, gold brocade this time, with lots of dangly bits on it. What's more, she'd brought that wretched little Mingle of hers along too. It sat in her lap, squeaking and protesting every time she swerved round a bend. But she still managed to stroke its fur and drive the sleigh one-handed, with a careless elegance he found infuriating.

'Now now!' said Mischa, the driving instructor, who was sitting behind them. 'Stop squabbling and let's get on with the lesson.'

They were in the practice run that led to the Sleigh Race meeting house. It was designed for intermediate drivers, with plenty of twists and turns, obstacles to steer round and several steep slopes. But it was still much easier than anything Nick had done before. Laughably easy. The whole thing was a joke, really.

'Right, would you like to try that again, Nickolai?' said Mischa. 'The way Krista just did it?'

Krista gave him a triumphant look. Nick snorted and took up the reins. Suddenly an ice bell chimed from the meeting house, a long grotto in the distance with a pillared entrance to let sleighs through.

'Ah! Someone wants me in the meeting house,' said Mischa. 'Probably about tomorrow's race. It's time to finish now, anyway.' He went to turn the sleigh.

'But we haven't had our full hour yet!' protested Krista.

'I must get back, Your Highness. We're behind schedule. I'll make it up tomorrow.'

Suddenly Krista shrieked. 'Oh, no! Where's my handbag? I can't find it anywhere!' She began searching around in a frenzy. 'I must have dropped it along the way! This is a disaster! I had my best silk hankie in it! The one Aunty Silvana gave me!'

Nick and Mischa exchanged glances.

'It's no good!' said Krista finally, huffing with resignation. 'You'll have to go, and leave us here. Nick's bodyguards can come and collect us, then they'll have to drive me around so I can look for it. It must be somewhere on the ground. I'm not leaving without it.'

She said this with such an air of authority that Mischa faltered mid-protest. 'But, Highness . . .'

'We'll be fine. Please do as I ask. Send Boris and

Olaf out to fetch us. See you tomorrow.'

She gave him a stern look and Mischa gave in with a sigh. She really was very pushy.

'As you wish, Highness.'

Reluctantly Mischa leaped out of the sleigh, bowed briefly to the princess and went towards the meeting house. As his figure dwindled into the distance, Krista turned to Nick with a mischievous smile. 'That got rid of him then, didn't it?' She reached under her cloak and pulled out the ridiculous handbag.

Nick gaped at her. 'But . . .'

'That was what's called a ruse, SB. So easy to fool these people, isn't it? Come on, let's go for a spin.' She went to take up the reins.

But Nick wasn't going to rise to it. Oh, no. He wasn't going to let her get him into trouble again. 'No, Highness. We shouldn't. It's illegal, you know it is,' he said piously.

'Ah, yes, but I'm the princess, silly. It's all right if you're with me.'

'Yeah, right, and I'll probably get the blame.'

'No, you won't. And it's only a little spin up the end, perfectly harmless. No one'll know. Boris and Olaf will be ages getting here.'

'You should be setting a better example, Highness.'

'*Royal* Highness.'

'Royal, most incredibly unbelievably royaller than royal, Highness.'

They glared at each other in stony silence for a few

moments, then both burst into fits of giggles.

'Oh, you are funny, Saviour Boy!'

Her cornflower-blue eyes seemed to fill his vision. Then his attention was distracted by something red and glowing that flickered at the corner of his eye. He turned his head sharply and saw it dive behind a pillar before flitting out again. It was *her* again – the stray Light Fairy from the other night! Nick's heartbeat quickened as he watched her spiralling tantalizingly towards him and away again. Krista's Light Fairy Petronella gave a slight squawk of disapproval.

'Friend of yours?' said Krista, eyeing the fairy curiously.

'No. But I think I've seen her before.'

'Where?'

'Oh, just around,' said Nick with a nonchalant shrug.

'Then she must be a stray. And you know what we're supposed to do about strays, don't you? Report them to the authorities. Then they get put in a phial in the Ice Chamber.'

'I think that's cruel. And you've gone very law-abiding all of a sudden, Highness. A moment ago you wanted to break the law yourself.'

She gazed back at him steadily, then grinned. 'Oh, very clever!' she giggled.

He felt a little surge of pleasure that he'd managed to get one over on her. Krista eyed the Light Fairy dubiously. 'You don't think she's a – you know . . . one of them, do you?'

'No . . . I think she's . . .' Nick hesitated. He didn't want to tell her what he thought about this strange little creature. But he felt more convinced than ever that she was trying to lead him to the Crystal Chronicle. He made to scramble out of the sleigh.

'Where you going, SB?'

'I just want to follow her a little way, see where she goes. On my own.'

'Oh, no you don't, not without me. You reckon she's some sort of messenger, don't you? I've heard your theories about the Cave of the Crystal Chronicle. I've always wanted to find that place, and it's my business as well, seeing as I'm the heir to the Kingdom. And believe it or not, I want this Mission to go ahead too!'

Nick looked at her, not knowing what to make of this. 'Aren't you scared about the claw thing I saw?'

Krista snorted. 'Poopsicles! It must have been a shadow. The light can play tricks with your eyes down in the mines. It's a well-known fact.'

'And what about the fact that we're not allowed to drive, or go down to the NetherWorld, or even out of the Kingdom? You're a member of the royal family, and it's the royal family that makes the rules.'

Krista shrugged. 'They're not my rules.'

Suddenly he saw her with new eyes. Maybe she was a rebel after all. 'You might get your hair and clothes messed up.'

'Oh, blow that. I've got loads more frocks at home. Come on, let's go together. Or are you scared?'

'No!' said Nick fiercely. 'That's the last thing I am!'

'Well, of course, you're only a commoner,' continued Krista carelessly, with a challenging sideways glance. 'You wouldn't dare, would you?'

Nick glared at her. In the background the fairy was swooping invitingly into the entrance of an offshoot tunnel. His fears about the claw subsided. He had to take the risk. The fairy would protect him, guide him, just like Elvina used to. And he didn't want Krista thinking he was a wimp. Grabbing the reins, he twitched his ears and the sleigh shot forward down the tunnel towards the forbidden darkness.

Into the Unknown

At first Nick and Krista were racing along the familiar tunnels and caverns of the known Kingdom. Luckily they were on its outer perimeters, so there was nobody about to witness their illicit adventure. After a while they began to spiral downwards, skirting the edge of the Moonstone mining complex, where the constant hammering of the miner elves could be heard echoing through the layers of rock. They passed several grottos containing trucks piled high with rare and precious minerals and glittering gemstones.

Nick kept his eyes firmly fixed on the Light Fairy flitting ahead. As he passed an alcove something glinting in the darkness caught his eye – a small silver claw hammer lying on the ground. He slowed to a halt and leaned down to snatch it up.

'What d'you want that for?' asked Krista with a frown.

'You never know, it might come in handy. I'm used to scavenging, done a lot of it in my time.'

Nick slipped the claw hammer into his belt and

drove on. The tunnels were growing narrower and darker now, leaving only the light of the fairy to guide their way. She spiralled along in the distance like a beacon. They seemed to be going steadily downhill, and the air was getting distinctly warmer and thicker.

They swerved round a sharp bend and began to cruise down a steep incline. Suddenly Nick's stomach lurched as the ground dropped away beneath them. Krista screamed and Snowflake set up a loud chattering noise and burrowed down the front of her satin bodice.

'Crumbling crystals! What happened then?' shrieked Krista.

The sleigh began to veer around, out of control. Nick gritted his teeth and commanded his ears to stay in contact, but it was like trying to drive through treacle. He looked around for the fairy, but she was nowhere to be seen.

'Um, I think it might be a good idea to turn back now!' cried Krista, her voice wobbling in fright. It was the first time Nick had seen her flustered.

But it was too late. The walls of the tunnel were undulating like heavy curtains. Nick's heart turned over in terror. Krista was screaming and clinging on to him. 'What's going on?' she shrieked.

'I think we've entered the NetherWorld!' shouted Nick.

They both cried out as the rocks sagged open into a yawning chasm. The sleigh began to plummet

'I think we've entered the NetherWorld!' shouted Nick.

towards it. It seemed to have passed out of his control. Nick's mind seized up in panic. How could he stop the downward plunge? A desperate idea came to him.

'Reverse thrust! Together!'

Both he and Krista gathered up the reins and rotated their ears backwards as hard as they could, trying to resist the downward pull. Gradually the sleigh slowed and they heaved a sigh of relief. Which immediately turned into a gasp of horror when they looked down.

Below them lay a lake of festering slime, hot and steaming. Huge, viscous bubbles glugged on it, and the heaving forms of many unspeakable creatures could be seen thrashing around beneath the surface, occasionally breaking above it with a soggy splash. Nick's flesh crawled as he looked at them. Great Ursus! What kind of life forms lived down here?

He pulled the sleigh level and saw a bank on the other side which looked relatively solid.

'Head for that bank!' he cried.

Steering chaotically they hurtled towards it and landed with a crash, tumbling out in a heap. After a few breathless moments they sat up on the bank, which felt uncomfortably clammy, and looked around.

'Flibbering frosticles!' gasped Krista. 'That was a close shave! Eeeuw! What's all this?' She looked at her hands, covered in slime, then down at herself, and her face filled with horror. Her beautiful satin gown was smeared with black, sticky gunge. 'Agghhh! Look at me! Look at my dress! It's ruined!'

'I thought you had plenty more at home,' said Nick sarcastically.

'Yes but – I didn't think it would be *this* bad down here!'

'What did you expect? A bed of snowflake flowers?'

Krista was feeling her head for her coronet. When she realized it was gone her face froze. 'Oh, Ursus! My tiara! It must have fallen off.' She began fumbling feverishly on the ground, squealing with anxiety. 'This is terrible! Mummy'll kill me! That was a present from Aunty Ulya! And my handbag! Where's my handbag?' She gasped again and renewed her fevered search, scrabbling on the soggy ground.

'So you really have lost it this time then?'

She whirled on him fiercely. 'Yes! And I'm glad you think it's funny, SB, but actually it's not. Mummy's a total dragon!'

'Oh, come on, Princess, that's the least of your worries now,' said Nick reasonably. 'At least we're still alive! And I did warn you that you might get messed up.'

He glanced about him nervously. He didn't much like what he saw. They were in a dark cave, hard to make out in the gloom, whose outlines seemed to be moving around like an image going in and out of focus. The ground felt very wobbly beneath them. They were on a central island, with a pillar in the middle reaching up to the ceiling, surrounded by the moat of bubbling slime. The whole place had a distinctly unstable feel about it, and it seemed to be revolving very slowly, like a giant merry-go-round.

'Well, I still think we should never have come. The best thing we can do now is get back in the sleigh and head home,' said Krista.

'No!' said Nick doggedly. 'I tell you, the fairy's a guide. She's been sent to help me. She's leading me to the cave.'

'But where is she?' protested Krista, glancing round. 'She's gone again!'

'She must be around somewhere,' Nick muttered with more confidence than he was feeling. 'Just give it a moment.'

Krista assumed her usual bossy, determined air. 'We must go back! Now! I command you! As your sovereign!'

Nick was not going to let some pampered, fussy princess stop him in his quest.

He said nothing. They glared at each other in silence, until a horrible gurgling noise came from nearby. They glanced round at the overturned sleigh and froze in horror. The bank underneath it was sagging like a wet blanket. The craft began to slide backwards, as if sucked in by a powerful vacuum.

There was a revolting glugging noise, and a long slimy tentacle reached out of the lake, with suckers all along it and a rubbery trumpet-shaped nozzle at the end. The tentacle suctioned on to the sleigh and dragged it backwards into the slime, pulling it down until it was swallowed up beneath the surface with a resounding gloop. The two of them stared hopelessly at the spot where their only method of transport had disappeared.

'Well, that's that then,' said Nick in despair.

'Oh, Ursus! What're we going to do now?' wailed Krista, all traces of the imperious princess vanished.

Nick's whole body filled with dread. What had they done? How stupid had they been? He should have listened to Vilmar.

'We'll have to try and head back on foot . . .' he said bleakly.

'But how are we going to get across that frightful moat?' cried Krista in a shaky voice. 'You shouldn't have brought me here! This is no place for a princess! You'll be in big trouble now!'

Fury welled up inside Nick. How dare she twist things like that! 'Well, it was your idea! You made me do it!'

'Did not!'

'Did!'

Suddenly there was a buzz and a squeak and the glowing shape zipped into view, hovering before them in a blur. She fluffed out her wings and chirruped at them. It sounded very encouraging. Nick felt light-headed with relief. 'There she is! I knew she wouldn't desert us!'

Down here where it was darker, she had a much brighter, more reddish glow about her.

'Oh, well, that's something I suppose, but what now, SB? We're in a frightful fix.'

As if in reply, the fairy bounced across the moat, darting aggressively at its viscous surface, making strafing noises. Slowly a reef of rocks rose up out of the slime, providing a series of lumpy stepping stones.

'Look! She's leading us to safety! Good girl!' cried Nick.

They scrambled up and ran across the stepping stones, trying not to look down at the heaving surface on either side. Disturbingly the reef sank back down behind them as they passed. The fairy squeaked and set off down a tunnel which seemed to have opened up before her.

Nick was struck by a sudden insight. 'Hey! She can control the rocks! Make them move at her command! She's leading us to the cave!'

'I still think we should go back, SB. Honestly, we can come another time.'

'What other time?' said Nick impatiently. 'When else will I get a chance like this? Come on, we've got this far. And we've got her to protect us now. Stop being such a – *girl*!'

And he strode off, pulling her protestingly with him.

'My outfit's going to be ruined! Mummy'll be livid!'

'Stop fussing and come on!'

They stumbled on, following the fairy through the murky passages. A dull red glow filled the whole place. Everything around them seemed to be shifting and changing shape. Krista did a lot of huffing and puffing at first, and complaining about how dirty her clothes were getting. She was looking more than bedraggled.

'Oh, look at all this slime! My shoes are getting ruined!'

'Take them off then!'

Nick ignored her constant complaints and after a while she gave up. She lagged along beside him, muttering grumpily under her breath, picking her way through the plodgy ground and holding up her skirts as they trudged after the fairy. Soon the air grew even hotter and stickier than before.

'We must be getting closer to the Vortex now,' said Nick uncomfortably, beginning to sweat in his robe.

'Oh, puffcakes! We're still miles away from it. I know my Elfin Kingdom geography, Saviour Boy. Remember, I grew up here.'

'I suppose you learned all that stuff at Elfin School, did you?'

Krista made a face. 'No, actually I have a private tutor. I'd much rather go to school with all the other kids, but it's not allowed 'cos I'm a royal. I sometimes think I'd love just to be like a normal kid, but I have to do all this official stuff. I don't have any real friends at all, apart from Mariska, and she just comes over and borrows my jewellery and never gives it back. You . . . well, you never know if people really like you for yourself when you're a princess.'

Nick felt as though a curtain had been whisked aside. Maybe they had more in common than he thought. As they followed the red glow through the gloom, a new camaraderie began to grow between them. Nick allowed himself to relax, feeling that with his new little Light Fairy friend accompanying them, they were safe. And as for that claw thing – well, there was no sign of it now. Maybe Krista was right; maybe it had been just a shadow.

The fairy led them deeper and deeper into the NetherWorld. They followed her through endless rolling tunnels, stumbling through pools of slime and tripping over ghastly outcrops of fungi.

They came at last to the banks of a wide river fringed by blackened trees. A stench of rotting vegetation assaulted their nostrils.

'Well, well. An underground forest,' murmured Nick, staring at it in wonder. The river wound sluggishly into its dark and dripping depths, overhung by branches glistening wetly in the gloom. 'Stinks, doesn't it?'

'So that's a *forest*, then?' said Krista, staring at it aghast. 'Yukkity yuk! Not the sort of place you'd want to go for a picnic, is it? Do they have them up on the surface?'

'Yeah. Loads,' said Nick. 'But they're beautiful, they don't look like that. They have proper leaves on, and branches which sway in the wind. And most of the time they're covered in snow that sparkles in the moonlight.' He sighed nostalgically, remembering his wild joyrides through the forest with the flying reindeer.

Krista looked wistful. 'I've always dreamed of going to the surface. You are so lucky to have lived up there.'

The fairy was buzzing purposefully at the rock face now, and a wide, dark tunnel opened out to their left. She beckoned them into it. They followed, and found it was swaying like the deck of a huge galleon. Slowly it settled down into a gentle rocking rhythm. They continued following the fairy along it, treading carefully.

'Where *is* this cave then?' asked Krista.

'I'm sure we're nearly there now,' said Nick hopefully.

Suddenly Krista stopped dead in her tracks and put a hand on Nick's arm. 'The tunnel's getting narrower.'

Nick saw to his horror that the walls were visibly closing in on them, as though operated by some gigantic machine. His heart began hammering in his chest.

'What do we do now?' Krista stammered.

'Run back the way we came?'

They turned – and saw with mounting terror that the walls behind them were closing in too.

'We're trapped!' shouted Krista. 'That beastly little thing has led us into a trap!'

With a flash of light the fairy appeared at their side, buzzing furiously. She darted at one of the walls and it suddenly burst apart, revealing an opening.

'No, she hasn't!' cried Nick with relief. 'She's come to our rescue! You go first, I'll follow.'

Krista started off down the newly opened passage. He went to follow. But without warning two projections shot out from the walls on either side of him, holding him in a vice-like grip and pinioning his arms to his sides.

'Come on, SB! Quick!' called Krista from the passageway.

'I can't! I'm stuck!'

Krista saw him and her face dropped. 'Oh, crustcakes! Hang on, I'll come and get you out.' She ran back and started trying to pull Nick free, but the rocks held him fast. 'How did you get into this fix anyway?' she muttered, as she tugged painfully at Nick's shoulders.

'The walls just closed in on me . . .' he gasped through gritted teeth. The rocks were pressing in on him harder now and he was finding it difficult to breathe.

'And where's the fairy? She's gone again!'

They struggled on in silence, Nick gasping in pain, until a terrible sound echoed down the tunnel towards them. They stopped dead and listened, breathing fast.

'What in the name of Ursus was that?' squeaked Krista.

Nick recognized it at once. It was the same unearthly roar he had heard that day in the mines. But louder this time, and closer.

'Go!' shouted Nick. 'You can still get away. Look, the passage is still open. I'll get out somehow. The fairy'll come back and help me.'

Krista hesitated, shaking her head and staring in terror towards the deafening noise that boomed down the tunnel towards them. Nick let out a hoarse cry as two enormous, glowing, cat-like eyes appeared in the darkness ahead.

'Nickolai! What's that?' Krista wailed.

Nick was so terrified he didn't notice that she had called him Nickolai for the first time. His heart was thumping in his chest like a jackhammer. It must be whatever owned that claw. You could hardly make it out in the gloom, but the size of the eyes, and the way they were spaced, gave you some idea of its enormity.

His voice came out in a raw scrape. 'I – I think it could be whatever it was I saw down in the mines . . . *now* do you believe me?'

He looked at her and saw that she was paralysed with fear. She nodded dumbly. Guilt and terror flooded into him. He had got her into this terrible danger. It was all his fault. The least he could do was make her go. 'Don't stay. Let's make sure at least one of us survives! Run, Krista! *Now!*'

'I'll go and get help, SB!' she stammered.

And with a stifled gasp, the Crown Princess turned and fled.

A Tight Spot

The rocks were squeezing the breath out of Nickolai till he could feel his ribs beginning to crack. The roaring of the beast grew louder, filling his whole head, and those terrible burning eyes loomed closer in the darkness.

This is it, he thought. *This is me, finished, after all I've been through, and those kids won't ever get their gifts on Solstice Eve . . .*

Black despairing thoughts raced back and forth through his head, then he remembered his Soulstone pendant. It wasn't much use in this situation, but it might help him meet what was obviously going to be a horrible death. One of his hands was squashed up against his chest; he fumbled down his front, pulled out the pendant and held it tightly in his hand, praying for deliverance.

Immediately his mind cleared and he began to think rationally. The claw hammer! It was an outside chance, but it was his only hope. With immense effort he reached towards his belt and pulled it out. He could feel the scorching breath of the monster gusting towards him now, like a blast from a furnace.

A new cave mouth had appeared, its entrance lined with huge white pillars, sharp and pointed at the bottom, dripping with . . . oh. A chill rippled his back as he realized that this was the monster's mouth, nearing him now, and those were its enormous fangs. Great Ursus! Was it possible for any living creature to be that large?

With a superhuman effort he began to hack away at the rocks pinning his arms and chest. He smashed at them frantically, badly gashing his arms in the process, and managed to clear a tiny space between himself and the rocks on either side. *Quick! Slip out before they close in again!* He wrenched himself free, ripping his clothes and his flesh, and ran as fast as he could.

Stumbling blindly down the tunnel he tried to shut out the terrible roaring noise . . . suddenly the wall gaped open to his left. A new tunnel! Thank Ursus! He shot down it – and gasped.

Barring his way was a huge four-legged beast. A tiny head wove around on its long rubbery neck. It plodded forward on enormous clawed feet, its bulk filling the tunnel. Its back seemed alive with movement, and a terrible squealing noise came from whatever it was that sprawled across it. In the gloom it looked ghastly, like some sort of dragon. Nick backed away, gibbering in revulsion, and turned to run . . . only to find himself face to face with another ugly brute – a bulky two-legged creature this time, a deformed combination of elf and goblin, with wavy ears and curly fangs.

A strangled scream came from somewhere. It sounded like Krista.

'Hang on to her tight, children!' said a warbling female voice behind him. 'What are you waiting for, you great lump! Come on, let's get them out of here!'

Nick's head began to swim and his senses dimmed. Behind him he was vaguely aware of the roaring of the beast, a loud gusting noise, and flames scorching his flesh. Rough, clammy hands gripped him and he felt himself being lifted up and jolted about as he was carried away, half conscious.

The dreadful noise faded out to a muffled roar, as though a soundproofed door had closed, barely audible through layers of insulation. Through glazed eyes he saw the tunnel ahead twisting and contorting, and the four-legged monster lumbering along with creatures lurching around on her back. He caught a glimpse of two long legs flailing, a flurry of skirts and a tumble of red-gold hair. The beast was carrying Krista! Were they friends or foes? A cluster of glowing lights, all of them dingy colours, flew ahead, darting at the walls, creating new formations and moving them aside to open new passages. The roaring sound blared out again, and another blast of heat scorched his skin. Then blackness closed in.

★ ★ ★

Grimgorr paced back and forth like a restless tiger. His huge tarry wings made a swishing sound as they folded and unfolded. His massive tail lashed around furiously, leaving deep score marks in the walls. He snapped his jaws at the red Light Fairy, snarling in rage.

'You let him get away!' he bellowed, gusting out a plume of fire which she ducked to avoid.

'No, I didn't!' snapped the Light Fairy. 'It wasss your fault, you great hulking idiot! You didn't move fast enough! And how wasss I to know those interfering busybodies would help him essscape!'

'Who are they, anyway? And why haven't I eaten them yet?' roared the monster.

'You didn't miss much; they're not particularly good eating. Once you've eaten elf meat you won't want any other. But you mussst eat elf boy firssst!'

'Then bring him to me! Feed me! I will not be denied any more! Arrrrrrghhhhh!' Grimgorr shook his head in fury and pounced on the nearest life form available. The fairy watched in distaste as he devoured a hapless invertebrate which happened to be minding its own business in the corner. 'Yeeuch! Bad food! Guh!' He spat it out on the floor. 'You're a bad, bad fairy! I've a good mind to eat you!'

She let out a spiteful sniggering noise and dive-bombed his massive ear, making him yelp. 'How many timesss do I have to tell you?' she hissed. 'I'm pure ssspirit essence! And you will do as you're told! If it

111

wasn't for me you wouldn't even exissst!' She zigzagged around in a state of fevered agitation, bashing against the rocks in her irritation. 'Damn and blast! What to do? What to do? How will I find another way of getting the brat down here?'

She stopped mid-buzz and hovered in the air. There was an ominous silence, becoming thicker and heavier with each passing moment. The beast quivered.

'Wait! My mistress is here again. She will tell us what to do!'

The darkness seemed to gather itself up into a ball. Then came the hissing noise, increasing in volume, swelling and wrapping itself around them. And out of its centre came the voice, deep and ancient, rumbling with pent-up rage, filling the air as though it were oozing in through the walls. The beast let out another roar of rage and pain as her voice pierced his skull.

'You have failed, yet again!'

'Misstress! What can I do? How can I stop him from eluding usss?'

'Listen very carefully. This will work.'

The fairy listened, hovering intently, while the disembodied voice issued more deadly instructions. When it had finished, it faded away as though it had never been there. The fairy quivered with new energy, pulsating with an even fiercer glow.

'Yesss! That is the answer! I have to leave you now, Grimgorr. I might be some time. If and when he returnsss, he will be all yours.'

And before Grimgorr could reply, she had streaked off.

Nick awoke on a cold stone floor and looked around. His ribs ached and his shoulders felt as though they'd been attacked by hammers. He was in a dark tunnel, but in the Elfin Kingdom again, for he could see a faint glimmer of phosphor lamps in the walls further along.

He couldn't believe he was still alive. He shuddered at the memory of that searing breath, those burning red eyes, those terrible dripping jaws. But where had the fairy got to? Why had she deserted him? A tremor of doubt came from deep within him. Maybe Krista was right. Maybe she wasn't just a stray Light Fairy, but one of the demon ones.

He sat bolt upright.

Krista! What happened to her? Nick felt sure it was her he had seen on the four-legged beast's back. But where was she now? He looked up and down the tunnel. No sign of anyone. She had deserted him too!

There was a scratching noise by his ear. He looked down and saw his little pink glowing friend, nestling on his shoulder. She fluffed out her wings and stroked his face. She hadn't deserted him after all!

'Oh, hello! It's you again,' he whispered. 'What happened to you back there?'

The fairy squeaked in a meaningful way, darted off and came back again. 'Ah, yes. Of course!' He understood what she was trying to tell him. She must have disappeared at the crucial moment because she'd gone to get help! From those strange-looking monsters who'd helped him escape.

Nick looked down at the fairy as she nestled under his chin, stroking her wings against him. 'You've brought me back safe! I knew you wouldn't desert me!' he whispered, rubbing his cheek against her soft wings. She made a little mewing sound. 'You'll stay with me now? Carry on looking after me?' She squeaked in agreement and fluffed out her wings again. She was so cute.

Then dark and ugly thoughts crowded into Nick's mind like invading slugs. It all seemed so obvious now. Krista had deserted him, but the fairy hadn't. This was all part of Krista's plan to usurp him. She had deliberately lured him down to the NetherWorld to try and get rid of him, probably knew a way out that he didn't. This fairy was his only friend.

Nick picked himself up, wincing with pain, and began to limp down the passageway towards the lights. The pink fairy fluttered around at his shoulder, following him. His ears twitched as the sound of marching feet and voices echoed down the tunnel towards him. As they came closer, he saw a group of palace guards, dressed in royal-blue uniforms. A luminous glow came from the Light Fairies clustered over their heads.

'Here he is! He's still alive!'

'Quick! Hide!' whispered Nick to the fairy. 'Else

they'll capture you and take you away from me!'

Without a sound, the fairy dived down his front and burrowed into his clothes to hide, just like Elvina used to.

A very old man who is very angry indeed is not a comfortable sight. Vilmar's wrinkled old face was white with rage, and Nick thought thunderbolts might shoot out of his ice-blue eyes any moment. Even Lenka had woken up and was cowering in the snowy depths of his beard.

'Do you realize how much danger you have put yourself in?' he whispered hoarsely. 'And the Crown Princess! Olga is in such a state of shock, she has retired to her chambers!'

Nick thought this didn't sound like a bad thing at all, but of course he didn't say so. He stood silently before the king, his knees shaking a little, but still defiant.

'I am only glad my dear departed wife Eva was not here to see it!' Vilmar continued in a quavering voice. 'My granddaughter has told me you have awakened some monster from the deep! You have been consorting with demons and mutants! Ursus knows what you may have laid the Kingdom open to now! A valuable practice sleigh has been lost. But most seriously of all, you have disobeyed orders! And led the princess astray!'

This was outrageous. *He* had led *her* astray? Nick felt

he had to protest. 'But please, sir, it wasn't my idea! She egged me on!'

'Nonsense! We all know what a headstrong and reckless nature you have!'

Nick felt a surge of righteous anger. 'Yes – and that's what saved the Kingdom!'

Vilmar blinked and straightened up indignantly. 'That is no excuse! Do not try that tactic again!'

Nick felt he had to defend himself. 'But I don't see why I should get all the blame for this. She did kind of talk me into it. And then,' he hesitated, knowing this was a slight distortion of the truth, 'she ran off and left me.'

Vilmar's face turned thunderous. 'Are you accusing my granddaughter of perfidy?'

'I don't know!' shouted Nick. 'I don't know anything any more! I'm confused. You've threatened to replace me on the Mission and I – I just don't know who to trust or what to think!'

Vilmar gave a sigh of deep regret. 'I'm afraid you leave me with no other alternative, Nickolai. For the time being, you are under house arrest! You are to be confined to your home until further notice. Until you have learned to control these impulses and behave rationally, your powers are a danger to the community. I suggest that once you have rested and reflected we meet again and review the situation.'

Nick nodded dumbly. There was nothing more to say. He became aware of the fairy tucked away down his front. He turned to go, and the palace guards stepped forward to escort him home. Vilmar called him back.

'And Nickolai – I suggest you use that pendant more often.'

Zak was beginning to despair of ever finding his people again. He had reached the familiar territory of their old hunting grounds now, not far from where the Golden City had risen up all that time ago. And still no sign of them. Only the empty and desolate wastes stretching all around him.

He stood on the ridge where he had watched Doransk mushrooming out of the earth, keeping an eye on its steady thrusting progress above the surface while straggling travellers passed by in their droves, heading towards it. He had felt terribly alone. Then he had met Nickolai, and felt he belonged again. But now he felt worse. Nickolai had gone back to his Kingdom; he was somewhere under Zak's feet, in another world, living his new life. And his own family? Where were they? Would he ever find them again?

On the horizon the city lay in ruins, a heap of charred and blackened lumps jutting dismally above the snow. At a loss for anything better to do he began to trudge towards it. The sun remained in the sky for most of the day now, drawing an elliptical shape in the high azure blue. The snow was blinding, and he had been forced to wear a strip of gauze across his eyes to shield them from the glare.

It took him several hours to reach the ruined city, and when he had finally passed through the derelict gates and begun to stumble amongst the blocks of fallen masonry and broken statues he was overwhelmed by a sense of desolation and loss. Memories flooded back of that glorious last night he had spent there, rejoicing at Nickolai's miraculous return from the dead.

Zak came across a giant blackened head whose features were worn and crumbled. It was a ruined statue of Magda, all its gold leaf fallen away. As he stared down at it, he felt something grow warm against his chest.

He felt for his tupilak, hanging on a thong round his neck. It was an Inuit charm, designed to ward off evil spirits. He gazed at it intently. He had made this charm several years ago when he was still a child, carved it from wood and decorated it with whatever he could find. It was an image of the ugly, twisted face of an old hag, with black chips of glittering stone for eyes, a hideous red mouth and pieces of fox fur glued on to represent a mass of straggling grey hair. It was only later on that he'd discovered he'd unwittingly carved an exact image of Magda, as Nickolai described her the night she had returned from exile to destroy the Kingdom.

Zak gave a start. The tupilak's eyes were glowing. It wasn't a trick of the light: the ugly face seemed to grimace menacingly. The thing began to grow warm in his hand, getting hotter by the minute. He shuddered; this must be a sign. Something told him his old friend was in trouble, that his age-old enemy was threatening to return and wreak her revenge on him.

He stared down at the snow under his feet, dazzling in the sun, and shielded his eyes. He knew what lay beneath. He'd spent many months with Nick in the dark, silent, dripping caverns under the Golden City, where they'd run a refugee colony of rebel urchins. And on that cataclysmic Solstice Eve, when Nick had destroyed Magda and her city and resurrected the Kingdom, he'd caught a glimpse of it as it came back to life. Nickolai was down there now amongst his long-lost people, making plans for his Winter Solstice Mission, probably unaware of the danger that threatened him. Magda had not been completely conquered. Some of her spirit still lingered on . . . or the tupilak would not be glowing and burning in his hand.

He had to get down to the Kingdom somehow, try and warn him! But how would he get down there? Zak remembered that sometimes the layers of ice creaked and shifted around, and the jagged ridges would heave and open up unexpectedly. He hated the idea of going underground, always had. It went against his nature. But he'd been there before, and he had to help his old friend . . .

He began wandering around, his eyes fixed on the

ground, hunting for some sign of movement.

After a few hours he began to despair. And then he heard it. A faint cracking sound, like an eggshell breaking. He rushed over to the place where the sound had come from, staring down at the dazzling white surface. A crack had appeared, just a sliver of darkness at first. There was a creak and a groan and the crack opened wider, like a smiling mouth. It stayed open.

Working at lightning speed Zak put his plan into action. He found a broken column and after much grunting, heaving effort he lugged it over to the crack and jammed it in there to keep it open. He pulled out his pickaxe, tools and ropes and began his descent, climbing down the newly created shaft.

Illusion and Betrayal

Ella was sitting by the fire, hunched and desolate, when Nick was shown back into their home. She looked up, her face stained with tears, and it seemed she had aged by ten years since Nick had last seen her. 'Nickolai! Thank Ursus you're safe!'

She rushed over and embraced him. Nick felt unable to control his own tears and buried his face in her neck.

After a while they sat down at the table together and the guards withdrew.

'What happened?' Ella whispered. 'How could you do it again? Put me through so much agony!'

Nick stared at her, filled with remorse. 'It was Krista's idea too, Mum. She said she wanted to find the Cave of the Crystal Chronicle as well, and we went to look for it.' Yet again, he didn't tell her about the Light Fairy. 'And then it all went horribly wrong, and now I've got the blame!'

From outside came the clamour of the town criers' bells. Needless to say, they had followed him home, and now Nick's bodyguards were trying to shoo them away. Above the hubbub, Nick recognized a shrill female voice.

'Oyez! Saviour turns to dark side! Danger to the community! He has been consorting with demons and monsters in the NetherWorld!' The voice trailed off down the passage.

Ella was white-faced with shock. 'And have you, Nickolai?'

'No, of course not, Mum! It's just that there's some weird stuff down there! And I wasn't making it up about the claw, I saw the creature it belonged to! He was enormous! But we managed to escape! I was just trying to find this crystal, so I can do what I have to do!'

She heaved a despairing sigh. 'Nickolai, you must leave it to others now. You have no choice. It's a good thing you're under house arrest, because now you won't get into trouble again! I can sleep at night, knowing you're safe! Because if I lost you again . . . I . . .'

Her face crumpled and dissolved into tears. Nick rushed round the table and put a comforting arm round her shoulders. 'I won't let you down again, Mum. But I don't want to let those kids down either!'

She looked up and dried her eyes, sniffing. 'Just sit tight and wait to see what happens. Promise me!' Nick looked away, his mouth in a stubborn line. 'Please, Nickolai! Keep yourself safe and try to cooperate from now on. I'm sure if you go and apologize, properly, to the king, and show him you've turned over a new leaf, you'll be back in favour in no time. And he will put an end to all these silly rumours.'

Nick flumped down on the chair by the fire. 'I don't know, Mum. If I apologize, they may never find the answer to this time problem! And then I won't be able to carry out the Mission.'

'Well, it looks as if you won't be anyway, the way things are going at the moment,' said Ella, jerking her head at the distant cacophony of town criers' bells ringing round the tunnels. 'Just bring yourself to say sorry, and that you won't do it again.'

Nick gazed moodily into the fire and said nothing. His mother sighed again, in defeat.

For the next few days, the Kingdom continued to buzz with wild speculation. Negative images of Nick played on the Crystal Chronicle plaque in Solstice Square with monotonous regularity. Everyone was waiting to see what would happen next. Ella hardly ventured out. The shopkeepers down the road missed her sunny presence, and her neighbours dared not visit her.

Nick stayed in his room most of the time. He came to rely more and more on the comforting presence of the fairy, who hovered around him constantly. He kept her hidden away from his mother, but she nestled on his pillow every night, and spent a lot of time burrowing in his red robe, which was usually lying in

123

a heap somewhere. With each day, Nick became more agitated about passing time, and more convinced that Krista would be in his place now. He longed to go to the workshop, to see what was happening there. She was probably sitting in Solstice Council meetings too. His ears would start twitching and have him groping for his pendant.

One night, after supper, he went into his room and his heart nearly stopped. Lying on his bed was an illusion of himself! The fairy was buzzing around it proudly. Nick gasped. He had left his red robe in a crumpled heap as usual, but now it had been laid out straight, and there was a faintly discernible shape underneath it, and an outline of his head, lying on the pillow. He gingerly felt around the whole optical illusion, and marvelled at it. There was nothing underneath the red robe but thin air, but anyone glancing at it would think that it was him lying on his bed.

His heart leaped with excitement. So this was what the fairy had been doing when she burrowed in his robe! She had been creating an illusion of him, so he would be free to escape from his home! He couldn't waste an opportunity like this. He crept to his wardrobe and found another cloak. It was dark-blue velvet with a hood, so he could disguise himself. Putting it on he tiptoed to his bedroom door, opened it quietly and peered into the living room.

It was empty. Ella must have gone into her room. He

glanced through the window and saw Boris standing guard outside the front door. The fairy squeaked softly and flew out of the half-open window. A few moments later he heard Boris's voice rising in irritation.

'Oi! Come back here, you pesky thing! I have to report you to the authorities!'

Nick peered round the curtains and saw that Boris was pursuing the fairy down the street, trying to do his public duty. She was creating a distraction so that he could get away! He slipped out of the front door and, pulling the hood of the cloak over his head, hurried off in the other direction.

'Is the boy still breathing?' enquired Moomsa, gazing down anxiously at the figure in its bedraggled furs.

'Yesh! Jusht about,' said Fangle.

'He still looks pretty bad to me,' she murmured anxiously. 'He must have had quite a fall down that shaft. And I only got him away from the monster in the nick of time.'

Fangle gazed curiously at the brown leathery face. 'Ish he an elf, d'you think? He hasn't got pointy earsh. And no Light Fairy.'

'No, silly, I think he's from the surface. Look at his face – it's weather-beaten.'

There was a tense silence in the cave as they watched the boy's inert face. Suddenly his eyes flickered open. What he saw made him think he was dreaming, and not a very nice dream at that, so he closed them again.

But Fangle and Moomsa were overjoyed.

'He's alive, children!' cried Moomsa. 'Look! The boy wakes!'

Her infants began cheering and squealing with delight, scampering around like puppies and waving their tufty heads. The dim blur of Peskies set up a shrill, high-pitched squeaking, and began doing a riotous dance around the cave in frantic formation. The boy cautiously opened his eyes and saw again the strange, dinosaur-like creature and her brood of identical infants, the rough, bodged-together giant with curly tusks and a domed head, and the strange cluster of glowing lights hovering in the background. They lit up what looked like a rather grimy, damp cave. No, he wasn't dreaming, unfortunately.

'Where am I?' he whispered in horror. 'Where is the Elfin Kingdom?'

'You overshot it, dear,' said the dinosaur creature. 'You are in the Lower Regions beneath the Kingdom. You are in the NetherWorld.'

The boy struggled up, wondering uneasily what the sticky film was that seemed to cover him. The dinosaur lady nudged him gently. 'All right, dear? Nothing broken? You've been unconscious for several days. You fell down a shaft. I managed to rescue you from the monster.'

Zak stared at her in alarm. 'Monster?' Then, like a nightmare suddenly catching up with him, confused memories crowded into his mind. Two massive burning red eyes, glowing in the gloom, a deafening roaring noise, scorching blasts of heat and a heavy pounding that shook the ground beneath him and seemed to echo through his soul.

'Yes, dear. But don't worry, you're safe now. We are in an underwater cave. He can't follow us here. And even if we look a bit . . . odd . . . to you, don't judge us on our appearances. We're friends.'

The tusked man spoke, spraying him liberally. 'You are the third pershon from above who has shtrayed down here and had to be reshcued by us recently. Can't think what you all shee in the place.'

Zak sat bolt upright and pushed down his furry hood. 'The third? What did the other two look like?'

'A boy and girl. About your age,' said Moomsa. 'Very nice-looking elves from the Kingdom above. The monster nearly got them too. At great personal risk, we rescued them and took them back up as far as we dared.'

The boy felt his heartbeat quickening. 'What did the boy look like?'

'Fair hair, blue eyes, pointy ears, of course. Dressed in red. Very twitchy boy.'

The boy let out a breath. 'Nickolai!' He began to struggle to his feet. 'I must get up there. I believe the boy you saw is my friend! I think he is in danger!'

Moomsa biffed him with her head and made him slump back down. 'Everyone is in danger, dear,' she warbled. 'And you're not going anywhere. There's a carnivorous beast out there. The NetherWorld is not a safe place at the moment.'

'And there ish an evil one, a demon,' continued Fangle. 'She has a shtrange and devilish glow about her. We have never seen her before. We feel she has come from the – the evil one from down there!' He nodded ominously at the ground.

'The Vortex?' said the boy incredulously. 'Magda!'

'Yesh! How do you know about her?'

'I was there when Nickolai defeated her and saved the Kingdom.'

'Well, dear, we think she's trying to come back. And this demon fairy is in league with her. She has created the monster. And she is probably up there now with your friend.'

'I knew it!' Zak let out a long breath. 'That's why I've come down here. To try and find him. I think he needs my help!'

Revelling in his new-found sense of liberation, Nick made his way towards the workshop. There were still a few elves scurrying to and fro, and it was a relief not to be recognized by them. One or two sleighs passed, including a delivery sleigh laden with parcels and provisions. It reminded him wistfully of Joe's old red-painted sledge back in Norsk. The only thing missing was the team of husky dogs, panting and yelping quietly as they pattered through the snow.

Nick slowed his pace and began to enjoy his

evening stroll. Now his absence was safely covered at home, he could afford to take his time, dawdle along, take everything in, look at shop windows, maybe even go in and browse! He didn't know the city well, since he had never been allowed out on his own. But he had spent hours poring over maps and longed to explore the place for himself.

There was a small parade of shops not far from his house, where people would purchase their daily supplies. The lights from the windows beckoned invitingly and spilled out on to the streets. He passed Aurora Interiors, a colourful shop selling elaborate home decorations. He lingered a while, looking at the display of intricately carved vases, goblets, chandeliers and gossamer lampshades. He came to Hublov's, a provision shop, whose window was full of pastries and sweetmeats. It was open late. His mouth began to water as he stared at the display of ice cakes, snow lollies, crystal crumble cookies and starlight syllabubs, glistening enticingly in the warm glow of the interior. But he didn't dare go in to buy something.

Reluctantly he went on, passing Kransky's, a shop selling sleigh accessories and bells, and a shop called Oracle Supplies that purveyed scrolls and maps. He wandered through the streets until he finally came out into the Hyperion Market. By day it was colourful and noisy, full of stalls piled high with foodstuffs. But all the stalls had packed up for the night and the place was deserted.

He slipped past the empty stalls and down Ursus Passage into Solstice Court, where all the grand houses stood. Their bluestone facades, covered in ice mosaic and ornate twisted pillars, glittered in the glow of the street lamps. Inside the houses Nick could see brightly lit rooms and elfin families settling down to chat by flickering firesides. He felt a pang of sadness. They led such normal lives!

He strolled silently across the square, past an ice statue of Queen Astrid the seventh and down Lower Ursus Passage towards Equinox Alley, a small tunnel that led to the side entrance of Equinox Plaza. The heavy metal door was shut. He loitered in an alcove until two workshop elves came out after a late shift. They left the door slightly ajar and a chink of light fell on to the pavement. Crossing the passage, he passed unnoticed through the door. He left it on the latch and tiptoed on to the main workshop floor.

The place was silent and empty now. In the dim glow, row upon row of machines stood still and waiting. On the conveyor belts, toys had been left in neat and orderly piles, ready to be worked on the next day.

Nick crept into the Arkfel Caves, adjoining the workshop, where the reindeer were to be housed the night before the Mission. Nine beautifully made icewood stalls ranged round the walls, filled with soft snow wool to keep the beasts comfortable. Sacks of lava nuts were stacked against the wall, and under a huge sheet stood his family sleigh. Nick lifted the corner: it was still there, the sleigh he had used to rescue the Kingdom. The silver bells and decorations gleamed – it was obviously being washed and polished on a regular basis.

He left the caves and made his way towards his workshop. His desk was covered with plans and drawings, still half finished. He leafed through them. Dolls, dolls, tiaras, handbags and more dolls. They had to be Krista's. There were a few scribbled notes lying about and he picked one up. There was an elaborate scrawl all over it. It was from Krista to Anatole.

'I like this ballerina bear,' it said. 'Please proceed to production immediately. HRH.'

So the princess had taken his place, was carrying out his work in his absence! The girl had actually been sitting at his desk! Giving out orders! Nick's stomach curdled with anger. He snatched the note, screwed it up furiously and hurled it on the floor. Then he slumped on the desk. After a while he fell into an uneasy doze, troubled by restless dreams.

He awoke early the next morning to the sound of distant voices and heavy doors being unlocked. The Plaza was opening up for the day. He'd better get out before he was seen. If he got home before his mother woke up then she wouldn't—

—he sat up straight, his heart hammering. Where was the fairy? He hadn't seen her at all since last night! He'd been so busy playing truant he'd completely forgotten about her!

A tremor of unease went through him; he recognized it from before, although he had ignored it. It came from deep within him, as though Elvina was trying to tell him something. Swiftly he crossed the workshop floor and slipped out through the side entrance just before the first elves came into the main area. Pulling the robe around him he hurried through the maze of streets back to his home. He passed several early-rising elves, catching disturbing snatches of conversation.

'I hear he's being kept under house arrest indefinitely,' said one elfin woman to another as they passed close by.

'Yes,' said the other woman, 'apparently the Solstice Mission plans are going ahead without him. Makes you wonder if he's necessary at all.'

Nick went very cold. He stood stock-still, shaking all over. Now his alienation was complete. He was an outcast. Completely usurped, his Mission taken over. What was he going to do now? Was it even worth being alive?

He stumbled on, scarcely feeling his feet on the pavement. As he rounded the corner of Ice Ridge Avenue, he saw Boris slumped outside the front door, dozing. Where was his little pink friend? She must be around somewhere. Maybe she'd stayed here to keep guard for him. He tiptoed past Boris, who was snoring quietly, crept up to the window and looked in. What he saw nearly made him faint with shock.

There, sitting at the table with his mother, wearing his red robe, was an exact replica of himself. Not just an optical illusion made out of thin air, but a real flesh and blood double. A talking, breathing, moving one. A mirror image, exactly resembling him in every detail. Like a twin brother.

The Net Closes In

The other Nick was staring thoughtfully down at his lava porridge, stirring it round and round in the bowl.

'I've been thinking, Mother,' Nick heard him say. 'I know that my pride and stubbornness sometimes get the better of me. And I'm truly sorry for all the trouble I've caused. I feel ready to go and apologize properly now, especially to Prince Ivan and Princess Olga, for putting their daughter in danger. And I want to make amends to the king and tell him I've turned over a new leaf.'

A wave of nausea swept over Nick and he clung to the window frame for support. He felt completely numb, disconnected from his body, as if his mind was floating around somewhere outside it. He saw his mother smile for the first time in weeks. 'That sounds like a good idea to me.' She ruffled his hair and started clearing away his plates.

Standing outside his house, looking in at himself, Nick's head began to swim. The ground beneath him felt as though it was falling away. This couldn't be happening. It must be a terrible dream. Why hadn't the fairy prevented it – and where was she? Feverishly he scanned the living room, but there was no sign of her.

Then it suddenly hit him.

Of course. That *was* her, sitting at the table. She was inside the red robe that cloaked the monstrosity that was his double. That's why she had been spending so much time burrowing into it! Somehow she had fed on its warmth and energy, taken possession of it, used it to create this living, walking, talking replica, made it flesh and blood.

How could he have been so stupid? She was not his friend at all. Krista had been right to suspect her. It was an evil spirit, a demon, not a stray or a messenger sent to help him. He should have listened to all the warnings. Why had he thought that he knew better than people who had lived in the Kingdom all their lives? And now this spiteful little creature had tricked him, led him into a trap; she had deliberately created the optical illusion to get him out of the way so she could carry out her plan, knowing he would seize the chance to escape.

He shuddered as the full implications hit him.

If demons were stray Light Fairies escaped from the Vortex, who had belonged to banished elves . . . then this one must be Magda's! She had taken over his identity, inhabited a replica of his body so she could carry out the Mission in his place! And then what? The outcome was unthinkable. His Mission would be taken

135

over by someone a thousand times worse than Krista, or anyone else in the Kingdom. His replica would prey on every child it visited, somehow use his body to suck the youth out of them, so the fairy could return to the Vortex and use it to resurrect Magda.

And after that? Magda's mask of youthful beauty would be restored. She would rise again and spread her empire across the globe, deceiving everyone. And every year, instead of him, she would travel the world in his flying sleigh. And instead of delivering gifts, she would prey on the children to keep herself young and beautiful. Childhood would become a thing of the past, and everything Nick had struggled to achieve would be in vain. He shuddered as he realized that only he knew about it.

A wave of panic engulfed him. Seized with a wild desperation he wrenched open the front door and burst into the living room.

'Don't listen to him!' he cried hoarsely, pointing at the replica of himself with a shaking finger. His mother was just emerging from the kitchen with a plate of snowberry cakes. There was a loud crash as she dropped it on the floor. Ella stood rooted to the spot and stared at him in horror. Her eyes had gone wobbly round the edges, as though they were being pulled in all directions.

'Ni—' she glanced from one to the other in bewilderment. Her Light Fairy Tilka cowered on her shoulder, twittering with anxiety.

The fake Nick feigned complete surprise. He stood up, pushed back his chair and stared at Nick as though he were an apparition.

'Who are you?' whispered Ella, white as a ghost.

'It's me, Nickolai!'

Ella began trembling all over and her mouth issued a soundless scream.

'Don't listen to that,' Nick jerked a shaking hand at his fake self, 'that *creature*! He's not real, he's an impostor! I'm the real Nickolai! Get him out of here! Call the guards!' He turned on his replica in fury. 'Get out! Leave this house at once!'

'Is this some sort of joke?' said the other Nick. 'What's going on, Mum? Who is this? You never told me I had a twin!'

Ella shook her head and began to cry. Suddenly Nick could stand no more. He lunged at his double and grabbed him round the throat. 'You're not real!' he screamed. 'You're an evil spirit! You're trying to take my place! Get out!'

To his horror, the other Nick felt solid and warm and real, but had an almost superhuman strength. His hands were like steel as he gripped Nick round the shoulders and pushed him away, hurling him down with incredible force. Nick's head banged violently on the floor and he lay there dazed for a minute. The face of his other self loomed over him.

Looking at him, Nick suddenly realized something. He had to seize his chance. 'Look, Mother!' he cried,

*Ella began trembling all over and her mouth issued
a soundless scream.*

pointing at the replica. 'His ears aren't moving! He can't be me! You know that's what happens when I get cross!'

A split-second, private moment passed between the two Nickolais, and a small, sly smile flitted across the replica's face. Then, to Nick's horror, his ears began twitching too, in exactly the same way. The impostor assumed an expression of righteous indignation and turned to Ella.

'Oh, yes, I'm angry all right, Mum!' he said dramatically, mimicking Nick's speech patterns exactly. 'I'm angry that this – *creature* can copy me in every detail! And no prizes for guessing where he's come from! He must be arrested immediately! Boris! Come in here quick!'

Nick gasped. This abomination had replicated him to such a degree that it was impossible to tell the difference! It was uncanny. Within seconds, Boris had barrelled through the front door, blinking anxiously. He had been fast asleep on his watch. When he saw the two identical twin Nickolais, one lying on the floor, the other standing angrily over him, his face drooped in shock and his jaw swung open.

'Great heavens – what – young sir—'

'Boris!' shouted Nick. 'It's me! Nickolai! The other one's a fake! I sneaked out of the front door last night, when you were chasing that stray Light Fairy, remember? She made an optical illusion of me lying on my bed, so I wouldn't be missed. And I stayed out all night! Then I came back and found this fake! The Light Fairy's done something! I left my red robe behind and she's somehow used it to make a replica version of me!' He turned beseechingly to his mother. 'Look at me, Mum! You don't believe that other one, do you?'

Ella looked from one to the other, her face a picture of anguish. 'I think – I think I must be in the middle of some sort of nightmare . . .' she said faintly. She was swaying on her feet.

Nick scrambled up and lunged at Ella, throwing his arms around her. He could feel her shrinking away and he clasped her tighter, trying to get through to her. 'Mum! Please, it's me! Please believe me! Don't turn your back on me!'

The other Nick strode forward and wrenched him away from Ella, who fell to the ground weeping in bewilderment and shock. 'Leave my mother alone!' he growled. 'Don't you dare touch her! She's *my* mother!'

'No, she's not! She's mine!' screamed Nick.

The replica hauled him up close, dragging him roughly by the collar, and stared at him eyeball to eyeball. Nick could feel his hot breath, the firm grip of his hands. 'I know who you are,' he said, breathing fast, 'and where you've come from. You should be arrested immediately. *You're* the impostor! *I'm* the one in the red robe! I've been here all the time. And you've come in from outside! Just walked in here, pretending to be me!'

Boris stared from one to the other, completely at a loss.

'No! Don't look at him! I'm the real Nickolai!' roared Nick.

'He's lying!' said the other one. 'Can't you tell? Tie him up!'

Suddenly Nick felt Boris's two beefy arms clamping around him from behind, and his arms were pinioned to his sides. He appealed in desperation to his mother. 'Please, Mum! Please believe me! Don't let them take me away!'

But there was a commotion outside and a babble of voices; a posse of palace guards poured through the front door and Nick was immediately surrounded. As he was dragged off, fighting and struggling like a wildcat, the last thing he saw was his replica's face staring back at him. A momentary glint of red gleamed in his eyes, then was gone. He moved over to Ella and put a comforting arm round her shoulders. She collapsed into floods of tears and buried her face in his chest, sobbing as though her heart would break.

'Oh, Nickolai! What's happening?'

Nick was frogmarched over to an official-looking sleigh and bundled into it. He stared numbly ahead at the uniformed elf driving the sleigh, ears twitching elegantly. As they glided through the streets, it quickly became apparent that the town criers were already on the case. Nick could hear their bells ringing all over the Kingdom, and their raucous cries booming down the tunnels.

'Oyez! New Nickolai drama!'

'Mysterious impostor assumes Saviour's identity!'

'Who is the real Nickolai? Identity crisis rocks Kingdom!'

A gaggle of criers bustled towards the sleigh and tried to follow as it swept through the streets, which were now full of wide-eyed elves, milling about in confusion. Nick leaned out of the sleigh, appealing to them in desperation.

'Don't listen to them! I'm the real Nickolai!' he shouted at them wildly, but they just stared back at him in perplexity and shook their heads. 'It's me!' he implored, trying to stand up in the sleigh. 'Can't you tell? Don't be fooled by the other one just because he's wearing my red robe! He's the impostor!'

But it was no good. The palace guards pulled him back down into the sleigh.

'I should keep quiet if I were you!' one of them whispered sternly in his ear. 'You're in enough trouble already and you're just making it worse.' And the driver urged the sleigh on.

As they passed through Solstice Square, the Crystal Chronicle disc showed two images of his face, side by side; one with the red robe, the picture of innocence, the other in the blue robe he had sneaked out in and was still wearing, with a distinctly shifty expression. With no other option than to give in, Nickolai slumped back in the sleigh and tried not to look at the suspicious faces of the elves they passed, their Light Fairies cowering against their owners.

He filled up with dread and despair. It was hopeless. He'd walked straight into the trap, an innocent fish swimming into a net. How could he have let such a thing happen again? How on earth was he going to convince everyone who he really was?

Yet again he found himself being accompanied along the sumptuous corridors that led to King Vilmar's stateroom. This time, though, he was being escorted rather more firmly. A million feverish thoughts whirled in his head as he tried to think what he was going to say. The solid silver doors swung open and the guards ushered him into King Vilmar's presence. The old king turned as he entered and stared intently into his face.

Nick's mouth went dry. 'I'm Nickolai!' he blurted. 'The real one! You've got to believe me!' Then he remembered his manners. 'If you please, Your Majesty.'

The wise old eyes, like chips of pure ice in wrinkled yellow parchment, searched his face. But the king said nothing.

Nick blundered on. 'I know the other one looks just like me and it's hard to tell the difference. But please believe me!'

'How can I be expected to know?' enquired Vilmar. 'I gather that the other one was at home, where he should have been. He is still wearing his red robe.

Whilst you – whoever you are – came in from the outside. You could have come from anywhere. Nickolai has been under constant house guard, confined to his home. He couldn't get out. He must be the real one.'

Nick felt desperation rising in a hot wave. 'But . . . I sneaked out for the night! I escaped! The Light Fairy got me out of the way! She created a distraction so I could sneak off without being seen, and then she created that vile, fake version of me! You must believe me!' he cried pleadingly.

Vilmar sighed heavily and for a moment Nick thought he saw doubt on his face. 'But nobody saw you leave, so it's your word against his. There is only one way to settle this. The two of you must come before the elfin court and speak for yourselves.'

Nick's stomach knotted into a cold lump. How could anyone in the Kingdom – even his own mother – know him well enough? He hadn't grown up here. There were no shared childhood memories. It was hopeless.

'In the meantime,' continued Vilmar, 'I'm afraid, to be on the safe side, both of you must be confined. Whoever is the impostor is a danger to the community, because he – or the spirit that resides in him – must have come from That Place.' He jerked his head downwards.

'Yes! It's Magda's emissary!' shouted Nick. 'And it's trying to take over the Mission! It's the one in my house, I tell you!' His ears were beginning to twitch with frustration. Vilmar's eyes flicked over them speculatively.

'What have I told you,' he admonished him, 'about controlling your temper?'

'Then I'm the one!' cried Nick, clutching at straws. 'You know I do this!'

'Oh, yes?' said Vilmar. 'I gather that you are identical in every detail though. You must go now, and let me ponder this a while.'

As Nick was led out, he missed the look of sadness and uncertainty that crossed the old king's face.

Nick was taken back along the corridors and tunnels that sprawled around the palace. As he passed a passage that led towards the royal apartments he came across Krista, accompanied by her two maidservants. She was cradling Snowflake in her arms, stroking his fur, and had obviously been waiting for him.

'So, SB,' she said casually. 'If that's who you really are. I gather there's been a bit of kerfuffle about your real identity.' Nick felt his stomach clench. This was the last thing he needed, more taunting from Krista. 'Well, we'll find out the truth tomorrow, won't we?'

'Yeah, and what about the truth about why we went down to the NetherWorld?' Nick shot back. 'It was both our decisions, but you let me take all the blame!'

She looked at him intently, narrowing her blue eyes. 'Are you the real Nickolai?'

From her perch on Krista's tiara Petronella made an affirmative sort of squeak.

145

'Of course I am,' said Nick wearily. Suddenly his rivalry with Krista didn't matter any more. 'But what difference does it make? Neither of us will be going on the Mission now. It'll be that fake version, sitting in my home.'

A puzzled frown wrinkled Krista's brow and she looked genuinely nonplussed. 'What d'you mean? Hey, SB, you don't think – you haven't been listening to – you've got the wrong—' Sudden insight flooded her face. 'Oh, crustcakes! I *warned* you about her! Oh, Nickolai, what have you done?'

Her face drained of colour and her eyes widened in horror. Snowflake let out a stream of chittering noises, waving his frondy whiskers at Nick. Krista stared down at the fluffy ball of white fur in her arms, then back at Nick.

The guard pulled him away. 'Don't talk to him, Your Highness. And don't let him touch your pet. You don't know where he's come from. He could be housing an evil spirit from the Vortex.'

As Nick was marched away, he glanced back and saw Krista staring after him with a perplexed and anxious look on her face.

A hush fell over the elfin courtroom as Nick was led in, still wearing the royal-blue robe. His replica, dressed in his red robe, was led in from another door and they were placed on a stand side by side, with a barrier between them.

Nick's eyes swept around the courtroom. The atmosphere was tense and Light Fairies trembled on their owners' shoulders. Sitting in the front row was King Vilmar, on a raised throne. Ranged on either side of him were Olga, Ivan, Krista and a row of white-haired Elders. Krista's eyes switched constantly back and forth from one Nickolai to the other, her brow furrowed, as if trying to distinguish between the two. Snowflake cowered in her lap. In the row behind sat his mother, looking haggard and anguished, a handkerchief constantly dabbing at her eyes. Her neighbour, Mrs Doblensky, sat next to her with a comforting arm round her shoulder. Anatole sat in the row behind, accompanied by several workshop elves. He looked at both defendants with a wide eyed stare, continually running his fingers through his shock of red hair.

The rest of the courtroom was filled with Crystal Chronicle town criers. They sat tense with expectation, occasionally glancing anxiously over at a long table at the back of the room, where they had been forced to leave all their confiscated bells in a clustered mass. When a decision broke, there would be an undignified scramble to the back of the room to grab their bells and scurry off around the Kingdom. Nick almost smiled at the thought.

He glanced to his right. His monstrous twin was gazing straight ahead, but the muscles on his jaw twitched. Nick willed him to look across. Finally he glanced sideways at Nick, returning his stare coldly; the

147

red light beamed out for a split second. Then he blinked dismissively and turned away.

'You must remain silent until you are spoken to, both of you!' said Vilmar sharply. 'You are here to prove your identity. One of you is the real Nickolai, saviour of the Kingdom, son of Ella Grishkin. The other is an abominable fake version, created by an evil spirit from the Vortex, a vile impostor with malevolent intentions. When identified, he will be considered an enemy of the state, possibly an emissary from the evil sorceress Magda. Once exposed as a fake, he will be placed in the Ice Chamber, according to the Elfin Book of Lore, until his body melts away to reveal his true essence. Then he will be placed in an Ice Phial with all the others.'

A gasp of horror ran round the courtroom. Vilmar held up his hand for silence and the buzz died down. 'I will commence by asking you both a series of questions. You, on the left, in the red robe. What is the name of Princess Krista's pet?'

Nick held his breath and Krista sat up expectantly, staring intently from one to the other. There was a brief silence, during which you could have heard a pin drop. Nick was sure everyone could hear his heart hammering in his chest. Then his twin spoke.

'Snowflake,' he said calmly. He looked at Krista and smiled. She didn't smile back. Snowflake set up a loud chitterwauling. The whole room erupted into a hum of speculation.

Krista stood up. 'Grandfather!' she cried.

'Silence in court!' boomed Vilmar. 'Only those who are spoken to may speak!'

Krista sat back down, looking very distressed. Nick felt tingles run up and down his spine. She knew it was him! Krista turned to Ella with an agonized glance and the two of them clasped hands. Nick felt a thrill of hope. They were on his side!

Vilmar turned to Nick. 'You, on the left, in the blue robe. What is the name of your Light Fairy, the one that is inside you?'

'Elvina!' said Nick quickly.

His replica glared at him. 'Of course you would know that!'

'Silence!' roared Vilmar. Lenka quailed from her position on top of his crown. He turned back to the replica. 'You, in the red robe. What are the names of the flying reindeer in the forest? The ones that will be coming up here on Solstice Eve?'

Nick allowed himself a ray of hope. How could his twin possibly know the answer to this?

But his replica smiled calmly. 'Rudolph, Comet, Vixen, Cupid, Prancer, Dancer, Dasher, Blitzen and Donder.'

Another buzz rose high in the courtroom like a swarm of bees. Nick felt as though he was being dragged down into a whirlpool. He turned angrily on the fake. 'No! You didn't know that! Not really! You must have some sort of telepathic powers! You've hacked into my mind and stolen it, along with my body!' He turned to the courtroom. 'He knows all my secrets! He can read my thoughts! He's stolen my memories! But he's still a fake! It's all an act!'

'No!' shouted the twin, sounding and looking exactly like him. He pointed an accusing finger at Nick and his ears began twitching madly, to illustrate how angry he was. 'Any questions you ask *him*, *he'll* know the answer to, because *he's* stolen *my* mind! You've got to believe me!' And with that the replica burst into passionate and noisy tears. Nick was astonished at his acting skills.

The courtroom was in uproar now. The fake Nick recovered his composure and both boys stood glaring at each other, one in blue, the other in red. Their faces were flushed, their eyes flashed angrily and their ears twitched nineteen to the dozen. Vilmar struggled to his feet and lifted his arms, trying to calm the hubbub.

'Silence in court!' he cried, raising his frail voice above the din. 'Or you will all be ejected!' A hush fell immediately. Vilmar looked at the two identical boys. 'And you two, control your tempers, both of you!'

In the tense silence, Vilmar turned to Ella. She stared back at him with a face full of agony.

'Ella, my dear,' he said kindly, 'you are his mother. We have not asked you yet. Who do *you* think is really your son?'

Ella opened her mouth but no sound came out. She shook her head, looking from one to the other. 'I –

150

think – that he,' she pointed at Nick, 'is the one . . . but . . .'

'Mother!' pleaded the replica hoarsely. 'It's *me*! You know it is!'

Ella's lips began to tremble. She let out a cry of anguish and collapsed sobbing in a heap. Mrs Doblensky comforted her.

'Then there is only one way to settle this,' said Vilmar. 'Before us stand two hot-headed young boys: one is genuine, the other a fake. They look and seem identical in every way. But the one who has the Soulstone pendant that I gave him is the real Nickolai.'

Nick's heart soared with new hope. Clever old king! Of course! The pendant! He still had it, hanging on a thread round his neck. He had forgotten all about it in the turmoil of recent events. He reached down into his tunic and froze with horror.

It was not there.

He turned to his replica and saw that his ears had stopped twitching. A small smile of triumph flitted across his face. He had reached down his front and his hand was clasping something. Slowly, he brought out the pendant. It swung on its chain, sending beams of unearthly light round the room.

Nick's insides shrivelled into nothing. This really was the end of it now. Careless and untidy as usual, he must have left the pendant lying around for this fake version to take possession of.

The creature turned to his audience, a pious

expression on his face. 'You can see I am the one true Nickolai,' he said calmly, 'because I have the great gift that our king gave me. I would never have let it out of my possession. I admit, the last few months have been difficult for me, trying to understand this new world I have found myself in. I know I have been impatient and wilful at times. But I see it all clearly now this terrible deception has occurred. You're my people – we have made a promise and we must keep it. I care more about the Kingdom and my Mission than anything else. Because that's what I have been born to do. I am Nickolai, the True North elf.'

There was a dramatic silence, followed by a general murmur of approval. This speech had obviously gone down well. Everyone wanted to believe in the new, improved Nickolai. It was so much easier, more convenient. Once more, Nick felt impotent rage rising up in him. Without his pendant he felt powerless to control his reaction to this terrible injustice. He started ranting hysterically.

'No!' he screamed. 'It's not true! It's all lies, an act! He's a puppet of Magda's, created by her evil spirit! They're going to take the Mission over in my place! What's wrong with you all? Can't you see what's happening? Look at me, Mother! Look into my eyes! The eyes you've known since I was a baby! It's me, Nickolai!'

The walls began creaking and hairline cracks were appearing. Cries of alarm rang out. Ella let out another cry of anguish. She stood up, leaning towards him. 'Nickolai! It is you!'

Nick was unable to restrain himself and tried to run out of the dock to hold her in his arms. But it was no good. He felt strong arms grabbing him from both sides. The courtroom swam before his eyes as he was taken away.

Vladimir, the Minister for Light, led the way, grim-faced and silent. As they marched through the endless passageways, Nick began to lose all sense of reality. Maybe the other Nick *was* the real one. Maybe *he* was the replica. He didn't know anything any more.

He kept going round and round in circles and ending up in the same place again – with the awful realization that his mother had not been able to save him. He put his hand over his heart, trying to imagine Elvina safely stored away. Was she still there? Maybe she'd deserted him too, in disgust at his stupidity. All along he'd been aware of those inner doubts, the quiet voice within. It had come from her. So why had he ignored it? Why had he chosen to listen instead to a stranger, who had seemed more real because he could see her with his own eyes?

Because he was a twerp, that's why.

Finally they reached a huge metal door, covered in a film of ice. Massive keys jangled in a complicated system of interconnecting locks that seemed to work in a chain reaction. The door swung open with a loud groan and a cracking noise. Nick saw, to his dismay, that it was as thick as a tree trunk. He shivered as he was led into a dark and eerie chamber. There was nothing in there except for icicle-encrusted walls, honeycombed with alcoves. In every alcove stood a transparent ice phial containing a dim light that seemed on the point of extinguishment, like an ancient star. In the centre of the chamber was a hinged ice casket with the lid open.

Vladimir turned to him. 'You are nothing but spirit; your flesh is just an illusion. When you are placed in here, the illusion will vanish. You will be reduced to your ethereal essence, and join the other phials in those walls.' He nodded at the alcoves.

There was nothing else for Nick to do but resign himself to his fate and go with dignity. He still couldn't quite believe it was happening. 'This is going to be the biggest mistake the Elfin Kingdom has ever made,' he said simply.

The guards went to manhandle him, but he held up a hand and climbed silently into the casket. When the lid closed, he lay there for a minute, breathing quietly. Through the ice walls of the casket he saw the blurred outline of Vladimir and the guards leaving the chamber and closing the door.

The Ice Chamber

The seeping chill crept through Nickolai. His breath was turning to icicles on his lips and nose. *I suppose freezing to death is better than burning to death*, he thought, in a dim and disconnected way. He became aware of something hard against his chest. The claw hammer from the mines . . . it was still there! He struggled to reach his belt and wrenched the hammer out. Maybe there was a slim chance . . .

In desperation he began to hack away at the ice. But his hands were frozen and the ice unyielding.

It's no good. I'm really done for now. With a groan of defeat, Nickolai slumped back down. Despair engulfed him. This wasn't just his defeat, it was the whole world's . . . the world's children . . .

An image of Magda smiling triumphantly at a row of blank, joyless young faces suddenly jumped into his mind and he convulsed with rage. He couldn't let that happen! His head jerked up and banged on the lid of the casket. And there was something right in front of his face.

The coffin wasn't made entirely of ice! Right next to his nose was a solid silver bolt. The hinges of the casket lid were made of metal! If he could just wrench them off . . . but his arm was stiff now with the cold. He blew on his fingers, his breath making puffs in the air, and grasped the hammer in clumsy hands. Gathering every drop of energy left in him, he began to work away at the hinge, hacking and picking. The silver hammer was ingenious, designed to prize out the tiniest gems embedded in the walls of the mines.

Come on, you can do it. He gritted his teeth. Gradually, with immense effort, he managed to loosen the hinge and pull it free. He pushed with all his might, but the lid of the casket was already beginning to freeze over. Summoning up more energy from a desperate place somewhere deep inside him, he heaved and finally shifted the lid sideways. Yes! The other hinge was slightly displaced. He moved round, changed hands and began to work away at the second hinge. His breath was filling the whole casket now and his hands began to warm up as he worked.

Finally he had it free. With one last effort he placed his hand in the gap between the casket and the lid, and pushed the whole thing away from him. At first it didn't budge . . . then slowly, with a groan, it began to shift sideways. Then there was a big enough gap to pass through. Freedom!

Nick felt like a stiff old man as he clambered out of the casket and staggered over towards the door. It was encrusted with ice and a freezing mist swirled around it. He scanned the surface. No handle, nothing but blank metal. Except, on the right-hand side, a keyhole. But of course, no key. Only Vladimir would have that.

Once again Nick was swallowed up in despair. He leaned against the door and sank slowly down into a sitting position, his head in his hands.

His ears twitched as he heard a faint noise from somewhere above his head.

He leaped up again, his heart hammering, and stared intently at the solid mass of grey metal. Yes, there it was again – a scuffling sound from inside the door – muffled squeaks and a long chittering babble. His eye was caught by movement. One sparkling whisker popped out of the aperture of the lock. Then another. They waved at him before retreating back into the depths of the metal structure.

Nick recognized the whiskers immediately. It was Snowflake! Which meant Princess Krista herself must be somewhere on the other side of that door! He allowed himself a small parcel of hope, wrapped up tight, and waited, hardly daring to breathe.

With much squeaking and squirming, the white fluffy thing scrabbled around inside the chamber of the lock, turning this way and that. Occasionally a paw or a tail protruded from the keyhole, then dived back in. His tiny paws scraped against the metal, manipulating the complicated system. Nick watched in fascination, making a mental note never to underestimate white fluffy pets again. After much scrabbling and squeaking there was a series of quiet clicks and whirring noises. Finally, a muffled *thunk* sounded from deep within the great metal structure. It shifted on its hinges and sprang open a crack. Then came the best sound of all – a familiar voice from the other side, whispering.

'Come on, Snowflake, we're going in!'

The door groaned as it was pushed inwards and Krista burst into the room, wielding an axe. They both jumped in shock.

Nick could hardly believe his eyes. This was not the Krista he knew. She was pale-faced, tense, but the most remarkable difference was her attire. She was dressed as a boy – in olive-green breeches, heavy shirt, leather jerkin and a pointed hat jammed on her head, with all her tumble of golden curls scooped up into it. All trace of jewellery had gone. And no handbags in evidence, except for a shoulder bag slung carelessly round her body. She looked amazing. Like a proper friend.

'Shivering icicles, SB! You've managed to get out already! I was just coming in to rescue you! How in the name of Ursus did you do it?'

Silently, because his face was too frozen to speak, Nick held up the silver claw hammer.

She beamed at him. 'Oh, clever old thing, well done!' She gazed round the chamber with an expression of horror and gave an elaborate shudder. 'Eeeuw! Don't like the look of this place at all. C'mon, let's get out of here.'

Nick stared at her dumbfounded, swaying on his feet. He felt stiff as a board and his teeth were clattering like piano keys. 'B–but Y-your H-highness! What – why . . . I thought . . .'

'Oh, do shut up, SB. You sound like a tap dancing class! Come on, let's get a move on.'

'But—'

She sighed impatiently and grabbed him by the collar. 'Just come! I'll explain in the sleigh.'

Putting her finger to her lips, she led him out, shut the chamber door with a thud and began hustling him away down endless corridors, passageways and spiral staircases, dodging guards and servants. She seemed to know every nook and cranny of the palace. Finally they emerged from a side door into a quiet street. Outside, Agnethe, also disguised in a borrowed outfit, was waiting at the reins of a battered old delivery sledge.

'Get in the sleigh!' hissed Krista. 'Before anyone sees you! And stay down!' They piled into the goods area at the back. With feverish haste Agnethe threw a tarpaulin over them, twitched her ears and set off down the street, whisking them along the back routes of the Kingdom. In the dark tent beneath the tarpaulin, Nick and Krista stared at each other. He was beginning to warm up now and his mouth was able to form a sentence.

'Your Highness – I – er . . .'

'Oh, do stop all this Highness nonsense!' said Krista briskly. 'We're past all that now. Listen, I've got an

159

escape plan. Are you all right, SB? You look a tad peaky. Bit chilly in there, was it?'

Nick groped for words, not sure whether to laugh or cry. 'But – how come you believed I was the real Nickolai? It was impossible to tell the difference! Even I was beginning to wonder!' He felt as though he had been given a whole new life. Krista had believed in him. He had completely underestimated her.

Krista snorted. 'Oh, grown-ups, they're just a bunch of idiots! *I* could see who the real one was. Maybe I know you better than you do!'

'But the other one was so convincing!' blurted Nick.

'Yes, but he wasn't bolshy and stubborn like you! The real Nick would never have been so humble. The fake one just said what people wanted to hear.' She gave another snort of contempt. 'But I knew straight away. And so did Snowflake, of course.' She patted the creature. He emitted a series of warbling noises and waved his whiskers about. 'He's a little star, isn't he? These rodents can squeeze into any space, you know. Proper little mechanics they are too. I'll tell you what finally did it though, in that courtroom,' she rattled on. 'The look on your face when you found your Soulstone pendant gone!'

'How come you know so much about that?' said Nick incredulously. 'Your grandfather gave me that in private.'

'Yeah, but he gave me one yonks ago. Grampy's in on this, by the way.'

Nick's mouth dropped open. 'What?'

'Oh, yes.' She smiled in smug triumph at his surprise.

Nick felt as though the conversation had just galloped off and left him far behind. 'But – if your grandfather knew I was the real Nickolai, why did he let me go down to the Ice Chamber?'

Krista sighed and began to explain patiently, as if to a child. 'Because he wants everyone to believe that the real Nick is the other one. And that the demon version is safely imprisoned. That's why I had to smuggle you out in secret. He couldn't give me the key, 'cos there's only one and Vladimir has it.'

'But why didn't he just say?'

Krista sighed again. 'Look, this is all very top secret. He's sent me to get you out so you can go down to the NetherWorld without anyone knowing. He can't let you go officially, because the NetherWorld is forbidden to all elves. And in the meantime he can keep an eye on the other one. He's under constant supervision. They'll lock him up the minute he tries any funny business.'

Nick felt as though he was floundering in a sea of bewilderment. 'You mean, he's giving me – sort of unofficial permission to go to the NetherWorld, to try and find the cave?'

'Yes – well done, you caught up. But he can't be *seen* to be doing it.'

Nick's mind was weaving. 'But why didn't he let me go before?'

Krista rolled her eyes. 'Because things have changed

now. That fake version of you has thrown everyone. It means we have a demon in our midst. Everyone's so paranoid about Magda after the Fall. People panic and overreact very easily, as you may have noticed. Sometimes it's best to keep things under wraps.'

'So . . .' said Nick slowly, trying to piece it all together, 'I'm on a secret Mission . . .'

'. . . to go and find the cave and get the crystal. Then the demon version of you can be dealt with properly, and you'll have what you need to do the Mission.'

Nick let out a long breath. He stared at Krista as if seeing her for the very first time. How he had misjudged her! The spoiled princess, obsessed with trivial things, was a complete front. Underneath it was a steely character, capable of serious action. She was the heir to the Kingdom, after all, and she would be running it some day. A girl like that, with her intelligence . . . of course Vilmar had been training her for her eventual role.

As Nick tried to process all this new information, he suddenly felt a terrible pang. 'But what about my mother? She didn't stop it happening!' He felt a lump rising in his throat.

Krista's face softened. 'She was in a difficult situation, Nick. Can you imagine how it must have felt to see a replica of your son walk in the door? And then the two of you start fighting!'

'But she let them take me away! She turned her back on me!'

Krista put her arm round his shoulder 'No, she didn't, silly! She tried to save you, then Grampy took her aside pretty sharpish. She's in on this too! Grampy's asked her permission to let you go – to do what you have to do. She's terrified of the risks, of course, but she knows you'll never be able to live with yourself if you let all those children down. So she said yes.'

Nick remembered the last time he'd seen her, standing in their living room with that monstrous replica comforting her. His stomach curdled. 'So she's got to pretend? Live a charade, acting as though he's her real son?'

'Don't worry. She's surrounded by guards, fully protected. We've made sure of that. She's a very strong woman, she'll carry it off.'

Nick felt as though he'd stumbled into a parallel universe. It seemed he'd misjudged everyone and everything. But now he knew that his mother loved him, believed in him, and that so did Krista and the king. They *were* on his side after all. The Elfin Kingdom worked in mysterious ways. He glanced at Krista in her jaunty boyish outfit.

'Hang on a minute – why are you in that get-up?'

'Yes, it's rather stylish, don't you think? I sort of borrowed it from the servants' quarters. Thought it would be more practical for the journey.'

His brain did another somersault. 'What journey? It's only a sleigh ride through the Kingdom for you.'

Krista looked sheepish. 'Er – yes, well, that's the bit

that Grampy *hasn't* actually given permission for, unofficial or otherwise. Wasn't exactly part of his plan. I'm coming with you!' She gave him a triumphant grin.

Nick shook his head. 'Oh, no! No way are you coming with me! It's far too dangerous for—'

'A girl?' she finished for him. She snorted again. 'Puffcakes! We're in this together. And I'm fed up with just being a princess. It's so boring! All that fussing over necklaces and hairdos and what I'm going to wear.' She sighed dismissively. 'And anyway, I don't think you realize how committed I am to this Mission, SB.'

Nick couldn't bear the thought of anything happening to this astonishing girl, now they'd started getting on. 'But – there's no need for you to risk your life as well! There's that terrible beast down there, and he nearly had me last time! I can't put you at risk again!'

She gave him a challenging look. 'Well, that's up to me, isn't it? And I reckon you're going to need help to find that cave. I'm coming with you, and that's that!'

One look at her face told him there was no arguing with her. He'd finally met his match – she was as stubborn as he was. He suddenly felt deeply ashamed that he'd ever suspected her of treachery. If they were going to survive this adventure, he had to clear the air between them.

'Listen, Princess,' he whispered in the darkness.

'Krista,' she reminded him.

'I've got a confession to make. For a while, I had these horrible suspicions about you. I thought that you wanted to take my place on the Mission. I was really jealous and paranoid. I'm sorry I ever thought that of you.'

Her blue eyes regarded him steadily under the gloom of the tarpaulin. 'That's OK, SB. I must admit I was quite jealous of you too, at first. I mean, one minute I'm the princess, OK, and we're celebrating Solstice Eve and you're this tiny baby and you and your mum have just won the race. Then this beastly witch woman appears out of a hole in the ground, with all these vile creatures from the Vortex. She had really bad breath, I remember. Yukkity yuk!' She grimaced at the memory. 'Then everything went dark and we all went to sleep. Then we woke up and everything was just as it had been before, only twelve years has gone by and all this stuff has happened. And you're suddenly the same age as me! And there's this big Mission and it's all your idea! And you're the centre of attention and you've done all this splendiferous stuff up on the surface, stuff I'd love to do and would never be allowed to because I'm a princess, all in a place where I've never been and will never be allowed to go. And I've missed it all!'

He looked at her and smiled sadly. 'You wouldn't have liked it, believe me. And I've missed out too. I'm in this place where I should have grown up, and I didn't.'

They smiled at each other. Nick knew with certainty that now the barriers were down they were going to be friends for the rest of their lives.

She took his hand. 'Well, there's no going back now. We're chums, OK?'

He blushed to his roots, hoping she couldn't see in the darkness. 'Yes. Definitely. And you can call me SB as much as you like.'

The sleigh lurched on, spiralling deeper and deeper, skirting the Moonstone mines and plunging further into the bowels of the Kingdom. Nick realized that the air was getting hotter. They had come to the edge of the NetherWorld. His heartbeat quickened with a delicious mixture of fear and excitement.

Agnethe slowed the sleigh till it came to a smooth halt. She lifted the tarpaulin off. Nick and Krista peered out and saw darkness all around them.

'This is as far as I can take you,' said the maidservant, glancing round with a nervous air. 'I'm still not happy about leaving you here, Highness. Are you sure you want to do this?'

Krista swung her legs over the side of the sleigh. 'Yes, Agnethe,' she said crisply. 'You work for me, and you do as I ask. That's it.' She kissed Snowflake's furry head and thrust him at her maidservant. 'Be a good boy, Snowflake. Please look after him for me, Agnethe. I'll be back. Come on, SB.'

She motioned Nick to clamber out of the sleigh. Krista turned to her maidservant. 'Go now, Agnethe! And try to delay the discovery of my absence as long as you can!'

'Your mother will have a fit, Highness,' said Agnethe, shaking her head.

'Oh, blow Mummy,' scoffed Krista. 'Tell her if she tries to dismiss you she'll have to answer to me when I get back. Now go!' She said it in such a commanding tone that Agnethe fell silent. Something about the princess brooked no argument now. Reluctantly Agnethe waved, turned the sleigh and shot away down the tunnel. Snowflake's squeaks of protest faded away.

The two adventurers turned to each other in a moment of silent comradeship.

'OK,' said Nick, a lot more bravely than he felt. 'Here goes.'

Hand in hand they crept along the dank tunnel, their hearts thumping in their chests, picking their way across the mushy ground beneath them. The place was already beginning to feel unstable.

'It all looks different from when we were last here,' muttered Krista. 'Pretty flaky place if you ask me.' She grabbed his hand. 'By the way, that beastie thing . . . any warning when he's going to attack, d'you think?'

'Not a lot, no. I really think you shouldn't come, Krista.'

'Nonsense!' she said. 'If you're going, I'm going.' She squeezed his hand rather tightly.

'OK, if you're sure.' Nick wasn't at all sure, but he tried not to think about the insanity of what they were doing. 'We'll just have to hope for the best.'

'So, where is this cave? Any idea where to start looking?'

'None at all,' admitted Nick. 'We'll just have to play it by ear.'

He flicked his ears, hoping to pick up some soundings of their whereabouts. Immediately everything began to shift around them; the walls heaved like a ship rolling in an unpredictable sea, and the tunnel lurched sideways into a steep curve. They screamed and began sliding down, then up again.

'Lean backwards!' shouted Nick, 'and try to dig your fingers and toes into the surface!'

They scrabbled desperately at the moist and crumbly rocks, but it was no good. Nick looked round and saw to his horror that they were sliding towards a dark ravine. Shrieking, they tumbled headlong, clinging to each other, until the ground beneath them gave way into black space. After a few moments of eternity, they landed with a splosh in what felt like a pool of warm treacle. A sulphurous stench filled their nostrils and steam rose gently from its bubbling surface.

They floundered around, treading water, trying to stay afloat. Next to Nick, Krista was gasping and spluttering, clinging on, threatening to drag him down.

'Just try and keep your head above the surface!' shouted Nick, struggling to support her. He saw the outline of a bank ahead of them. 'Look – there's land over there! Come on – swim towards it!' he cried in panic, as their combined weight threatened to pull them under.

'What does "swim" mean?' gasped Krista.

Nick realized with a shock that she didn't even know what swimming was. In the underground caverns of the Kingdom, everything was frozen solid. 'OK!' he said breathlessly. 'Hang on to me and I'll pull you along!'

He turned on his back, hooked his hands under Krista's armpits and began to swim towards the bank, trying not to think about what might be lurking below the surface. To his immense relief he felt no thrashing limbs. He continued dragging her through the heavy slime until he felt something solid underneath him. 'It's all right!' he cried. 'You can put your feet down now! Just wade the rest of the way.'

Krista stood upright, swaying uncertainly, and staggered through the syrupy water until they both reached the bank and clambered out, throwing themselves down. The ground squelched and sank beneath them like a pillow, but remained relatively firm. Krista lay gasping for breath for a moment, then sat up and looked down at herself. She was covered in slime.

'Eeeuw! Thank Ursus I didn't wear a ball gown!'

'It's going to be pretty mucky down here, so you'd better get used to it.'

Krista's Light Fairy fluttered around her anxiously, squeaking in alarm. In the dim glow Nick thought the princess looked rather blotchy. Suddenly he felt a stinging sensation on his left arm. He looked down and froze in horror.

A large slug-like creature, about the size of his thumb, had suctioned on to his forearm. It was a sickly translucent colour and made horrible sucking noises. He retched in shock and revulsion as he watched his own blood course steadily into it, filling it up and making it swell visibly. He screamed at the top of his voice and tried to pull it off, but it had latched on, clinging to him like a magnet. The glistening creatures were all over him, fastening themselves on like leeches.

Krista started screeching hysterically. He looked up and saw that she was covered too. That was no blotchiness he had noticed a moment ago. She was frantically trying to pull the creatures off, her face transfixed with horror.

'Aghhhhhh! Yuk! Help! They're everywhere! What are these creatures, SB? They're revolting!'

'Don't ask me!' Nick cried hoarsely, tearing desperately at himself. He could feel them stinging him all over now. He looked up and a spasm of horror lurched down his spine. More and more of the white pulsating creatures were crawling out of the swamp towards them, inching up the bank in a slow and steady tide.

The Swamp

Nick and Krista scrambled up the bank, backing away, trying to pull off the leeches. But the revolting things continued squirming towards them with relentless determination. Nick's stomach heaved as he watched them.

'I think I'm going to be sick!' gulped Krista, trying not to retch, hanging on to every shred of her self-control. 'Look at them! Hundreds and hundreds of them! I can't bear it! The blasted things won't come off! What are we going to do, Nick?'

Nick's mind raced feverishly. 'I'm blowed if I'm going to let these creatures suck the life out of us when we've only just got here. We'll have to think of some way of repelling them.'

Krista snorted. 'What do you suggest? Maybe we could ask them politely to leave us alone?'

Nick was grasping at straws. 'Come on, think! What could possibly put them off?'

'Ursus knows! Salt? Acid? Ice? Fire? None of which we have with us. Ugh! Get off, you horrible things!

How dare you?' She tore at the slugs.

'Some sort of chemical thing might put them off . . .'

Krista gasped and her face lit up. 'Hang on a minute! I think I might still have my perfume bottle in my bag! It's quite a strong substance, made from essence of snowberry and icicle flowers. We could try spraying that on them.'

Nick remembered the flowery fragrance that always seemed to linger round the princess. He smiled in spite of himself as she rummaged around in her shoulder bag. Girls always seemed to need to carry stuff around with them. But then her face dropped.

'Oh, blithering blisticles! I think it must have fallen out in the swamp!' She looked at the scummy water then back at Nick.

He groaned. She obviously wanted him to go in and get it. 'No way, Krista. If you expect me to go back in there . . .'

'But it's our only chance!' she pleaded.

Sighing heavily, Nick flung off his sodden blue cloak, squished through the jellied mass of crawling slugs and plunged into the water. He dived under, feeling the syrupy liquid close in all around him. It streamed into his nostrils and ears in a most revolting way. He held his breath, groping for the perfume bottle. More slugs were swirling around him.

The swamp wasn't too deep, so he lunged further and started rummaging around on the bottom. His fingers touched a solid shape sticking out of the mud. A large flute-shaped glass bottle. He grasped it, pulled, and it came away easily. He thrust himself up to the surface.

But something large and snake-like was tugging him back down, winding itself around his leg. It tightened its grip and pulled harder. His flesh crawled in horror. The writhing limbs of some octopus-like creature were everywhere. He caught a horrifying glimpse of a large, flabby mouth, bristling with teeth, and several pairs of black beady eyes ranged around a tiny head. Above him he heard the muffled sounds of Krista's screams.

'Come back, Nick! Now! There's something else in there!'

As if he hadn't guessed. He wrenched himself free, gasped for air and looked around. The water was full of thrashing limbs and tentacles. Much, much worse than the slugs. Dropping the bottle, he began to swim towards the bank as hard as he could, but the creatures were wrapping themselves around him with tenacious force.

He came up for another desperate gulp of air. Krista's voice echoed in the cave above the sploshing noises.

'Here!' she called. 'Try fighting them off with this!' He looked up and saw she was holding the axe she had brought with her to the Ice Chamber. 'Catch!'

Wondering whether this girl was a liability or a godsend he raised an arm to catch it, preparing to duck. The axe glinted in the reddish gloom as it sailed towards him. He reached up and – thank Ursus! – fielded it in his slippery grasp. At least she hadn't sliced his arm off. He felt a sharp tugging movement as something huge wrapped itself around his waist and he hacked fiercely at it, heedless of hurting himself. The thing slackened its grip, releasing a cloud of black blood that swirled around him. With desperate strokes Nickolai began to swim back to shore, stabbing at the monsters, lashing out at them on all sides as he flailed through the water.

He finally neared the bank, where Krista reached towards him and hauled him out. With shock, he noticed that the slugs were all over her.

They collapsed, panting with terror and revulsion. The creatures in the swamp subsided under the surface, but the army of slugs had surrounded them now, a tide of glistening, pulsating whiteness.

'Did you get the perfume bottle?' she asked breathlessly, staring at him with wild eyes.

He couldn't believe it. 'No – funnily enough, I had other things on my mind! We don't know if it would have worked anyway.'

'What are we going to do now?' wailed Krista. The stinging was growing unbearable. 'It's no good,' she groaned, pulling a slug off her cheek. 'They're going to suck us dry! I'm beginning to feel faint already!'

'Shhh!' hissed Nick. He sat up, his ears twitching alertly.

'What is it?'

'I can hear something!'

From behind layers of rock, a muffled babble of children's voices floated towards them. The noise grew louder, echoing across the cavern. There was a huffing noise, and the rock face on the other side of the swamp sagged and gave way. A tunnel opened up. Waddling clumsily towards them came a strange dinosaur-like creature, with a mass of movement on her back. Nick recognized her immediately.

'It's her!' he whispered. 'That weird creature from last time.'

'Oh, my – yes, she rescued me, I remember now.'

The creature's tiny head swayed about as she swung her long neck to and fro to scold the row of caterwauling infants on her back. 'Quiet, children!' she rapped out in her strange croaky voice. 'We'll find out where the noise is coming from in a moment!'

She stopped as soon as she reached the bank on the other side and gazed across the swamp at them. 'Oh, lordylumps! It's those youngsters from above again! Well, twiddle my scales, whatever next?' She peered at them intently, and her beady little eyes took in the situation immediately. 'Ah. Swampworms. Hang on a moment. Soon sort that out for you.'

She took a deep breath and her scaly flanks ballooned like a pair of bellows.

'Great Ursus! What's going to happen now?' cried Krista in alarm.

The creature exhaled explosively, blowing out a

plume of fiery blue gas. It gusted towards them and enveloped them in a vaporous cloud. Surprisingly, it didn't smell of rotting vegetation, or sulphur, as you would have expected in a place like this, but of something far cleaner and sweeter. More like peppermints, or violets. As the gas swirled around them, the swampworms began to shrivel up. The ones already suctioned on to Nick and Krista's skin began to shrink, until they released their grip, curled up into balls and fell one by one on to the soggy ground.

Nick saw to his immense relief that the swampworms were retreating hastily over the bank, squirming backwards and diving for cover in the slimy water. The creature blew another blast of blue gas across the swamp. There was a violent movement and the underwater monsters turned tail and fled, leaving a stream of bubbles as their limbs thrashed around in their haste to get away. The cave went quiet and the surface settled down to a gentle simmering calm.

'How did she do that?' said Krista wonderingly. 'Jolly clever, don't you think?'

'Fossil gas!' replied the creature. 'Works every time. Now stay there, dearies, I'll be with you in a moment. Hang on tight, children.'

With a resounding gloop she dived into the swamp, her long body slicing through the surface, and swam steadily towards them. The half-submerged babies gurgled noisily. Moments later she hauled herself up the bank. The babies came up one by one, popping above the surface and gasping for breath as their mother shook herself like a dog. Nick and Krista recoiled as swampy slime sprayed all around them.

As soon as they saw the two young elves on the bank, the baby dinosaurs squealed in delight, leaped off their mother's back and scampered towards them. In moments, Nick and Krista were surrounded by the weird little creatures. They swarmed around them, snuffling like eager puppies, vying for attention. Petronella let out a shriek of alarm and buzzed anxiously above Krista's head.

'Down, children!' cried the dinosaur sternly. 'Don't crowd them!'

The babies backed off obediently and sat in a circle, regarding the two strangers with unblinking eyes, wagging their tails furiously.

'Sorry about my children,' said the creature. 'They get a little overenthusiastic.'

Nick and Krista gaped at the ring of baby dinosaurs, at a loss for words.

'Well, they're an improvement on the slugs,' muttered Nick, not sure what to make of these new life forms. They were miniature versions of their mother, with scaly skins, long necks and a wavy crest running from their heads all the way down to their spiny tails.

'Actually, I think they're quite cute!' said Krista. She reached down and tickled one of them under the chin. He squealed with delight and the whole crew burst into a babble of excitement, surging forward for more attention. 'Go on, Nick.'

Gingerly Nick reached out and patted the nearest one on the head. 'Er, hello, little – er – thing . . .'

The dinosaur lady waddled forward and biffed the babies out of the way with her head. 'Run along now, children, out of my way!' She craned her neck down and planted her strange reptilian face right in front of them, revealing a snaggle of teeth in a lipless mouth, which was presumably her version of a smile.

'Hello, dearies,' she warbled. 'Moomsa's the name. Rescuing's the game. I try to look after people round here, especially those from above unfortunate enough to stray into these regions. It's a hobby of mine, really. This is not a very good place for anyone to be wandering around in. Pleased to meet you.'

There was a stunned silence, then Krista remembered her manners. 'Awfully pleased to meet you too,' she said politely, holding out her hand then retracting it hastily as she saw Moomsa's large reptilian claws. 'I'm the Crown Princess Krista, heir to the Elfin Kingdom, which as you may be aware is situated above us. Thanks awfully for getting rid of those ghastly creatures for us. And thanks also for rescuing me last time. I seem to remember something of it, but not much.'

'Don't mention it, dear,' said Moomsa. 'I heard your voices. Had to come and investigate.'

Nick began to wonder if he was dreaming. Then he

remembered his manners, scrambled up and brushed himself down (which was a fairly pointless exercise, since they were both still covered in slime). 'My name's Nickolai,' he said, attempting a courteous nod.

'And not just *any* Nickolai,' Krista cut in. 'He's *the* Nickolai! Saviour of the Kingdom!'

Nick glanced at her swiftly to see if she was being sarcastic, but her face seemed to be shining with pride.

'Oh, how nice, dearie,' warbled Moomsa. 'Very clever of you.'

'Don't tell me you haven't heard of him?' gasped Krista in astonishment. 'He's frightfully famous!'

'Can't say I have, dear. But I'll take your word for it.'

Krista looked almost put out. 'And he's a toy maker extraordinaire! You should see the things he makes!' Nick glanced at Krista again, in pleasant surprise. An unfamiliar warmth spread through him.

'How delightful!' said Moomsa. 'I don't know what toys are, but I'm sure my children would love them.'

Krista was cooing and making silly faces at the baby dinosaurs, who were now huddled together staring at them curiously. 'Oh, look at them! Bless! What delightful children you have,' she said to Moomsa, all princessy charm. 'Are they all yours?'

'Oh, yes,' said Moomsa proudly. 'Give me no end of trouble, but I love them dearly. Say hello, children!' The babies responded with a series of unintelligible gurgling noises. 'Aren't they sweet!' she crooned.

'They're enchanting,' agreed Krista.

'Yes, quite charming,' said Nick. The sense of unreality was overwhelming him now, but at least they were safe for the time being.

'Well, dearies, I think it's time we got you out of here,' announced Moomsa in a matter-of-fact way. 'Come along now. I'll take you to our refuge.'

'Where's that?' enquired Nick, still watching the babies, who were now wandering around on the bank, sniffing and snuffling at wormy things in the mud.

'It's an underwater cave, a safe haven where those amongst us who are civilized take refuge from the monster. He doesn't seem to like water.'

Both young elves stiffened at the mention of this and stared at her. Nick's heart clenched with terror again, remembering the terrible roaring, the dripping fangs and those glowing red eyes coming towards him.

'You mean, that big beast thing you rescued us from last time?' he croaked.

'Yes, dear – he's new round here. Not sure where he's come from, but I think it's something to do with that demon Light Fairy. The red job. Not a good sort at all.' She shook her frondy head and her crest rippled all the way down her back.

Nick shuddered. 'Yes, we know all about her. She's probably created the monster to destroy me.'

'Yes, you're probably quite right, dear. They're all in league with that she-devil from below.'

Krista shifted closer to Nick and grabbed his arm. He could feel her quaking against him. 'Have you seen him lately?' Her voice came out in whisper. 'The monster?'

'Not today, no, dear. But every time I spot him he seems to have grown a bit bigger and sprouted some new feature. I think this demon fairy has somehow made him out of fossil remains buried in the rocks down here – from some of the planet's most terrifying beasts of prey I shouldn't wonder. He has very highly developed tracking skills and a keen sense of smell.'

Nick shuddered again. Moomsa looked straight at him. 'I can sense your emotions are very strong, young man. He will be able to detect you easily. So keep your feelings in check.'

Instinctively Nick reached for the pendant and remembered it was missing. Yet another part of his evil replica's plot, to leave him as vulnerable as possible.

'Come along now, hop on. There's enough room if the babies squeeze up. I can offer you the only safe passage round here.'

Moomsa made a strange clip-clopping sound in her throat and the baby dinos scampered over and clambered on to her back. She jerked her long neck at Nick and Krista and swung it round to indicate her back. With a certain amount of trepidation they climbed on and settled between the little creatures. They set up an immediate clamour, jostling and wriggling, squabbling over who would sit closest to the new passengers. Moomsa's hide felt rough and scaly, but she was reassuringly warm and solid.

'This is most comfortable, madam,' said Krista graciously. 'And thanks awfully for offering us a lift.'

'That's quite all right, dearie. Now sit tight and enjoy the ride.'

Moomsa headed towards the nearest rock face. They felt her body swell underneath them as she took a deep breath and released an enormous blast of fossil gas. The rock face fell open and the strange entourage set off down the heaving tunnels, with only Petronella's glow to light up the gloom, and the babble of baby dinosaurs echoing all around.

The Law of the Jungle

The next few hours seemed like a strange dream to Nick. It was the most bizarre experience of his life so far. They rode along on Moomsa's back, sandwiched between baby dinosaurs, as she continued her stately progress through the NetherWorld. The whole place was lit by an eerie reddish glow. Petronella huddled on Krista's shoulder, watching the passing landscape, which seemed to be in constant heaving turmoil.

Occasionally, hideous faces seemed to leer at them out of the rocks, only to retreat again into the dark mass. The infants along Moomsa's back kept up a constant stream of gibberish, which only she seemed to understand. They wriggled and squabbled constantly, trying to clamber on to Nick or Krista's laps, or sit on their shoulders, until a bark of anger from their mother called them to order.

Moomsa seemed to know how to navigate the place and released regular blasts of fossil gas at the rock faces to open them up into new tunnels. When the ground suddenly dropped from beneath them, she was ready for it.

'Whoopsidaisy! Here goes!' she called out, as they lurched sideways, then plunged downwards at sickening speed. The tunnel began to sway like the deck of an old tub steamer in a storm. 'Hang on tight, everyone!' With amazing agility, Moomsa scuttled up and down the sides of the tunnel as it swung to and fro. Her great reptilian claws gripped the surface, defying gravity. Her passengers clung on tight, the babies shrieking with excitement as the chaotic ride went on.

Eventually the rocking movements slowed down and they continued on their way. After a while they noticed fleshy outcrops of fungi growing out of the walls, waving folds of rubbery growth as they passed. Moomsa huffed at them if they crept too close and they recoiled immediately. They came at last to the banks of the river. It oozed past them and wound sluggishly into the underground forest, where dripping branches overhung the banks on either side. The water shone with a dull metallic gleam and swirling masses of debris floated past on its surface. A foul stench of decay wafted through the air.

'We are now entering the jungle region,' announced Moomsa, as though they had arrived at the high point of a particularly nice excursion. 'But first we must cross the River Yolgulus.'

Nick gazed down into its murky depths, feeling very disinclined to enter yet another piece of slimy water.

*Nick and Krista clung on for dear life
as they lurched along . . .*

He hadn't enjoyed it much last time.

'I'm not sure I fancy another ducking,' said Krista.

'Looks like we've got no choice,' muttered Nick.

'Oh, frazzle my fronds, we'll be across it in no time,' said Moomsa heartily. 'Hang on tight!'

As she descended into the river the water rose steadily over them, covering their feet, their knees and their upper legs, until they were waist deep. It was unpleasantly warm and sticky on their skin. Moomsa swam with slow and steady strokes until they reached the other side. She clambered up the bank and shook herself out. The babies coughed and spluttered as they emerged one by one.

'Right – here goes, me dearies!' croaked Moomsa. 'Jungle tour coming up!' She wheeled around and plunged into the dense vegetation. Nick and Krista clung on for dear life as they lurched along, deeper and deeper into the heart of the strangest world they'd ever encountered. Never in a million years could Nick have imagined that such a hot and humid hellhole existed under the icy wonderland of the Elfin Kingdom.

All around them a raucous din echoed from the depths of the jungle: strangled cries, blood-curdling shrieks and nasty slithering noises. There were constant scufflings and skirmishes in the undergrowth, and occasional glimpses of hairy legs, tentacles and writhing limbs.

'Did you have any idea what this place was like?' Nick whispered to Krista, who was sitting in front of him with a particularly determined dinobaby settled on her lap. She turned her head to look at him. Her cap had been abandoned now in their wild goose chase through the NetherWorld, and her mane of curly hair kept blowing in his face, a pleasant reminder of the cleaner air above.

'No, actually. No one ever talks about it up there. Taboo subject. It's weirder than I could ever have thought possible. But at least we're still alive.'

The time ticked by as Moomsa crashed through the undergrowth at a fair pace, keeping close to the riverbank, which was overgrown with tangled roots and nasty squelchy things. Long tendrils reached towards them and trailed across their faces. Giant plants loomed out of nowhere, with yawning red mouths and sticky tongues, snapping ferociously at passing insects. The passengers ducked every time one came near.

'This place is getting worse by the minute,' groaned Nick, as something swooped past them, squawking loudly in their ears. They caught a fleeting glimpse of a monkey's face and a bird's body.

'Oh, take no notice of that, it's a bird monkey,' said Moomsa. 'They love showing off.'

'Are you sure these things can't get us?' gasped Nick, ducking as a large black whirring insect flew past his nose, making a sinister droning noise.

'I'll look after you, dear,' Moomsa called gaily over her shoulder.

Moments later a huge mottled snake dropped down

from above and coiled itself around Krista's waist. She screamed as it tried to lift her off Moomsa's back. The babies began squealing with fright.

'Nick! Help!'

Nick's stomach lurched in fear. He grabbed on to Krista's legs, but the snake was yanking her up with incredible strength. Moomsa's head snapped round like a whiplash and blew a gust of fossil gas at the python. Immediately he released his grip, dropped to the ground and slithered off into the undergrowth. Krista spent several moments gasping for breath.

'Great Ursus, Moomsa!'

'Don't worry, my dears, you'll soon get used to it,' said Moomsa in a comforting voice.

'Er, we weren't exactly planning to stay that long,' said Nick. 'We're in a bit of a hurry, you see. I need to find – actually I was wondering if you could tell us—'

'Shh!' hissed Krista, digging her elbow into his chest. 'Just let things take their course for a while. It's rude to pester people and we're lucky to have been rescued. We can ask her about that when we get to the refuge.'

They came to a large bulge in the river, where the water swirled around towards the middle like a plughole. It looked deep, dark and very dangerous. The young elves gazed at it apprehensively.

'Don't tell me,' said Krista. 'We've got to go down there?'

'We'll be in the cave before you know it,' said Moomsa. 'Ready for the dive?'

'No!' shrieked Krista. Nick realized she had lost her nerve completely. She was as white as a sheet and shaking all over. 'It's no good!' she wailed. 'I can't bear going underwater!'

Nick felt his agitation rising. 'I said you shouldn't have come!' he cried hotly. 'This is no place for girls!'

'Oh, yeah?' stormed Krista, turning on Nick and squashing the baby behind her. 'Well, if you think girls are so useless, who was it rescued you from the Ice Chamber?'

Nick felt helpless and panicky. They had to go along with it and there was no turning back now. 'I didn't want you to come,' he said lamely. 'But we've got to do it! And—'

Nick was cut off as the jungle din rose to a deafening crescendo. Squawks and shrieks of alarm echoed all around. The ground began to shake beneath them, and something could be heard crashing through the trees in the not-too-far distance. Whatever it was sounded gigantic. The pounding grew louder and closer, until they heard the unmistakable sound of giant paws thundering along the ground towards them.

Moomsa let out a long gurgling cry of alarm. 'You've alerted the monster!' she cried. 'You silly boy, getting all het up like that! He's sensed you! There's no time to lose! Hold your breaths, close your eyes and hang on tight!'

189

Without further ado she took a flying leap and dived into the river. They wrapped themselves around her scaly flanks and clung on like limpets as the rank water swirled around them, pouring into their eyes and streaming up their nostrils. They spiralled into darkness. Pressure closed in all around them, filling their ears with muffled underwater sounds. A powerful force was sucking them down, then they were being pushed along a tight channel. After an infinity of this there was a popping noise, like a cork being pulled from a bottle, and sudden silence. Something closed behind them with a gentle thwock. Moomsa landed heavily and they were tipped off her back, tumbling on to a hard surface.

Nick took a breath, opened his eyes and saw a small cave. It was dank and rather dismal, but at least it was relatively dry. In front of them stood the strange half-elf with the domed head and the curly tusks, who had rescued Nick last time. He towered over them, a rough-hewn giant of a man. But he looked friendly enough.

'Welcome to our humble home,' he said in a gruff, snorty sort of voice, spraying spittle all over them through his fangs. 'Itsh not much, but itsh all we got. Pleashe join ush for shupper. My name is Fangle. And I believe you know each other.'

He waved a lumpen hand towards the corner, where a dark-haired figure in bedraggled furs crouched over a fire, cooking something.

Nick recognized Zak immediately. His familiar brown face lit up when he saw Nick and creased into a smile. He leaped up and ran towards Nick with his arms outstretched.

'Flying fishbones!' he cried. 'It is you, Nicku! I thought I'd never see you again!'

Nick's heart somersaulted with joy. 'Zak! How did you get down here?'

The Quest Thickens

Nick and Krista's clothes had dried surprisingly quickly in the humid air, although they still felt uncomfortably clammy. But Nick hardly noticed in his joy at seeing his old friend again. Zak looked weary and weather-beaten, but he was still his old self. Nick introduced him to Krista who, to his annoyance, seemed utterly fascinated with him. Zak told Nick everything that had happened since the last Solstice, and Nick interrogated him about Joe and Hannah, and all the people he'd grown up with in Norsk. 'And the flying reindeer. What about them? Are they still there in the forest?' he enquired anxiously.

'Yes. Think I saw one just as I was leaving, flying above the treetops. Don't worry, they'll be coming. They won't let you down.'

'And what about your people? Have you seen any sign of them?'

Zak's face clouded over. 'No, not a fishbone.'

'So why did you come down here?' asked Krista, who was staring at him goggle-eyed.

Zak brought out his tupilak and showed it to her. She stared at the strange, home-made object.

'Crystalcakes! What's that?'

'It's my lucky charm,' he told her. 'I made it myself, to ward off evil spirits. It turned out to be a replica of Magda, didn't it, Nicku? The old hag version, under that mask of beauty. It started to grow warm and I knew it was a sign – it always warns me of danger. I just had a feeling that Nicku was in trouble. So I found a crack in the ice, climbed down it, and landed up here. And then this terrible roaring beast was coming towards me, and Moomsa came, and got me out in the nick of time.'

Krista continued staring at him in wonder. 'Gosh. So you spend your whole time living up there on the surface? In all that ice and snow? How do you survive?'

'Oh, there are ways and means,' said Zak nonchalantly. 'My people are very resourceful.'

Krista let out a long admiring breath. 'Gosh, you must be terribly clever people, you Inuit.'

Zak shrugged modestly and Nick felt even more uncomfortable. He didn't want the princess to be *too* impressed with Zak – and, anyway, he was itching to get on with the Quest. Time was ticking on, anxiety was gnawing at his guts, and he was bursting with questions. He was haunted by Magda's beautiful but evil face, restored by stolen youth, and images of blank-faced children waking up on Yuletide morning, not even caring what was in their stockings. His replica would probably leave lumps of coal instead.

'Er – Moomsa, Fangle, I'm – *we're* – on a very important Mission. We're trying to find . . .'

Krista shot him a warning glance and he trailed off. 'Wait for the right moment!' she hissed. Nick made a superhuman effort to control his impatience.

'Dinner's ready, dearies,' called Moomsa, chivvying her infants towards a trench dug out of the cave floor. Fangle began dishing out something hot and smelly and they fell upon their food like ravenous puppies.

Then Moomsa, Fangle, Zak, Nick and Krista settled down in a circle round the fire. Dinner turned out to be lava nuts and pigfish, considered to be something of a delicacy in the NetherWorld. It could be caught in the many creeks and backwaters, and Fangle assured them it was quite harmless if you cooked it straight away. He served their dinner with great ceremony, on crude platters made out of some beaten metal retrieved from the river.

Nick and Krista stared at the gooey mixture on their plates with immense distrust.

'Eat!' commanded Fangle. 'It'll put hairsh on your chesht.' He tapped his own, which resembled a shaggy hearthrug.

They exchanged amused glances and took a tentative bite. Surprisingly it didn't taste too bad at all, rather like salty chicken. Fangle began chomping heartily, spilling food down his front. Moomsa ate in a more ladylike manner, craning her long neck down to eat straight out of the bowl.

'It is very kind of you to invite us to dine with you,' said Krista, 'in your cave, which is most charming. And to share with us what little you have.'

'Oh there'sh plenty more where that came from,' said Fangle heartily, spitting food everywhere. 'And there'sh blitherbug pudding for afterwardsh. Yum!'

Krista let her plate drop and stared at Fangle with a horrified expression. '*Blitherbug?*'

'Yesh! Thoshe black hairy inshect things flying around in the jungle,' said Fangle cheerfully. 'Make a droning noishe. Delishous when you fry them in a little rock-shalt butter and sugar cryshtal. Crunchesh them up a treat.'

Krista's face went green and Nick nearly gagged.

'Come on, you two,' whispered Zak. 'You'll get used to it. And we've got to eat.'

Krista smiled weakly and forced more food down. 'So, are you both from round these parts?' she enquired. Her childhood training in polite dinner conversation had been very rigorous.

'Yes, dearie,' said Moomsa. 'We're NetherWorld citizens. I myself derive from a noble and ancient race.' She preened with pride. 'Unlike my companion here.'

Fangle began to bristle. 'Fungushrot and pishwash!' he spluttered. 'I don't give two shlugs what my originsh are. But I do know I have shome elfin blood in me.' He flapped his large wavy ears, which Nick thought bore only a passing resemblance to an elf's ears.

'Twiddletosh!' exclaimed Moomsa. 'You know you've got goblin blood in you. I mean, let's face it, the rock you came from was pretty low down in the strata, near the Vortex.'

Fangle threw down his plate with a clatter and glared at her with flaring nostrils and flaming eyes. It was not a pretty sight. 'How dare you!' he snorted furiously, spraying food all round the cave. 'I don't know exactly what kind of rock I came from, but I am not a goblin! And my Light Fairy is not a demon! Torquil may be a bit wayward, but she's not one of *them*!'

The baby dinosaurs, who had been sleeping in a twitching mound in the corner, woke up and began whimpering in alarm.

'Oh, look now, you've woken the children,' tsked Moomsa. 'And we've got guests too! What will they think of us?' She swung her neck round to stare at them. 'Don't take any notice of our squabbles, dearies. We like each other really. The truth is, we're all of us strange mixed-up creatures down here. The stray Light Fairies who slipped down here on the night of the Creation created us all out of the rocks. The results were somewhat haphazard, as you can see. I'm not sure where my fairy is. I think I may have swallowed her by mistake.'

'Yesh! At leasht *I've* got one!' muttered Fangle furiously.

'So where is she?' asked Nick, glancing round. 'And the other ones?' He remembered the dingy glowing swarm that had flitted around their rescuers last time.

Fangle glowered. 'The Peshkies? We keep them in a shafe place, only let them out for a short while after shupper.'

Moomsa gave a warbling sigh. 'They are quite a handful. Mischievous, but quite harmless, strays with no owners. Lost souls, all of them. But the red ones, well, they're a different matter. They're demons. They are the Light Fairies who've escaped from the Vortex, from banished elves. And when they touch the rocks down there, they turn them into goblins.' She looked pointedly at Fangle.

He glared back at her. 'I tell you, I am not a goblin!'

Krista gave a delicate shudder. 'Yes, well, we know all about demons and goblins. And occasionally we get stray Light Fairies up in the Kingdom too. This is one of the reasons we're down here.'

She threw a meaningful glance at Nick and he took this as his cue. 'I think it's time I explained our reasons for being here,' he began. He took a deep breath and told their hosts the whole story, right from the time when Magda returned from exile to destroy the Kingdom, up to the present moment. When he'd finished Fangle and Moomsa shook their heads and tutted loudly.

'Well, what a story!' murmured Moomsa.

'Bad bushinesshh, eh?' muttered Fangle.

'We've been watching that demon fairy for some time,' said Moomsa heavily. 'Knew she was a bad lot. And then when this monster appeared we knew it was her doing. She's obviously a servant of Magda, the evil Queen.'

Everyone shuddered as if her presence was around them.

'Yes,' Nick continued in mounting agitation. 'The consequences are too awful even to think about. So we've got to find this Cave of the Crystal Chronicle as soon as possible because I need the original crystal to carry out my Mission – and to undo all this terrible damage. But we're running out of time now. We've got to sort it all out before Solstice Eve.'

Pessimistic murmurs and much head-shaking came from their hosts. Fangle made a strange whistling sound through his teeth. 'Shounds like an imposhible Mission! And what about the monshter? He'll hunt you down the minute you try and leave thish cave!'

'And even without him in your way, you'd never find the cave you speak of,' warbled Moomsa. 'Not if it lies at True North. No one can ever find that.'

'But I thought with my special powers I might be able to pin it down!' cried Nick. 'I thought people like you might have some idea where it was!' Krista shot him a warning glance, but he felt as though he was trying to hang on to a tiny thread of hope that kept ravelling out of his reach.

'No, dear, not us. However,' Moomsa sat up straight, 'there is one possibility . . .'

Nick leaned forward. 'What's that?'

She began weaving her tiny head around thoughtfully. 'Yes . . . if you could resurrect one of the Ancients . . .'

'Oh, pwishtush!' spluttered Fangle. 'Not another of your nonshenshe theories.'

Moomsa snorted in indignation and looked down her nose at him. 'I'll have you know that the rock I came from contained fossils from a proud and ancient race of creatures, a race that roamed the earth many, many thousands of years ago.'

Zak gasped. 'Sedna's toenails! I thought you looked familiar! You mean dinotuks, don't you? My grandfather used to tell stories about them.'

'I've never known our proper name,' said Moomsa dreamily. 'All I know is I have some of that blood in me. They died out eventually. But after them came more creatures, who were stronger and cleverer than us. Tall and magnificent . . . wonderful tusks . . . great foragers and navigators they were. If you could find the remains of one and bring it back to life, it might lead you to the right place.'

Nick's ears twitched in suspense. 'Where should we look?'

'Up above,' said Moomsa, waving her head at the ceiling. 'They lived much further south than here, in warmer climes.'

'But that'll take ages!' exploded Nick, ignoring another reproachful glare from Krista. 'And we haven't much time. Why can't *you* do it, Moomsa? You're an Ancient One.'

Her long face took on a solemn expression. 'Not really, dear. I'm a mixture.'

'Hah!' said Fangle. 'She's not as posh-fangled as she makesh out! It'sh worth a try, anyway. But you'll shtill have to evade the monshter, whatever you do.'

There was a heavy silence in the cave as everyone digested this information. Nick groaned at the enormity of the task ahead of him. It really was looking like an impossible Mission now.

'I say!' cried Krista. 'Does this mean we've got to go up to the surface? To the world above?'

'Yeah, looks like it,' said Nick gloomily. 'But I don't know if we're going to be able to carry this off, Krista. I was hoping we could just come down here and find the Cave of the Crystal Chronicle somehow. Now it looks as if it's not going to be that simple. And if we've got to go up to the surface and start hunting around for ancient remains . . .' He subsided into a heap of despond.

But Krista was quivering with anticipation. 'I don't care! We've got to try. And I can't wait to see it! The surface! I'll be the only elf apart from you who's ever been up there!'

'It's very cold,' Nick warned her. 'Isn't it, Zak?'

But Zak had gone very quiet; he was thinking

deeply, staring into the meagre fire. Suddenly he jerked like a puppet and leaped up. 'I think I know what Moomsa's talking about!' he cried. His black eyes were shining with excitement. 'I found something like that on my way up here! It was a pair of tusks sticking out of the frozen mud! They looked like this!' He made a shape with his arms. 'They were huge, like young trees! Sedna knows what was lying beneath the surface, but maybe they belong to one of them! I'm sure I can find it again!'

There were cries of enthusiasm all round. But Nick still felt sceptical about the whole plan. 'This is all very well, but how do we resurrect this ancient relic? And how do we get up there? The king has put a magnetic lock on all the rocks in the Kingdom, even down here, so no elf can bust their way out.' He turned to Moomsa. 'Can you come with us? Open the rocks with that fossil gas?'

She shook her frondy head. 'Oh, no, dear. I'm not taking my babies and I won't leave them behind.'

Nick slumped in despair again.

'But there are other ways and means,' she added.

'What are they?'

'Ah, yesh. About time you met them,' said Fangle. 'It'sh time for their evening outing.'

He stood up and shambled over to a small opening in the cave wall. He pulled out a rock wedged in the hole and a stream of luminous flying creatures flew out, scattering everywhere. All of them glowed with a lurid greenish-brown or purplish tinge, like dim stars. Petronella gave a squeak of alarm and dived down Krista's front.

'There you are,' said Fangle, waving his hand at the seething mass. 'Meet the Peshkies. Shtrays with nothing better to do than caushe mischief.'

Everyone watched as they bounced off the walls with anarchic glee.

'Somehow you're going to have to find a way to tame them, dear,' said Moomsa kindly. 'And if you can get them on your side, you'll find them the best allies in the world. They can move the rocks and help you find a way up to the surface. And when you find your ancient relic – well, if they can bring dead rocks alive, there's no knowing what they might be able to do.'

Nick stared at the swarm of Peskies, who were now zigzagging round the cave like a nest of crazed hornets. The buzzing noise was deafening.

'Besht of luck,' chortled Fangle. 'You're going to need it.'

Secrets

The whole Kingdom was thrown into chaos when the news broke out that the Crown Princess Krista had gone missing. Search parties scattered to all corners of the city, which was sealed off and patrolled day and night. Rumours ran riot and town criers rushed around, clanging their bells and shouting out conflicting theories.

'Oyez! Princess goes missing!'

'Oh nay! Princess feared dead!'

'Heir to Kingdom kidnapped by goblins!'

'Princess escapes to surface!'

'Who is responsible? Let the people decide!'

A news embargo was quickly imposed and the town criers' bells fell silent. Instead of transmitting news pictures, the Crystal Chronicle disc in Solstice Square played bland elfin tunes and showed soothing images of dancing Light Fairies. The square no longer thronged with elves, but stood silent and empty; occasional passers-by would hurry through, speaking in nervous whispers. A hush settled over the ice streets and tunnels, grottos and alleyways, courtyards and marketplaces; all were quiet and deserted, as the elves lived in daily fear and anxiety.

Up at the Ursus Palace, a pall of doom hung over the glittering corridors and staterooms. The servants passed to and fro like ghosts, speaking in low voices. Olga was nowhere to be seen, Ivan was grim and stony-faced, and Vilmar looked another hundred years older. His whole body seemed to have shrunk to a fragile wisp; he shuffled around the palace, hunched in deep thought, his ancient brow knitted in a constant frown. He was shut away in council meetings all day and into the night.

In all this turmoil the Solstice Mission faded into the background. As far as the populace was concerned Nickolai was carrying on with his at work at the Equinox Plaza.

But Anatole knew better.

It was a small nagging doubt at first, but with each passing day he became more and more convinced that something was amiss. This Nickolai who came to work every morning wasn't his usual self, somehow. And there were more palace guards here now, posted all around the Plaza. Nickolai couldn't move a muscle without several of them materializing at his side in an instant.

Anatole stood watching him now, inspecing a toy which he'd invented from his memories of the Golden City above. It was a golden statuette of Queen Magda, which had started out with black eyes that glowed like coals and a head that swivelled, emitting tinny proclamations. At the flick of a switch she turned into coal, then back again into gold. Except now, that seemed to have changed.

'This is definitely one of my favourites,' said the boy who was supposed to be Nickolai. 'One of my best, don't you think, Anatole?'

'Yes . . .' said Anatole distractedly, watching closely. He suppressed a jolt of surprise and felt prickles of shock run down his spine. For a split second he thought he had seen a strange red gleam in the boy's eyes. He looked again and saw that it had gone. Maybe he had imagined it.

'Yes, well, I think this one's ready to go into production now. Let's give it another test run.' He pressed a switch and the whole thing went into operation again. The model statue of Magda in her golden robe sprang into action. The eyes sparkled like diamonds, instead of burning coals. It swivelled its tiny head, but instead of screeching out the usual messages it began to sing sweetly. 'Follow me and I will show you true happiness and joy,' it sang. 'In my Kingdom every child will have a lovely toy . . .' Anatole waited for the statue to turn into coal, but it didn't.

The workshop elves looked at each other in puzzlement. Anatole scratched his head, making his gingery mop of hair stand up on end. 'You know, it's

205

funny,' he mumbled vaguely, 'but it seems different from before.'

The Nickolai boy smiled a smile that didn't quite reach his eyes. 'Oh, yes, I made one or two design modifications. Don't want to scare the bra— little kiddies, do we?' His smile stayed on his face, but his pupils had a hard line round the edges. 'Anyway, let's not get distracted by unimportant details. No pressure, but we've loads to do . . . bizzeee bizzzeee bizzeeee . . .'

His voice made a strange rasping sound as he said those last words, reminding Anatole of a buzzing insect. Warning bells began to ring inside his head and a sudden flash of insight told him he was in the presence of evil. He felt as though he was suffocating. He made an excuse and loped quickly away, resolving to request a private audience with the king.

With mounting despair, Nick watched the Peskies cavorting round the cave. They were impossible. Just when they seemed to have settled down they would scatter again, flying in a thousand different directions like a swarm of bees. Fangle had been trying to teach him how to communicate with them.

'Feshtering fungushrot, you're not trying hard enough, boy!' cried Fangle. 'Try again. And conshentrate this time!'

Nick wished Fangle wasn't such an intimidating hulk – but he meant well, even if it was a bit disconcerting being sprayed every time he spoke.

'Come on now, boy!' trumpeted Fangle, his tiny eyes boring into Nick. He flapped his ears in encouragement. Nick closed his eyes and tried to imagine what the fairies were thinking. If anything. All he could hear in his head was a white noise, the fizzing babble of a multitude of squeaky voices speaking in a language he didn't understand. He tried to formulate some sort of command. *Cluster together!* his mind said. The fairies continued fizzing around, completely ignoring him.

'Try to relax your mind, you bone-brained elf!' woffled Fangle. 'And shtop twitching thoshe earsh. Look – watch this!'

Fangle composed his untidy bulk, closed his eyes and furrowed his massive domed brow. Slowly the fairies stilled their restless movement and gathered together obediently. Fangle opened his eyes, fixed them beadily on a point in the wall and waved a craggy hand towards it. The Peskies hesitated, then flew over and clustered round a spot in the rock face. They began darting at it repeatedly. After a few moments, a small fissure opened up. The fairies immediately stopped buzzing and the opening closed again.

Everyone gasped. The cave went very quiet.

'Gosh!' breathed Krista. 'You did all of that without saying anything.'

'It'sh not as easy as it looksh,' said Fangle sourly. 'Usually takes yearsh of practice.'

He flapped his ears in encouragement.

'It's all very well, but I can't hear what you're thinking!' protested Nick.

'Yesh. But they can!' Fangle explained.

'This is really stupid!' Nick cried. 'If only I could move the rocks the way I used to before. I just twitched my ears and they moved! But now there's this flipping magnetic lock on them.'

'These things are sent to try us, dear,' sighed Moomsa from her corner, where she was trying to clean her unruly heap of infants with a long rasping tongue.

'I did try to persuade Grampy to lift it,' said Krista. 'But he refused. Kept going on about security of the Kingdom. So that's it and all about it.' Petronella gave a twitter of agreement and flew up to sit on Krista's head.

'Well, these delinquentsh aren't subject to the rules of the Kingdom above, sho you're going to have to get them to do it for you,' said Fangle robustly. 'You can't always have thingsh your own way. Now, keep those earsh still and use the power of your mind.'

'Why don't you try holding my tupilak?' suggested Zak, who was sitting cross-legged on the floor next to Krista. 'It's good for focusing the mind. I use it when I'm hunting, and it helps me make a connection with the animal.'

Krista let out a sudden gasp. 'No, hang on a mo! I've got something better! In all the kerfuffle I completely forgot!' She pulled a pendant on a silver chain out of her front and held it up. The milky stone swung to and

209

fro, glowing in the firelight. 'My Soulstone! Grampy gave me one too, remember? It's supposed to help you communicate with the cosmos or something. I've never used it much.'

Nick remembered his own, which was probably still hanging round the neck of his replica, back in his home. He'd never really taken it that seriously either.

Krista held it out to him. 'Go on, you can borrow it.'

'It's worth a try,' said Moomsa.

Nick sighed and took it from her. It might just work.

Looping it round his neck he felt its coolness on his skin. He clasped it in his hand, closed his eyes and concentrated hard, trying to send out feelers from his mind to the dingy swarm of lights. Suddenly, to his amazement, the hubbub of tiny voices seemed to be making sense. It was as though a mist had cleared, and the sounds were touching on the edge of understanding. Not words so much as unformed woolly thoughts, vague urges, like the babbling flow of a river. The voices seemed to be saying, *Give us something to do!*

Encouraged, Nick half opened his eyes and through slitted eyelids saw that the glowing mass of Peskies had subsided into a wavery body of dim light. They hung in the air expectantly, as though waiting for something. A shiver of excitement ran through him. He'd got through to them! He tried to hold the moment, but the intensity became too much. His thoughts skittered away like beads from a broken necklace. The Peskies scattered and zigzagged around the cave in a riotous swarm. He had lost the connection.

Nick groaned and slumped to the floor. 'I give up! I can hear them now, but they're not listening to me!'

Fangle gave a snort of impatience.

'Oh, come on, SB! I'm dying to get up to the surface!' groaned Krista.

Zak leaped up and grasped him by the shoulders. 'This is not the Nickolai I know! You never used to give up so easily!' His black eyes flashed. 'Come on, Nicku! Keep trying!'

Anatole bowed low and approached the throne. His steps faltered as he saw the king. The change in him was shocking. Vilmar was so frail and hunched it seemed as though he would fold up and disappear. His eyes were hollow and sunken, and his cheeks looked almost transparent.

'My dear fellow,' he said in a quavery voice. 'What brings you here? Shouldn't you be in the Plaza? You are nearing completion on many of the production lines.'

'I wanted to see you, sir. I dare not speak of this to anyone else.'

A shadow crossed Vilmar's face. 'Come here, young man.' He gestured for Anatole to sit at the foot of his throne.

'It's about Nickolai, Your Majesty,' began Anatole.

Vilmar stiffened. 'And what would that be?'

'I don't think that one in the Plaza is him,' Anatole said bluntly. Tact and diplomacy had never been his forte.

Vilmar started in shock. He hadn't realized how observant the young man was. 'What makes you say that?'

'It's his eyes. They've got a red gleam in them. I've seen it several times now.'

'It's probably just a reflection, my boy. There's plenty of coloured Light in the Plaza.'

Anatole hesitated before continuing. What he was saying went against a ruling by the highest court in the realm, presided over by Vilmar himself. 'No, sir, it was coming from him. His eyes are cold and hard, and they've lost their sparkle. He's trying to hide it, but after a while you start noticing little things that the real Nick wouldn't say or do. And he's doing something awful to the toys in the workshop. Changing them. I think he's putting a spell on them, maybe to affect the children, hypnotize them into thinking Magda is a good thing. I think this is all part of some bigger plan . . .'

Vilmar seemed to fold up into himself a little more. He sighed heavily. 'This is a most serious statement you're making, young man. You are challenging a state decision. According to the elfin court, the real Nickolai's identity was proven beyond a doubt and the impostor was sent to the Ice Chamber.'

'But it isn't him!' cried Anatole vehemently. 'You've made a terrible mistake! I know him well enough! You sent the real Nick to a living death in the Ice Chamber! And that fake one's doing awful things! He may even have done away with the princess too!'

He waited for a wrathful reply to fall upon him, but it didn't. Instead Vilmar put a comforting hand on his shoulder. 'You have shown yourself to be much, much more intelligent and astute than most elves your age – but then, that is why you are in a position of such responsibility. I am proud of you. Can you imagine how the gravity of this situation has weighed on me since that day in the courtroom? I have hardly slept since! Now, I am going to tell you something that may comfort you a little. But it's a state secret, a secret of such importance that you must tell no one, do you understand?'

Anatole nodded.

'It's something that only I and one or two others know, and it's vital to everyone's safety that no one else finds out.' He took a deep breath and his voice shook slightly. 'The other Nickolai – the real one – is not in the Ice Chamber. My granddaughter helped him escape!'

Anatole's mouth dropped open into an astonished 'O'. 'Escaped! From the Ice Chamber? But where is she? And where is the real Nickolai?'

Vilmar's frown lines deepened. 'They are both on a secret Mission, in the NetherWorld. I had to let

Nickolai go, or the Solstice Mission would fail, but I could not be seen to permit it. He was supposed to be going alone, but unfortunately my wayward granddaughter disobeyed orders and went with him. She is as reckless and headstrong as he.'

'They are in the NetherWorld? The forbidden regions?' The colour drained from Anatole's cheeks.

'Yes. They are looking for the Cave of the Crystal Chronicle, to obtain the original crystal. He needs it to carry out the Mission.'

'So what about this other – Nickolai? The impostor? He must have the demon inside him, yes?' Anatole's pale eyes looked frightened.

'It's all under control. He is being watched very carefully. This is why a blanket of secrecy has been laid over the whole matter.'

Anatole stared blankly into space, trying to take it in. 'It's a risky game, sir. That other one – he may cause damage.'

'We have contained the situation,' said Vilmar. 'And now you know the truth you can help in the surveillance operation. Make sure Nickolai's original toy designs keep going ahead, and report back to me on a regular basis. And do not allow your doubts and suspicions to show. We do not want to alert the abomination.'

Anatole bowed. 'Yes, Your Majesty. It will be an honour to serve the Kingdom.'

Vilmar patted him on the shoulder. 'You are a loyal

citizen. I know I can rely on you. All we can do now is hope and pray that they both come back safe.'

Nick gathered himself together, clasped the Soulstone pendant tight and concentrated hard. This time the Peskies stayed hovering in an expectant mass. *Hold there!* Slowly, he swung his arm to point at a spot in the wall. The fairies flew over and clustered round it. *Now open the rocks*, he told them silently, in thoughts that weren't even formed into words. The Peskies began to dart at the wall in a concentrated swarm. With a creak and a groan, a small fissure began to open up, wider and wider, until it became a gap big enough for him to pass through. The fairies hovered, waiting for the next command.

There was a light pattering of applause, and Nick turned round to see Zak, Krista, Moomsa and Fangle beaming.

'Yesh! You've done it!' cried Fangle. 'You've won them over! You're ready to go up to the shurface now!'

The motley crew stood at a conjunction of three tunnels, the young adventurers preparing to take leave of their underworld hosts. Fangle handed Nick a small drawstring pouch made from the mottled skin of some reptilian creature. It contained all the Peskies except for Fangle's own Light Fairy Torquil, who nestled in the hairs on his chest.

'Now, lishten to me carefully,' snorted Fangle,

bringing his craggy face up close to Nick. His small eyes gleamed fiercely. 'Theshe are very precious to me, these Peshkies. Make sure you bring them back shafe. And get them back into the pouch when they've finished a task, or they'll just shcatter to the four winds.'

Nick wiped his eye and nodded. 'Yes, Fangle, I'll bring them back safe. And thanks ever so for the lessons. I wouldn't have been able to continue the Mission without your help.'

Fangle enveloped him in a hearty embrace, squashing Nick's head against his hearthrug of a chest.

Krista could barely conceal her excitement. 'Goodbye, and thanks awfully for all your help and hospitality. We won't forget this, up in the Kingdom.'

Petronella was peering doubtfully out of the top of her shirtfront, obviously not keen on the idea of going up to the surface.

'Yes, we'll never forget your kindness,' said Zak. He went to rub noses with Fangle and Moomsa, then thought better of it.

A chorus of sobs and whimpers came from Moomsa's back, where her infants were sitting in a dejected row, snivelling loudly.

'Oh, look, they don't want us to go!' cooed Krista, and she went up and patted their tufty heads one more time.

'They'll miss you dreadfully, dearies,' said Moomsa. 'They've become quite attached to you all. And I shall miss you too. Do try and come back to visit.' She dipped her head and nuzzled her departing guests with her rubbery nose. The wavy frill on her crown trembled with emotion. 'You take care now. And good luck with finding the Ancient One.'

After more sad goodbyes their underworld friends turned and lurched away down the tunnel, Moomsa plodding along, occasionally swinging her head round to look back, Fangle treading with his oddly dignified, lumbering gait. The three adventurers watched them go.

'Super people,' sighed Krista, 'although I can't see them at a palace ball.'

'Come on, let's get out of here,' muttered Zak. He seemed uneasy and his eyes darted around anxiously. 'I don't fancy meeting that monster again.'

'OK, let's find a good exit point.' Nick began to scan the rock face, looking for a suitable place. He opened the drawstring bag and the Peskies fluttered out. Taking hold of the pendant he prepared to command them.

A sound in the distance made them all freeze.

'What's that?' whispered Krista.

It was a slow and steady pounding at first, faint as a heartbeat, but gathering momentum. They glanced at each other.

'It's him, isn't it?' said Zak, looking grey underneath his brown skin.

The sound became louder and more distinct, a

thundering of gigantic paws. Then a blood-curdling roar echoed towards them.

'Quick, SB! Open the rocks!'

Trying not to let fear engulf him, Nick focused his mind in a single command and pointed at the rock face just above them. The Peskies gathered in formation, swooped up towards the ceiling and hovered there. Nick closed his mind against the din and willed them to start making an opening. *Come on.* The pounding noise was getting closer and closer, and the ground was shaking visibly now, as though a demon were rocking the foundations of the earth.

'Hurry!' cried Krista, her voice rising to hysteria.

'It's hard to concentrate!' said Nick through gritted teeth.

Krista and Zak clung together, watching anxiously while Nick continued willing the fairies to do his bidding. At last they began darting at the rock face. A small fissure opened up in the surface, then the edges sagged and closed up again, like a piece of loose material.

'It's too unstable here!' said Zak, his voice almost a scream. 'Try another place!'

Nick scanned the surface, but it all looked the same. He screwed up his concentration and willed the Peskies to attack the rock with more concentrated force. They dived repeatedly at the surface and the fissure gaped open once more to reveal a long, twisting shaft, snaking upwards into infinity. It undulated like a flabby tube and looked impossible to crawl along.

'How are we supposed to get along that?' whispered Krista in horror.

'We'll have to try!' muttered Nick. His heart was fluttering in his chest like a trapped bird. Time was running out. It was pitch black and the horrible pounding noise was filling his ears.

He was not prepared for what happened next.

Suddenly, the rock face behind them melted and collapsed. Their faces lit up as a gust of fiery gas shot towards them, scorching their hair and blasting their faces. A thunderous roar shook the world around them and echoed along the newly formed tunnel with a resounding boom.

'Sedna's teeth! It can breathe fire!' hissed Zak in terror. 'And melt rocks!'

Nick turned to look behind him. His heart lurched into his stomach when he saw what was bounding towards them with frightening speed. It was hard to make out in the gloom, because the creature was as black as night. But out of the darkness loomed a large panther's head, two burning red eyes, fangs as tall as pillars and two giant black paws, unleashing curved claws as long as sleighs.

Escape to the Surface

Nick, Krista and Zak stood rooted to the spot, numb with terror. The sheer scale of the creature was hard to take in. They could feel his hot breath, and the pounding of his giant paws filled their heads, as though there were no other sound in the world. The Peskies hovered around Nick, squealing in fright; his friends clutched at him in helpless horror.

Nick's feet squirmed; he must take control of the situation.

'Come on! Get into that opening, fast!' He glanced up at the fissure in the wall above them. 'You go first, Krista, we'll give you a leg up.'

Krista was staring down the tunnel, speechless with shock. Petronella gave a squeal of fright and dived down her front. She dragged her gaze away from the monster as the boys hoisted her on to their shoulders and shoved her into the saggy opening. 'Try and brace yourself with your hands and feet!' Nick called anxiously. Her legs flailed around as she hauled herself along.

'Go on, Zak!' Nick cried hoarsely. Zak clambered on to Nick's shoulders and scrambled into the opening. Through the undulating sides of the shaft he caught fleeting glimpses of Krista's slender body lurching around. He felt another scorching blast and glanced round. His heart almost stopped.

The huge, ferocious face was almost filling the tunnel now; you could see the individual rows of teeth ranged along the inside of its mouth, each one sharp as a dagger and taller than a fully grown man.

Zak reached out and hoisted Nick up into the shaft, moments before the monster's jaw snapped at the air beneath his feet. The Peskies swarmed in after him.

Nick began crawling up and away, his heart thumping painfully. He glanced down and saw a small section of the beast's terrifying face framed in the opening below him. Any moment now and there'd be another blast of that awesome firepower.

Quick. Close it up!

His mind was so paralysed with fear it seemed to have gone blank. He screwed it up into a ball and silently communicated his will. The Peskies buzzed around the opening and closed it with a dull sucking sound, shutting out the creature's snapping jaws. At once they were enveloped in thick, soupy darkness.

'Keep pulling yourselves up!' he called through the muffled silence. He could see their bodies wriggling along the twisting shaft ahead of him, scrabbling at the sides as they tried to get a grip. The fairies surged ahead of them in a glowing mass, veering this way and that as the tunnel twisted and turned like a snake. Moments later there was a roaring sound and a wave of heat passed through the rocks close by, scorching their skin.

'That was close,' shouted Zak. 'He nearly got us!'

'Just keep on moving!' Nick instructed, hoping against hope that the next blast would miss.

The Peskies flitted on, forcing their passage with lightning speed. The violent fire-blasts came without warning, but each time the fairies diverted the tunnel's course at the last moment. The strange convoy continued in this way for some time, squirming along the shaft as it zigzagged around, narrowly avoiding each blast of firepower. It was terrifying and exhausting, like being in a battle zone.

It must have been some time before the fire-blasts subsided. Gradually the rocks became more stable and felt cooler to the touch. They had reached the icy regions of the Upper Kingdom. The Peskies began to slow down and led them along further twists and turns, opening up more passages through the rocks until they emerged at last in an open space.

It was a large grotto, rugged walls streaming with moisture. The dim light from the fairies threw up the twisted shapes of stalagmites and stalactites. The adventurers sank to the ground, now reassuringly solid, panting with exhaustion. They were safe, for the time being at least.

Nick noticed a faint glimmer of light filtering down from above. 'Look! The surface!'

Krista stared at him breathlessly. 'Yes, but how do we get up there, SB?'

'There's no way up to the roof,' Zak pointed out. 'And no way out.'

'Wait – I've had an idea.' Nick held his pendant, closed his eyes and connected with the unruly swarm. He visualized what he wanted them to do. The Peskies started flitting round the cave, checking the place out. Suddenly they grouped together and dived towards a wall. They made a series of sharp, darting movements, and slowly an extraordinary sight began to materialize.

One by one a row of rough hands emerged from the rock face, palms turned upwards, ranged up the side of the cave. They jutted out like gnarled stumps, creating a rudimentary stairway leading to the roof. The hands beckoned at the children, inviting them.

'Well, shivering syllabubs!' breathed Krista. 'A living staircase! Is there anything these Peskies can't do?'

'Actually, they were doing what I told them to,' Nick pointed out. 'Wait and see what they do next. You'll like it.'

The fairies were clustering on the curved roof of the cavern now. They formed into an arrow shape and dived at it in a concentrated mass. A round, fat face began to take shape in the rock, with a grinning mouth and a bulbous nose. The mouth smiled wider and stretched open, pulling the rock apart. There was a splintering sound and fragments of ice and rock tumbled to the floor. A jagged opening had been created to the outside world, framing an oval of blue. Bright sunlight flooded into the cavern and an icy blast of cold Arctic air rushed in.

'At last!' breathed Zak, gazing up at the hole in the roof. 'Home! I was beginning to think I'd never see it again.'

Nick turned to Krista, who was gazing up in awe. 'There you are!' he beamed. 'The surface. The place you've always wanted to see. Are you ready to go up?'

The Land of the Midnight Sun

Zak was the first to emerge into the open. He threw his arms wide as though he was greeting an old friend and gulped in lungfuls of fresh air. 'Great bears alive! That's better!'

Nick came up next and helped Krista clamber out of the rough opening on to the surface. The hole closed up behind them immediately, and he stowed his pouch full of Peskies away in his belt. After the tropical heat of the NetherWorld the Arctic cold slammed into them and snatched their breath away. They stood silently for a few moments, blinking in the unfamiliar daylight. Endless white expanses of snow stretched for miles around, glittering in the sunshine. Horizons beckoned from afar, ringed with distant mountains and jagged ridges of ice. A vast canopy of blue sky arched overhead, streaked with passing clouds.

Krista stood as still as a statue, silenced by the grandeur. The biting wind tore at her hair and clothes, and her tumble of golden curls glinted in the sunshine. Eddies of snow whirled around her. Even in her boyish clothes she still looked like a princess, an ethereal being who had strayed into the real world. Petronella crept out from under her tunic and peeped out at the scenery. She warbled in alarm and disappeared, never to be seen again in daylight.

'So! Welcome to the land of the midnight sun!' cried Zak, waving a fur-covered arm at the scenery as if he had created it himself. 'My home!'

'What d'you think then?' asked Nick anxiously. Suddenly it was really important that Krista was impressed.

'It's beautiful,' she whispered. Tears filled her eyes, although it might have been the wind making them water, Nick wasn't sure.

'Is it like you imagined it?'

'Better!' she breathed. 'A thousand times better! The light!' She gazed up at the sky. 'And the blue! Where does it all end?'

'It goes on for ever. No one knows where it all stops. But during the winter the sky is dark all the time and the stars come out. It's like a carpet of diamonds, but above your head instead of under your feet.'

'I can't wait. All our streets and things are named after the heavens. Now I'll actually get to see them!' She turned to Nick. 'If I'd never met you I'd never have seen this place, SB.'

The enormity of his responsibility towards her suddenly hit Nick like a sledgehammer. She was an elfin princess who'd grown up in the lap of luxury, pampered and cosseted all her life, and here she was, in zero temperatures, shuddering with cold. Her teeth were chattering and her skin was turning blue. What was the point of the Mission if he didn't return with her safe and sound? He wouldn't want to carry on if she wasn't there with him as his friend.

He sprang into action. 'For Ursus' sake, what are we thinking of? We've got to get this girl protected against the cold! And me! Or neither of us will survive!'

Zak's face fell in alarm. 'Too right, Nicku. Let's see what we've got here.' He heaved his sealskin rucksack off his shoulders and began to pull out an astonishing collection of Inuit equipment, somehow carefully packed and squashed into the space. There were rolled-up furs, polar-bear hoods, sealskin boots, a selection of tools and cooking equipment, and a hide tent. They bundled themselves up in furs.

'You look like an Inuit girl now, Krista!' said Zak.

'Better? Feeling warmer now?' asked Nick. The two of them regarded her like a pair of anxious parents.

She had stopped shivering. 'Yes, I'm fine. Now stop fussing.' She looked down at herself and did a twirl. 'Quite stylish, I suppose. The furs do pong a bit though.'

Zak gave a snort. 'So what? They'll keep you warm. They're made from animal skins. You'll get used to it.'

'Yes, of course. I insisted on coming along, so I'd better get on with it, hadn't I?' She glanced around. 'And look at all this snow! Isn't it splendiferous?'

Taking a few experimental steps, she examined her footprints. 'What amazing stuff! How fun to have grown up with it everywhere!' Nick and Zak exchanged amused glances at her childlike delight. She kicked a few sprays up in the air, picked it up and sniffed it, then made a snowball and threw it at Nick. A small snowball fight ensued, until Krista stopped dead and pointed over to the left. 'What's that over there?'

They followed her gaze and saw a heap of charred and blackened stumps scarring the horizon like a row of rotten teeth. A shudder passed through Nick as he looked at them. 'That's what's left of the Golden City of Doransk. Do you really want to see it?'

'You bet!' said Krista enthusiastically.

They gathered up their belongings and set off towards the ruins. Her enthusiasm began to wane a little as they trekked across the wastes. The going was rough and despite the fierce sun a biting wind still blew across the landscape. When they finally passed through the derelict gates of what had once been Doransk, a bleak and desolate scene met their eyes. Blocks of fallen masonry scattered the ground and the broken remains of statues and columns lay crumbling into dust. Most of it had been covered over in drifts of snow and layers of ice; the old city was gradually being buried under the harsh onslaught of the elements, obliterated from the face of the earth.

Nick stared at the deserted city, memories flooding back of the strange times he had spent here. It all seemed like a dream now. They began to show Krista round, reminiscing about their adventures, describing how it had once been: the magnificent avenues and parks, the grand squares with their sparkling fountains and jewel-encrusted pavements, the old marketplace with its colourful stalls, the hill where Magda's gleaming castle had overlooked the city in all its splendour; and finally the grim, cheerless compounds where all the newcomers had been herded to live in shanty huts.

'What a place it must have been!' said Krista in amazement.

'It was a fool's paradise,' said Zak. 'Made of fool's gold. It ruined our lives!'

'All that glitters is not gold, that's what Joe told me, and he was right,' said Nick. 'You wouldn't have liked it, Krista, once you realized what it was really like underneath. The Elfin Kingdom is the real thing.'

They came at last to the scene of Nick's final confrontation with Magda in the main square of the city. A huge head, from Magda's biggest statue, lay on its side. The nose had caved in and the eyes were black sunken holes. They stared at it for a few moments and Zak let out a stream of Inuit curses, fumbling for his tupilak. Nick shuddered, and felt sure he could hear a faint echo of her voice rumbling up from beneath his feet, a deep heavy hissing sound. He shook his head; he must have been imagining it.

'Do you really think her demon fairy is trying to

resurrect her and take over the Mission?' whispered Krista.

Nick's face darkened like a shadow blotting out the sun. 'Yeah, probably, but she'll do it over my dead body!' He looked up at the sky. He could tell by its position that the sun would soon begin its downward slope towards the eternal night of winter, and he felt the relentless surge of time pressing on. The urgency returned, rising up in his chest.

He began to feel a gravitational pull inside him, the same as he had felt last time when he and his friends were travelling to the Pole in search of the Golden City. Except this time it was pointing south. It was like a natural compass inside him, pulling him towards his destiny.

'That reminds me. This isn't a joyride, it's a serious quest. We've got to find this Ancient One and get back here before the Winter Solstice. And we haven't much time!'

Zak slapped him on the back. 'First things first, Nicku. We need rest, shelter, a fire and food before we set off. Hey, where are you going?'

Nick was striding around with an air of great purpose, hunting through the piles of rubble.

'What are you looking for?'

His face alight, Nick turned to his friends. 'I've just had an idea! I was wondering if there was an old sledge lying around. There must be loads that got left behind. I thought—' He stopped and scratched his head.

'Well, I was hoping I might be able to use the forces to power a sleigh, like I did before. Then we can travel much faster.'

Krista sighed. 'You can't keep harking back to the past, SB. You have to deal with things the way they are now.'

Nick waved his arm wildly at the horizon. 'But – surely I can use my ears to power a sleigh up here? It's not against the law, and I did it before.'

Krista gave him a look of weary patience. 'You were using your family sleigh last time, remember? Book of Elfin Lore, Rulebook two, section one, rule number twenty-three. Only elfin sleighs, made from the Kingdom's precious minerals, can connect with the forces. An ordinary sleigh wouldn't work. So, no can do I'm afraid.'

Nick stamped his foot in the snow with frustration. 'Oh, blasting bugholes! There's always some boring little obstacle, isn't there?' His shoulders slumped as yet another spark of hope was squashed at birth. How on earth were they going to do it in time?

The journey was long and arduous. The sun shone round the clock, but provided little warmth against the biting winds. It beat down on them mercilessly, blinding them with its glare. Krista trudged resolutely along, keeping her eyes fixed on Zak as he led the way. Nick could tell she was finding it tough, but she brushed away all his concerns and refused to complain, or give in to exhaustion and cold. He began to realize that she was made of much sterner stuff than he'd thought. *What a girl!* he mused. You could search the world over and still not find a friend as special as her.

On and on they trekked, through the endless daylight, over the vast wilderness of ice and snow, while the sun circled slowly overhead like a bird of prey, watching their every move. They traversed huge ridges and troughs and passed under giant archways of ice that glittered in the sun like magnificent entrances to some forgotten city, but which led only to more endless, empty terrain. Nick guided their way like a walking compass, and Zak helped them navigate over the pits and troughs and ridges, always aware of the pitfalls.

Occasionally they would see a polar bear in the distance, its yellowish shape rising up against some towering precipice of ice, or etched sharply against the blue horizon, regarding them intently across the empty wastes. But apart from occasional sightings of bears, Arctic foxes, caribou and seals their journey proceeded without incident, through the never-ending days.

They hunted and fished, and Krista turned out to be quite good at it. They stopped at regular intervals to eat and rest in the hide tent, even though the sun still shone. But Nick found it hard to sleep, his mind plagued by restless thoughts. How long would it take them to get to where Zak had seen the tusks? Would they ever find them? And if they did, would they be able to resurrect the Ancient One? How long would it take them to get back up to the Pole? Would they return in time to stop his replica in the Kingdom carrying out his evil scheme? And what about the monster? Where was it now? Would they be able to defeat it and find the Cave of the Crystal Chronicle, so Nick could accomplish his ultimate Mission? Talking of which, where was everyone else in the world? They hadn't seen a soul for days.

Finally, after days of weary travelling, they saw a small line of figures on the horizon, moving at speed. The faint baying of dogs carried across the still, cold silence.

'Look!' cried Nick excitedly, pointing at the distant figures. 'People!'

Zak's face broke into a smile when he saw them. 'Yes! Some of *my* people! They must be following the caribou herds! I'll call them!'

He put his hands to his mouth and let out a shrill, piercing whistle that shot across the wastes like an arrow. The group of figures stopped, turned and raced towards them in a flurry of swishing blades and yapping dogs. As they drew closer they could see there were about ten Inuit in all, with several sleds drawn by husky dogs and a deer slung over a pole. In moments they were surrounded by a clamour of friendly brown faces and panting huskies, wheeling around excitedly. There was much greeting, chattering and rubbing of noses. Zak babbled away in his Inuit language, his face intensely animated. Then he took on the expression of a disappointed child. Nick knew at once that Zak had enquired after his family, but that there had been no sightings of his people.

After much gesticulation and chat the Inuit produced a sled laden with provisions, big enough for all of them to ride on, drawn by four sturdy husky dogs, and they continued their journey south at much greater speed, to Nick's relief.

Every time they came across a new tribe, Zak would make the same enquiries after his family, only to be met with the same disappointment.

As the weeks wore on, the sun began to dip in the sky a little more every day, making an ever increasing loop towards the horizon. The shadows grew longer, stalking them across the snow. Soon a faint sprinkling of stars began to appear for a while in the western sky, and they knew that autumn was approaching.

It was on an autumn morning, when dawn silvered the horizon and a grey light spread across the landscape, that they finally reached the Great Frozen Sea, cresting a ridge to find it spread out before them. Broken up into ice floes, it stretched as far as the eye could see like a giant jigsaw, its massive blocks jostling each other constantly. Distant icebergs rose above the horizon, their jagged white peaks poking up like icing on a cake.

They stopped the sled and gazed silently across the vast expanse.

Krista stared at it despondently. 'Well, here's the thing. How on earth are we going to get across that lot?'

Zak slapped her heartily on the back. 'There'll be a tribe along in a minute. The Nenet fish along this stretch. Then we can trade the sled in for a kayak.'

Sure enough, before long they ran into a small band of Inuit fishing at the edge of the icy sea, who dropped their nets and rushed towards them with effusive greetings. After the customary back-slappings and nose-rubbings, the sled and dogs were traded in for a kayak.

They were ready for the journey across the sea. Nick, Zak and Krista clambered into their newly acquired kayak with all their supplies, preparing to push off into the half-frozen ocean.

Krista glanced around nervously. 'Is this thing big enough for all of us? It's not going to overturn, is it?'

Zak grinned at her. 'I've been kayaking since I was five. Just relax.'

They readied themselves to set sail.

'One two three, away!' cried Zak.

Nick pushed their kayak away from the shore with his oar and the small craft cruised out into the icy water. It felt reasonably stable and everyone in the boat steadied themselves. They began to paddle smoothly, following Zak's instructions as he steered at the helm. Day had broken now and the sky hung grey and leaden above them, heavy with pot-bellied clouds. The

It seemed the gound itself was bellowing with rage.

shore receded as the boat sliced through the water with surprising speed. They were heading towards a wide gap between ice blocks when a commotion broke out behind them. Dogs yelped and cries of alarm shattered the peace. Nick turned to look, and froze.

The Inuit on the shore were scattering in terror. Just behind them, something was stirring underground. There was a deafening rumble from below. The ice was heaving and trembling, as though a huge force was pushing its way up from underneath.

'It's him!' cried Krista. 'He's followed us!'

'Keep paddling!' shouted Zak. 'We must get away!'

'But what about the Inuit?' protested Nick.

'There's nothing we can do. Paddle as fast as you can!'

The shore shook with violent tremors. It seemed the ground itself was bellowing with rage. Slowly the gigantic underground force pushed its way up, throwing out mounds of dislodged ice, blasting melted snow everywhere. There was an almighty roaring noise and a plume of fire rose high into the air. A hole blew open in the ground. Out of it came something so dark and unspeakable it was hard to comprehend. A giant black paw emerged over the edge of the rim, extending long sharp claws. The giant paw stretched further out of the gaping hole and clamped down heavily on the ground.

Nick gulped in shock. The monster must have tunnelled all the way here, using his firepower like a blowtorch, melting everything in his way. Another giant paw emerged from the hole and began to tear at the ground, scoring long deep gashes.

'Just keep on paddling!' screamed Zak, furiously gouging at the water in front of the kayak and aiming for a crack in the ice.

But they couldn't tear their eyes away. Seeing their predator slowly revealed in broad daylight was far worse than catching mere glimpses of him in the gloom of the NetherWorld. The head rose up first, a massive snarling panther head, coal-black and gleaming in the sunshine. Two red eyes glowed in the black face, burning with such hatred it made Nick's blood run cold. The great jaws were pulled back into a ferocious snarl, revealing those impossibly long, sharp fangs. Two black pointed ears twitched and rotated. The giant whiskers came out next, springing from the opening like thick wires and vibrating dangerously, sending out visible waves.

The creature hauled himself out of the fractured ground with the lithe grace of a cat, muscles rippling in the sun. Finally the rest of him emerged – a gigantic vision that blotted out the scenery: huge haunches, powerful legs, taut and gleaming, and a long tail, which unleashed itself and lashed around furiously, cracking like a whip in the cold air.

The red eyes scanned the area and alighted on the terrified crew in the kayak. They glowed like stoked embers and sent out terrible beams of scorching light.

The travellers stared in disbelief.

'What on earth is it? What kind of species has it come from?' whispered Nick.

Zak's eyes were black holes in a grey-brown face. 'I don't know. But if that demon fairy has created it out of fossil remains, my guess is it's a sabre-toothed tiger, mixed in with lots of other things. She's created a monster out of all the worst prehistoric beasts of prey she could find!'

The monster lifted his huge head and let out a deafening roar, then slunk rapidly to the shore, crouched low against the ground. He drew back at the water's edge with an angry snarl and began pacing restlessly back and forth along the shoreline, bellowing with rage.

'He's coming to get us!' screamed Krista, hysterical.

Nick suddenly remembered what Fangle and Moomsa had told them. 'He doesn't like water,' he yelled, 'so he can't follow us! If we paddle fast we might be able to get away! Out of the reach of the fire!'

Desperately they heaved at the oars, trying to propel the boat as fast as they could. The beast bellowed again and let out a long column of fire which shot across the surface towards them.

'Duck!' shouted Nick.

They threw themselves down, making the boat rock wildly. The plume of fire shot across their heads, narrowly missing them. Nick peered above the rim of the boat and saw that the beast was still pacing back and forth, beside himself with frustration. Then he stopped and steadied himself, quivering on his haunches like a cat about to pounce. A small flame of hope leaped and flickered. 'Maybe we *can* get away! Pull!'

But his hopes were dashed a moment later when the monster did something totally unexpected, something Nick had not been able to see in the darkness of the NetherWorld. The black beast licked his lips and leered horribly. Then with a measured, creaky flourish he unfurled a pair of enormous tarry wings that opened to a span of terrifying breadth, casting giant shadows across the landscape. They crackled horribly in the silence. Nick's head began to swim in terror, as the giant cat-bird rose into the air and began swooping towards them.

Mighty Beasts

Like an angel of death the monster flew towards them. The mouth gaped open and the talons stretched out, ready to claw them out of the water. Surely there was no hope for them now?

'So the wretched thing can fly!' whispered Krista. 'Moomsa said he kept sprouting new features! What are we going to do, SB?'

Nick's mouth went dry. His heart was thumping wildly as he watched the beast swooping towards them, a dark and unstoppable force. In a few seconds he would snatch them up and swallow them whole, boat and all, in one almighty gulp.

There was only one slim chance of survival, but as an alternative it was unthinkable: throwing themselves into the icy water, where the creature couldn't get at them. But they would freeze to death in moments. They were between the devil and the deep blue sea.

'We have to try and keep him at bay while I think of something!' Nick gasped.

Zak began rummaging frantically in the bottom of

the boat. 'Got loads of whale harpoons,' he said, fishing some out and handing them round.

They took aim and threw a shower of harpoons at the beast as he lunged towards them. One brushed past his whiskers with a twang, making a loud humming noise. The others just bounced off harmlessly, like tiny darts on a giant dartboard. But Krista threw one that went straight up his nostril and got stuck. It must have caused the monster pain, for he yelped and withdrew momentarily, snarling ferociously, trying to shake it out.

'Good shot, Princess!' shouted Zak.

'They always have a weak spot, monsters!' she yelled in triumph.

Nick looked at her admiringly. But the beast recovered and began looming towards them again.

'Water! We've got loads of it here!' called Krista. 'How about we try and get some out of the sea and throw it at him?'

'It's worth a try!' Zak dived into the bottom of the boat again and brought out some buckets and cooking pans. Desperately they dipped the buckets over the edge of the boat into the icy sea and as the monster drew closer hurled the water over him, spraying his face and eyes. He recoiled, howling, and drew back a little in mid-air.

'Come on, keep it up!' cried Nick.

But the beast quickly recovered and wheeled around, preparing for another attack.

'It's not going to keep him off for long!' Zak cried in panic.

'Just keep chucking the water at him and try and fend him off till I think of something better!' gasped Nick. Desperate thoughts were whirling around in his head. How else could they disable the creature? Maybe damage his wings? Force him down into the sea? He looked round frantically and in the distance saw a familiar Arctic sight: a whale's tail, breaking above the surface and flipping over lazily.

A wild thought came to him. He turned to Zak. 'Have you got any more harpoons? And a rope? Really strong rope?'

Without a word Zak rummaged around and brought out more harpoons and a coil of rope.

'Tough as steel. Made from fishgut. I've caught fully grown seals and walruses with this gear,' said Zak, handing it to him. Nick grabbed it and threw the rope round his shoulder. The monster had arced round and was storming in for the counter-attack. He loomed nearer. His jaws opened wider, filling their vision. The boat shuddered. There was a crunch, and loud splintering noises tore the air. The boat had been sandwiched between two ice floes that had crashed into each other. A spout of water shot up from the collision and spurted into the beast's face, drenching the enormous muzzle and eyes. He began thrashing around in mid-air, while the huge leathery wings flapped uncontrollably, trying to lift him away. It gave them a little more time.

Now was the moment to put his plan into action. Nick glanced at the grey giant in the waves, powering towards them. Their boat was being squeezed relentlessly between the two great slabs of ice.

'Out of the kayak! Now! Leap on to the ice floe!' The other two looked at him in bewilderment. 'It's our only chance!' he screamed in desperation. 'The boat's about to be crushed! Jump out now!'

They scrambled out of the kayak and leaped on to the slippery ice. 'Run to the other side!' Nick instructed. 'And stay together!'

The beast was recovering now, preparing for another lunge. The floe lurched, producing another spurt of water which shot up in front of him, making him recoil. Nick glanced round and his heart leaped with hope. The whale was nearly upon them now, breaking through the ice floes like the massive hull of a ship. There was a loud honking noise that echoed around the ocean like a ship's foghorn. The whale was signalling his support.

'Look!' cried Zak. 'It's the qammiq! The qammiq that helped us last time!'

'I know!' shouted Nick. 'And I reckon he's going to help us again! Stay here!'

'Where are you going, Nicku?'

'Hey, come back, SB!'

Before they could stop him, Nick was running across the ice floes, leaping from one block to the other, luring the monster away. He could hear the swishing noise of giant wings flapping overhead, feel his hot breath, hear the growling snarls coming from those jaws.

'Come and get me then, you horrible creature!' Nick cried, taunting him. 'You can't catch me!'

The beast roared in rage and lunged at him. He looked up and saw the claws stretching towards him, ready to snatch him up. Nimbly he ducked out of the way and leaped across to the next ice floe. He heard the beast bellowing in rage behind him.

The whale's shiny grey bulk heaved out of the water, now alongside. If he could time it right . . . a shadow fell over him. The creature was right overhead. He glanced up and saw his great scaly green underbelly. Beneath the viscous skin he could just make out a black beating heart, pulsing away like a giant pump. If only he could use his harpoon to spear it! But it was too risky; he might miss, and he needed the harpoon for his plan.

The whale reared up in front of him. He seized his chance. The monster was bearing down on him again. He continued running, ducking and diving, leading him away, at the same time uncoiling the rope from around his shoulders. He attached the harpoon to the end of it and, taking aim carefully, waited for his moment.

As the monster lunged at him again, he hurled the harpoon. It sang through the air and – yes! – hooked itself into his right nostril. He held his breath, hoping it would hold fast. The beast pulled away, but the harpoon stayed stuck. The more he pulled, the more firmly it embedded itself in his sensitive tissue. The beast had been ensnared!

He roared in rage and pulled away, dragging Nick into the air with him. Nick was jerked upwards and began dangling over the ice floes, swinging like a pendulum. He unfurled the rest of the rope and looked down. The whale's tail was breaking above the surface. Using his weight like a ball and chain he slid further down the rope, swung himself towards the mighty qammiq's tail and launched himself at it, pulling the rope with him. The rope caught round the giant's tail. Nick swung clear, then lurched back. He began to spin round and round the whale's tail on the end of the rope with dizzying speed. His plan had worked – the rope was wrapping itself around the tail like string round a bobbin. There was a judder as it pulled taut and Nick was jerked sideways like a puppet. He clung on to the rope by his fingertips. He had connected the two beasts! Like a circus acrobat on a high wire, he pulled himself up and along the rope, hand over hand.

A black bulk of fury thrashed above him and the great wings flapped and strained, engulfing him in gusts of wind. The whale was honking loudly, heaving around in the sea below, sending up huge gouts of water from the hole in his head. It was spraying the monster, distracting him; he was writhing in agony, twisting and turning in mid-air, trying to pull up and away from the whale and the spouting seawater. Nick gritted his teeth and clung on to the rope; he was being drenched in brine and the rope was getting slippery.

Glancing down he saw an ice floe edging into view. Time to bail out. He let go of the rope.

And fell.

Nickolai plummeted through the air like a stone. If he landed in the sea he would freeze in moments. He could hear screams in the background, and roars of rage and pain from the beast above. He landed with a bone-crushing thump on a cold, hard, slippery surface that lurched with the impact of his fall. Thank Ursus! He had landed on the block of ice. Shaken, but not injured, he scrambled to his knees and saw the whale's tail, still thrashing about in the water, attached by the rope to the beast's nostril.

The rope slackened then pulled taut repeatedly as the battle raged on. The whale wrenched the monster this way and that, dragging him down towards the sea. The monster tried to fly up, flapping his great wings, hauling the whale out of the water. It was an epic tug of war between two mighty beasts, pitching their strength against each other, and it seemed to go on for hours.

Finally, with a loud honk of outrage, the whale plunged under the sea in a mighty dive, creating an enormous down-swell, dragging the beast with him. Roaring and screaming horribly, the monster fizzled and steamed, sending out a sulphuric stench. The line snapped at last under the strain, and the whale swam off, waving his tail in a gesture of defiance, before plunging beneath the waves. The beast continued to flail around, bellowing horribly, until he finally slipped under an ice floe and sank beneath the waves. Black smoke belched out from the place where he had gone and bubbles rose to the surface.

Somehow Nick made his way back to the ice floe where he'd left his friends. The boat had been smashed to pieces like matchwood, and its fragments bobbed about in the water. But Zak had managed to rescue his sealskin rucksack and some of the equipment from the boat. He had also managed to catch a fish, which he was now cooking over a fire.

Krista sat hunched in her soaked furs, staring at Nick in wonder, as though she was seeing him for the first time. 'I still can't believe you did that, SB! You were amazing! I've never seen anything like it.'

Nick felt himself blushing. It was embarrassing, but nice at the same time. He shrugged modestly. 'Oh, well, had no choice really. Had to do something, eh?'

'So d'you think he'll come back? The monster?' said Krista through chattering teeth, glancing nervously at the place where the enormous thrashing beast had been swallowed up by the waves. 'Or have you finished him off?'

Nick really didn't want to think about that right now. 'I hope so! But we've still got to get across the water. And now we've got no boat.'

'And only one fish,' said Zak dismally, waving the stick with the fish on the end of it. 'Look. It's reducing as I cook it. There'll hardly be enough.'

They glanced at the fish. 'Oh, dear,' sighed Nick. 'Shame there's nothing bigger round here.' He suddenly felt the Peskies junketing around in the snakeskin pouch tied to his belt, where he'd secured them after they'd emerged on to the surface. Muffled squeaking noises erupted from within.

'I think they want to come out,' said Krista.

'Better not,' said Nick. 'They might fly away.'

'No, they won't,' said Zak. 'They're devoted to you now. I think they're trying to tell us something.'

Tentatively Nick untied the pouch and released the Peskies. They swarmed out in a mass, glowing against the grey sky, and flew over to the paltry fish on the end of Zak's stick. They buzzed around it purposefully, and before their eyes the thing began to grow. It expanded until it was the size of a prize sea bass, and Zak's stick began to groan under the weight of it.

'Wow! That's incredible!' cried an astonished Krista. 'They can make things grow, as well as moving them!'

'Shame we didn't know that before,' said Zak. 'But at least we won't starve tonight.'

After their meal Zak pitched the tent, driving his metal spikes into the surface of the ice floe. They huddled in there, bobbing about on the waves, dozing fitfully through the night.

It was at dawn that they were awoken by a babble of voices in the distance, the sound of oars plashing against the waves and clunking noises on the blocks of ice. Krista peered out of the tent.

'I say!' she cried, pointing in the distance. 'Look! What frightfully good sorts these Inuit people are!'

Nick and Zak peered out of the tent and saw several Inuit boats approaching them across the frozen sea, navigating between the ice floes. As they drew level, animated conversation took place between Zak and his people. He turned to them, his face alight.

'They saw everything. They're grateful that you've saved them from the monster! And now they've offered to escort us over the sea!'

The fleet of Inuit kayaks took them to the southern rim. On the other side another sledge and team of huskies were provided and the expedition continued. To Nick's relief, Krista was bearing up well under the rigours of life in the Arctic. Her pale skin was looking somewhat weather-beaten now, but her fragile beauty remained intact. Nick marvelled again at her toughness. When he'd first met that frivolous princess at his Homecoming Ball, he'd never in a million years have imagined that she'd turn into this feisty girl who could withstand ordeals like this. How wrong you can be about a person, he thought.

They travelled on.

The brief Autumn Equinox had passed and winter closed in, cloaking them in darkness. The sun had slipped below the horizon, not even returning for a brief glimpse. The nights stretched out and joined up into one endless pattern. Only the phases of the moon lit their way. Nick became even more anxious as the true depths of the night heavens were revealed in the inky blackness overhead. Vast constellations spread a thick carpet of light above them, twinkling in the velvety darkness. They camped under the stars, and after dinner they would lie by the fire gazing up at the galaxies.

'There's the Great Bear, look, lying over the pole. And Polaris, the Pole star. I used that to navigate when we were travelling up here before.'

'The Ursus Palace!' said Krista. 'That's what it's named after!'

'And there are the seven sisters, the Pleiades!' said Zak, who knew his astronomy better than anyone.

'That must be what the Seven Sisters quadrant is named after, in the east part of the Kingdom, where all the tunnels meet!'

The map of the heavens spread above them, guiding their way. Nick marvelled at it all, but still there was the nagging doubt gnawing away at him. Time was ticking by and the Winter Solstice was approaching. Again the haunting images of children all over the world, waking up on Yuletide morning with their childhood stolen, came back to plague him. He found it impossible to sleep during their short rest breaks; fidgety and restless, always anxious to keep moving on.

At last the ice-packed wilderness began to give way to open scrubby tundra, covered with the first snows of winter. The trek continued until one night, they came out through a narrow gorge cut between two rocky ridges and saw a barren plain stretching before them. It glistened eerily in the moonlight, grey and desolate. In the distance could be seen what looked like the curved, bare branches of a tree growing out of a cleft in the ground.

'There they are!' cried Zak excitedly. 'I knew my sense of direction was right! I knew I'd find them again!'

They began trudging across the plain towards the tusks. The closer they got, the taller they loomed, soaring out of the ground in two curved arcs like a pair of saplings. Nick's apprehension mounted. Would they belong to an Ancient One after all? Would it be a complete set of remains? And would the Peskies be able to resurrect it? When they drew level with the giant tusks, the three friends gathered round and stood in silence. It was an eerie sight.

'We'd better start digging – carefully,' said Nick.

Armed with pickaxes and shovels, they began the excavation. The carcass was in a very shallow grave, but it took several dark days to unearth what lay beneath the covering of silt and frozen mud. They worked round the clock, digging deep into the permafrost that lay under the surface, revealing layers of frozen ice. It looked like crumpled folds of material, thrust into waves and ridges, recording centuries of underground movement.

Slowly a giant carcass began to emerge. At first came a huge domed head, from which the tusks grew. Then a long trunk was uncovered. Gradually the rest emerged – a massive body, covered in shaggy dark-brown fur, a round belly, a long sloping back, a rump, ending in a bushy tail, and four powerful legs.

At last, as the moon rose over the hill, casting long shadows across the landscape, the entire carcass lay fully exposed in the creek: the perfectly preserved remains of a magnificent woolly mammoth, frozen through the ages in the prehistoric ice.

'Holy Sedna!' exclaimed Zak. 'That's Jarkov! He's one of our animal gods.'

The three adventurers fell silent. Nick's heart began to race.

With trembling hands he stepped forward and stood in front of the huge form lying motionless in the ditch. He took out the pouch, opened the strings and peered inside. A dim glow shone out from it. He held Krista's Soulstone pendant tightly and began to transmit silent thoughts to the creatures within. Faint squeaks came from inside the pouch as the Peskies began to stir from their sleep. Slowly they flew out of the pouch in a straggling mass and hovered in a cloud of dim Light, glowing faintly in the darkness. Nick pointed at the mammoth carcass.

The Peskies began to shimmer more brightly. They flew to the body and hovered over it in a clustered ball of Light. Spreading out, they began passing over the inert form, touching every part of it. An eternity seemed to pass as the three friends stood in a circle, watching as the fairies worked their magic. But the carcass remained motionless and silent.

A cold lump of despair made its way into Nick's stomach. Maybe this wasn't going to work after all. 'It's not going to happen,' he groaned in disappointment. 'It's not working.'

Krista grabbed his arm. 'No, look!' she whispered excitedly. 'I think I saw its tail twitch!'

'A trick of the light,' Nick replied gloomily. 'Or maybe the wind.'

'She's right,' said Zak. 'Look again.'

Krista *was* right. There was a definite twitch in the tail. Encouraged, the Peskies went into a frenzy of activity, swarming around the huge form as it began to show signs of life. Nick caught his breath as the tail flicked again and the great limbs began to stir. The whole body quivered, sending a ripple through the fur.

Finally it moved, in a slow and deliberate way. The great shaggy, domed head lifted off the ground, raising its tusks and extending its long leathery trunk. The huge beast struggled up and rose slowly to his feet. He lumbered majestically up the side of the ditch to the top of the ridge and towered over the landscape, outlined against the pale disc of the moon. The Peskies hovered over his head in a halo of light, making a low humming noise.

He shook his rug-like coat, raised his head and let out a long, trumpeting roar that echoed all around them in the silence.

Jarkov

Jarkov took a deep breath and his brown flanks swelled and deflated like a giant balloon. He let his trunk drop to the ground and swung his head about to take in his surroundings. When he saw the figures standing in front of him, he froze. Two puzzled little eyes stared at then from under a shaggy fringe.

The three adventurers stood perfectly still, fighting the urge to back away and run. It had suddenly occurred to them, all at the same time, that he might not like what he saw, and charge at them. He was a daunting sight, his massive bulk towering over them, the breeze gently stirring the long hair hanging from his belly.

Nobody spoke. Nobody could guess what might be going on inside that great hairy head as he stood there watching them.

But Nick couldn't suppress a wave of elation as he stared at the magnificent specimen. He had brought a prehistoric creature back from the dead. Him and the Soulstone and the Peskies he had managed to tame.

Whatever happened next, at least he had achieved that.

'Great bears alive!' murmured Zak at last, daring to break the silence. 'The Ancient One! You've done it, Nicku!'

'He's beautiful, isn't he?' breathed Krista. Petronella had finally crept out of hiding and sat perched on her shoulder, making nervous cooing noises. 'But a tad scary too, don't you think?'

The creature grunted. Encouraged, Nick took a step towards him. Zak put an arm out to stop him.

'No, wait. Let him make the first move.'

They waited in the silence that enveloped them all. Only the wind could be heard, sighing gently in the background. Suddenly Jarkov caught sight of the swarm of glowing shapes hovering above his head. He jumped and let out a cry of fear, shaking the fur all over his body. He swung his great tusks around in distress, trying to swipe at them.

Panic shivered through Nick. He must keep the beast calm, get the Peskies out of his hair. They had done their job now. He grasped Krista's Soulstone pendant and concentrated. To his great relief, the Peskies flew over and surged around him, looking very pleased with themselves. The beast stared at them incredulously, his great head swivelling as his eyes followed their movements. Nick willed the Peskies into order until they settled down, gathered into a ball and dived into the pouch. He waited till the mammoth had calmed down and held the Soulstone pendant even more tightly, hoping it would help him make contact with the beast. He closed his eyes and tried to imagine what was going on inside his head.

Nothing.

He tried again, stilling his mind and shutting everything out, sending an invisible line of thought towards the massive creature.

Again, nothing.

He mustn't lose hope. They'd got this far.

Then like dawn breaking, light began to seep into Nick's brain. It must be inside him, for all around them was the darkness of the Arctic night. It was light from another place, or another time. It filled his head with a hazy yellow mist. The mist began to clear and a vivid picture gradually came into focus. He saw verdant forests, bathed in sunshine; green hillsides dotted with rocky outcrops; lush pastures thickly carpeted with grasses and bright-yellow flowers, nodding in a warm and gentle breeze. He could almost smell and taste them.

Was he imagining it? Was it just a picture his own mind had conjured up? No, it was too definite. With a thrill Nick realized that he had connected with Jarkov's mind. He had been transported back through time. This must be how the Arctic Circle looked all those centuries ago!

All of a sudden, Jarkov jerked and let out a cry of terror. Painful images began to flood into Nick's brain: a blood-curdling roar just behind him; headlong flight across the grasses, heart thumping in panic and terror; a fleeting glimpse of long sharp fangs and terrible claws and a piercing pain in the back leg, as something long and sharp sliced straight through it. These were Jarkov's last living moments; he had been trying to escape from a beast of prey, something fierce and savage. There was a struggle, then a dark fog enveloped him as he hurtled headlong into the ditch and everything went black.

Nick came out of his trance and saw Jarkov still standing in front of him. But now the beast was staring directly at him, and there was recognition in his eyes. Shivers ran up and down Nick's spine as Jarkov held his gaze. He pawed the ground with one elephantine foot, and took a tentative step forward. Nick took an equal pace forward. Jarkov plodded towards Nick for a few more steps, then stopped and lifted his trunk. He let out a long trumpeting sound. Nick saw that his tusks curved around towards each other at the front in a graceful arc, creating a circular space.

'You are some kind of shaman, Nicku!' whispered Zak. 'He's chosen you as his guardian in his new world. You'd better go to him!'

Very slowly, one step at a time, Nick trod softly towards the mighty mammoth until he came close enough to feel his warm, grassy breath. He stepped inside the two curved tusks, which encircled him like an embrace, and their eyes met head on. He drew closer still, and put his hands on either side of the

Shivers ran up and down Nick's spine . . .

creature's hairy trunk. Laying his head against him, he smelled the comforting animal smell, felt the warmth of his shaggy brown hide. He began willing him to understand what he wanted. He felt his own natural compass inside him, straining like the needle of a dial pointing in the direction of north.

True North . . . he whispered inside his head, trying to communicate in thoughts rather than words. *Help me find it. Take me there.*

Suddenly he felt something coiling itself around his waist. He was being lifted in the air, and the world turned upside down. For one terrible moment he thought Jarkov was going to hurl him down on the ground like a rag doll, but the next he found himself sprawled on Jarkov's long hairy back. He gasped in surprise. The mammoth's back was soft and warm, like a huge uneven armchair, sloping down sharply towards his tail.

Nick crawled up and settled himself on Jarkov's neck, between the domed head crowned with tufts of brown hair and the fleshy hump just behind it. He breathed a sigh of relief and heard cheers and whistles breaking out behind him. He looked down and saw his friends staring at him in astonishment. Krista was gaping in wide-eyed wonder and Zak was grinning from ear to ear.

'Have you told him where you want him to take you?'

'I've tried,' said Nick, 'but I'm not sure if he—whoa, boy!'

His words were cut off as Jarkov galvanized into action. The great beast wheeled around and set off purposefully, plodding along in a slow and steady gait. Nick swayed and lurched on Jarkov's back as he began lumbering towards the ridge between the mountains.

'Come on, quick! You'd better hop on!' Nick called over his shoulder. Zak and Krista gathered up their belongings and hurried up behind.

'Pull yourself up by his hair!' shouted Nick jerkily, as Jarkov's stride quickened.

Zak leaped on to Jarkov's flank, grabbed a handful of shaggy fur and hauled himself up. He turned and reached down to Krista, grasped her hand and yanked her up too. In a few moments they had scrambled on behind Nick, and all three of them straddled the long sloping back. They shuffled up and clung on to each other, swaying with the mammoth's movements.

'Just sit tight and enjoy the ride!' called Nick.

Krista let out a squeal of joy. 'I can't believe we're doing this! Here's one to tell the grandchildren!'

Nick wondered briefly if any of them would survive long enough to have grandchildren, and who he would have them with. Then he suddenly knew who it would be.

The moon rose to its fullest spate and the stars hung overhead as the mammoth swayed majestically across the plain towards True North, carrying the three adventurers on his back. The Great Bear shone brightly in the sky ahead, an illuminated astronomical diagram of a spoon lying on its back. Much higher up, to the right, the Pole star twinkled faintly, like a small silvery ball that had just been hurled from it. It lay directly over the North Pole, and Jarkov was heading straight towards it.

Jarkov plodded along at a relentless pace, eating up the miles with surprising speed. Every so often they would lurch and cling on to each other as Jarkov stopped to graze off the tundra which poked out of the snow in sparse clumps. As the endless night of the Arctic winter wore on, they straggled over countless ridges and gorges towards the Arctic Ocean. The snows were falling fast and leaden clouds gathered over the mountains. They pulled their furs around them and huddled together for warmth.

At regular intervals Nick would bend down and lay his head against Jarkov's bony skull. The great beast would draw to a slow and measured halt, allowing his passengers to slide off his back. He would wait patiently while they set up camp for the night, lighting a fire and foraging in the frozen ground to find some grazing for him. Eventually enough grasses and roots would be dug up to feed the creature and settle him down for the night. He would sink on to his front knees, roll over on his side and go to sleep. Nick, Zak and Krista would eat some of the dried fish from Zak's supplies, then snuggle up together in the curve of Jarkov's belly, using his long hair and the warmth of his body for shelter. They would fall asleep to the comforting beat of his great heart thumping away inside his chest.

But still Nick slept fitfully, gazing anxiously up at the stars. When the Great Bear lay over the Pole upside down the Winter Solstice would be upon them. It was already beginning its slow turn in the sky. Would they make it in time? And what about the monster? The demon Light Fairy must have endowed him with fantastic powers. A beast like that was not easily put down. But he hardly dared voice his fears to the others. As far as they were concerned he was dead and gone.

They journeyed north, and Jarkov continued to lumber over the ridges and troughs with grim determination. Nick's eyes were fixed constantly on the horizon, or on the stars above. The moon hung in the sky all the time, moving through its phases like a magic lantern show. By the time they reached the shores of the great ocean the sea had already frozen over, a mass of solid ice interrupted by jagged ridges and troughs. The ghostly grey and white seascape stretched on for miles, shining in the moonlight.

Undeterred, Jarkov stepped on to the frozen sea and began plodding over the uneven surfaces until they reached the towering ice cliffs that fringed the Northern Rim. They entered the great polar ice cap through a cleft in the cliff face, and the strange caravan continued over the frozen wastes.

Then the blizzard set in. It went on for hours. It drove against them like a fierce white blanket, filling their eyes and ears with bitter snow, ripping at their faces and trying to wrench their furs off them. They were forced to take shelter in the lee of a mountain ridge and the snow piled up around them, blanketing them against the cold. Jarkov's body provided some protection and Zak packed the snow into a makeshift igloo and lit a fire to keep them warm. If it hadn't been for his Inuit survival skills they would have perished.

After a while the sky cleared. They dug themselves out of the snow cave and found themselves at the top of a gorge between two enormous cliffs of ice. A glacier swept down the valley in a curved swathe, like a frozen carpet. Beyond lay the Arctic plains of the Pole itself. The moon shone eerily on the icy wilderness, making a path for them to follow.

'Look! The Pole! We made it, Nicku!' shouted Zak.

Nick smiled, but something in the back of his mind rang a warning bell. What was it? A sound, a movement? Or just some instinct?

They were halfway down the gorge when his ears began to twitch.

'Do you hear what I hear?' whispered Nick.

Krista returned his frightened stare, white-faced. 'Um – I'm trying not to listen,' she gulped.

The sound was distant at first. A muffled roar, followed by a deep rumbling noise. The ground began to tremble.

The mammoth ground to a halt. He began flapping his ears and glancing round uneasily. As the tremors increased he let out a snort of alarm. Suddenly the sky lit up as a plume of fire and steam burst through the surface at the top of the gorge and rose into the night.

'He's come back again!' wailed Krista. 'Oh, Ursus! I really thought you'd managed to finish him, Nick!'

Nick tried to send soothing thoughts into Jarkov's brain, but the mammoth let out a bellow of fear at the sight of the fiery geyser spouting over their heads. Nick glanced about feverishly for possible ways of escape, but the solid walls of ice towered above them on either side. They clung on tight as Jarkov began lurching underneath them, his great shaggy body quivering in terror. Horrible crunching noises split the air as the ground at the top of the gorge began tearing itself apart. The column of fire was scorching its way through the ice. A massive chasm gaped open and the travellers groaned in horror.

A gigantic black paw emerged from the crack and clawed at the snow. The head emerged, and the burning red eyes turned their fierce gaze down the canyon towards them. It let out a deafening roar, so loud it must have been heard on the equator.

In answer came an equally loud chorus of bellowing, snorting noises that echoed round the gorge. Dark shapes appeared at the top of the ridge. Nick gasped in terror and disbelief.

The monster was not alone.

Battle of the Titans

There seemed to be hundreds of them, thundering down the slope, making the most appalling noise. It bounced off the walls of the canyon and assaulted their eardrums.

'Crumbling crystals! They're not exactly easy on the eye, are they?' muttered Krista. 'I don't think I'd like one of them for a pet.'

'This isn't funny,' Nick retorted, gulping down his fear.

They were indeed so ugly it made you wince to look at them. Built like tanks, with square bodies and short powerful legs, they had black woolly coats and oblong heads, with several horns ranged along their snouts. Their snarling lips, flecked with foam, were pulled back to reveal rows of sharp teeth. Nasty yellow eyes glared out of their horny skulls. The three adventurers stared at them aghast, trembling with fright. Their imaginations couldn't have dreamed up anything worse.

'Where on earth did they come from?' said Nick

in a wobbly voice. 'And what in the name of Ursus *are* they?'

Zak's eyes flicked across the abominations hurtling towards them, mouthing silent prayers and grasping his tupilak as though it could ward them off. 'I think – they're another of that demon Light Fairy's horrible experiments with ancient fossil remains. They look like woolly rhinos – but with extra bits added on.'

'But how did she manage to do it, when she's living inside my fake body? I guess she must leave it at night and escape somehow!'

'Well, however she's done it, she's created them to help the monster destroy you, SB!'

The clamour increased as the army of rhinos poured down the gorge, a monstrous regiment of fighting machines, designed to ram anything in their path to oblivion. Far above them the great black beast hauled himself out of the chasm and towered over the landscape, blotting out the stars. He raised his head and let out another unearthly roar, releasing a blast of fire that ignited the sky for miles around. Then he began prowling down the slope towards them, haunches gleaming in the moonlight. Any moment now and he would unfurl those enormous leathery wings, rise in the air and swoop over his army.

Jarkov began bucking and rearing underneath them, his whole body quivering. The jaws of death and defeat seemed to be closing in. What chance did they stand against this onslaught?

But then Nick remembered the Mission, and all the children who would be waiting for him to arrive on Midwinter's Eve. And Krista, the princess of the Kingdom, whom he'd led astray. He had to do something. A wild idea gripped him. It was worth a try. Nick turned to his friends. Their faces were ashen with terror and their eyes filled with despair.

'I've got a plan.'

They gaped at him.

'It'd better be a good one, SB.'

They turned their reluctant gaze back to the advancing tide of rhinos, and the beast at the top of the gorge, preparing for his descent.

'Where's that pickaxe? And the ropes?'

Zak stared at him in bemusement. 'What do you want them for?'

'You'll see in a minute.' He took off the Soulstone pendant and handed it to Krista. 'Here. You'd better have this back – I'm sure if I can get through to Jarkov, you can.'

Her mouth dropped open. She was trembling with fright, trying not to show it.

'But don't you need it?'

'I'll have to do without. Just get him away from here and stay out of the way.'

They continued staring at him in bewilderment. He quickly explained his plan to them. Krista was shaking all over with terror, but she put the pendant round her neck and nodded.

Quick as a flash, Nick and Zak slid off Jarkov's back. Krista grasped her pendant, urged her mount forward and turned him to face the bottom of the gorge. She galloped off with him down the slope. Her hair flew out wildly behind her as she rode him, clinging on to his shaggy fur. With the thundering of rhino hooves rushing towards them, he and Zak sprinted over to the side of the gorge and began to hack their way up the sheer cliff face of ice, gouging out holes for their hands and feet, using the pickaxes and ropes and hooks as grappling irons.

Higher and higher they climbed, scrabbling frantically, till they were halfway up. They slung their pickaxes over their backs and looked down at the gorge below. The rhinos were stampeding in a dark tide, coming closer to where they had begun their climb. Nick had to time it just right. He and Zak exchanged feverish glances.

'Not yet!' Nick shouted above the din. He waited a few more moments, watching intently.

The rhinos were right underneath them now, a roiling sea of woolly bodies. 'Now!'

With lightning speed they abseiled down the side of the cliff face and dropped on to the surging mass. They began tumbling along with them, balancing on their backs like acrobats. The pounding of hooves filled their ears and they could smell their hot stinking breath. Further down the gorge Nick could see Krista astride Jarkov's back, trying to stay on as he bucked about wildly. He had to stop the stampede before it reached them. There was a swishing noise from further up the gorge and a blood-curdling roar, and he knew that their predator must be spreading his wings, ready to take off.

It was time to act. Balancing to stay on the back of the rhino bucking underneath him, he took out the pouch containing the Peskies and opened the drawstring. They burst out with an angry humming sound. He sent out a silent message to them, hoping he could do it without the help of the pendant. In a matter of moments they were buzzing around the rhinos' heads like a swarm of bees. Yes! It had worked – he'd got through to them! Maddened by the glowing creatures that darted in their faces and zigzagged in front of their eyes, the rhinos broke their stampede and began running around in circles, crashing into each other like giant boulders. The Peskies continued taunting the beasts, luring them to the side of the gorge. The boys jumped free of the herd and watched as, one by one, they slammed against the cliff face, ramming their huge horns into the ice. Momentarily stuck, they thrashed around in a frenzy, bellowing in rage.

A shadow fell across them. The monster had caught up. He was hovering right overhead, his lips pulled back in a ferocious snarl, ready to release a blast of fire.

'Let's go!' shouted Zak.

Nick grabbed his sleeve. 'No, wait!'

The next few moments seemed to go into slow motion. The beast took a deep breath and exhaled explosively. The blast of fire roared out of his mouth. At the same moment, the two boys ducked and ran off. The blast of fire hit the rhinos full-on and enveloped them in a gout of flame. Black wool fizzled and the smell of burning flesh filled the air. Their bellows of agony bounced off the cliff faces. It was a gruesome sight.

'Run!' shouted Nick, pulling Zak away. They hurled themselves down the gorge, rolling, tumbling and slithering on the ice. The shadow passed overhead again and fear clutched at Nick's heart. The monster, unaware that they had escaped his fire-blast, had swooped on ahead of them, dark wings spread to their full span, heading straight down the gorge.

Nick hoped Krista had been able to get Jarkov out of the way. He glanced around for them. Where were they?

Their view was blocked by something dark and massive which filled their vision. They stopped dead and their gaze travelled upwards.

Jarkov had grown to a gargantuan size – he was of truly mammoth proportions. His back was level with the top of the gorge, and around his head buzzed a glowing halo of lights. A tiny figure far above them waved cheerily. It was Krista, still sitting astride his back. Nick felt a surge of admiration and relief.

'Great Ursus! She's a genius! I'd forgotten the

Peskies could do that!' he gasped. 'She's got through to them and made them grow Jarkov, like they did with the fish! Why didn't I think of it?'

'She's a pretty smart girl, Nicku!'

'Of course she is!' replied Nick. 'She's going to be running the Elfin Kingdom some day!'

Ahead of them, the monster stopped in mid-flight, flapping his leathery wings to stay aloft, momentarily puzzled. His giant head swivelled this way and that.

'Cooo-eeeeee! Up here!' called Krista.

His red gaze travelled upwards and took in the vast bulk of the newly enlarged mammoth standing in front of him. His jaw gaped open. It was the first time he had encountered any creature bigger than himself.

'Surprise!' crowed Krista triumphantly. Her laughter echoed around the gorge.

The monster blinked in shock. Hovering overhead like a bird of prey, he hissed and spat, then started a low rumbling growl of displeasure. Nick held his breath, wondering what Krista would do next. Suddenly Jarkov lowered his trunk and dipped it to the ground, sucking up mounds of snow like a giant vacuum cleaner.

'Great bears alive! She's turning him into a water cannon!' cried Zak.

Nick felt a thrill of elation at Krista's quick thinking. He and Zak waited in silence, watching as the monster snarled angrily and flapped towards the girl astride the giant mammoth. He opened his mouth to breathe fire, but drew back when he saw Jarkov's mighty trunk raised and pointed at him.

He hovered uncertainly, then roared in fury. Jarkov answered him with an equal bellow of rage. He was vibrating with a new kind of energy. Nick suddenly remembered the fleeting glimpses of claws and fangs in his vision of Jarkov's last moments. Jarkov had been killed by a sabre-toothed tiger! Somewhere inside that great shaggy head dim memories must have been awoken of the predator which had ended his previous life. And now he was out for revenge.

The two titans squared up to each other, ready for the final showdown. Their moonlit shadows fell across the snow. The monster's red eyes sent out scorching beams, his great muzzle pulled back in a horrible leer. His jaws opened wide, revealing the impossibly long fangs projecting from his mouth. He filled his lungs and released an almighty blast of firepower.

Jarkov was ready. He blew out a tidal wave of melted snow that engulfed the monster completely. The capacity inside the mammoth's trunk must have been phenomenal, and it was too much for the beast. He fizzled and smoked and thrashed around in the air, twisting in agony. Then he plummeted to the ground and landed heavily on his back, revealing his livid-green underbelly. Bellowing in anger he slithered further down the gorge between Jarkov's mighty legs.

'Come on up! The view's great from here!' shouted Krista from far above them.

They looked up at Jarkov's towering flanks, like the side of a massive hairy mountain. Her face peered over the edge.

Nick suddenly had a premonition of disaster. It had all been too easy. The monster wouldn't be beaten without a fight. The battle wasn't over yet. And Krista, his best friend Krista, was up there on her own. He must get up to her now.

'Come on, Zak! Slightly bigger climb this time!'

They scrambled up and leaped on to the mammoth's foot. It was the size of a large igloo. Slowly they began climbing up his leg, using his long shaggy coat to pull themselves up, until they reached his shoulder. Krista peered down at them. She was sitting in the dip between his head and his fleshy hump, which was considerably larger now. They scrambled up the last bit and clambered on behind her.

'Are you all right?' enquired Nick anxiously.

'Yes, I'm fine,' she said impatiently. 'Aren't you going to congratulate me on my brilliant stroke of genius? Getting the Peskies to make him bigger? I knew he wouldn't be able to blow out enough water the size he was.'

Nick was about to speak when Zak pointed down the gorge. 'Look! He's recovering!'

Jarkov had wheeled around, manoeuvring his massive new size in the tight space of the gorge, and faced down the slope. The monster was scrambling to his feet, preparing for the counter-attack, shaking his head and roaring with rage. Nick's heart lurched with fear.

'Go, Jarkov!' he cried. 'Finish him off this time!'

Quivering with the desire for revenge, the great mammoth lowered his head and charged down the slope. Nick and his companions clung on desperately as they lurched around on his back, winding their arms and legs in his long hair.

The impact when the two giants clashed together was earth-shattering. Jarkov rammed into the monster, sinking one of his tusks into his side before he had time to pull away. Black blood gushed out. The beast let out a horrible high-pitched scream. He lashed out at Jarkov, tearing a huge gash in his leg, but Jarkov was undeterred. He lunged again, impaling him on a tusk, shaking his head and hurling him though the air. The black beast landed with a sickening thump and rolled over and over to the bottom of the gorge, foaming at the mouth.

Jarkov thundered after him. By the time they reached the wounded beast he was struggling to his feet. Roaring with rage he flapped his wings to try and lift himself off the ground. But one of them was broken and he slumped back down. He crouched low, poised to strike back, snarling ferociously. Black blood gushed from his wounds, darkening the snow. He took a deep breath and opened his jaws to blast them again. But Jarkov was ready with another wave of water which doused the flames. The monster fizzled and squirmed in agony, roaring horribly. A foul-smelling smoke filled the air.

The beast rolled on to his back with his legs pawing at the air. His underbelly was exposed, green and viscous and slightly transparent. Nick saw again the dark pulsating heart in his chest. He was seized with a fierce desire to destroy this monster once and for all.

But the beast still had some fight left in him.

With an agonized snarl of rage he dragged himself up, opened his wings and rose raggedly into the air. Then he swooped towards them and, with one swipe, reached out a gigantic paw and snatched Krista off Jarkov's back before plummeting downwards again. She sailed through the air, enclosed in the great black paw, his claws curling around her like the bars of a cage.

'Nick!' she screamed.

He couldn't let this happen! Krista's cries of terror echoed jerkily round the gorge. The beast lay snarling on his back, waving Krista around like a trophy. Then he brought her up close to his gaping mouth. The jaws opened wide and the fangs towered above her. He was about to devour her.

'I'm coming, Krista!' yelled Nick.

Jarkov dipped his trunk to the ground, snorkelled up some more snow and blew another gout of melted water all over the beast. He shook his head in fury and slumped again. But still he didn't drop Krista; she was held fast in his paw, jerking around in the air like a puppet.

Nick leaned down and put his head against Jarkov's skull, desperately transmitting one final request. He scrambled over Jarkov's domed head and down on to the long hairy trunk. The wounded monster was beginning to struggle upright again for a final fight-to-the-death counter-attack. Nick had to act fast.

Jarkov lowered his trunk over the beast and Nick ran along the hairy bridge till he was right over the black beating heart. Then he leaped off and dropped on to the monster's underbelly, landing with a dull thud. The monster's red eyes flared open and he let out a roar of rage, dropping Krista, who plummeted to the ground with a scream. Lashing out his paws, he tried to claw Nick off his stomach. But Nick ducked, missing the huge claw by a hair's-breadth.

He had seconds to spare before the beast recovered and killed him. Summoning up all his strength, he took the pickaxe off his shoulder and swung it down into the beating heart under his feet with all his strength. There was a horrible squelching sound as he felt it sink in. Black blood spurted up all around him like a stricken oil well, rising high into the air. Nick was drenched in it; thick black rain, hot and stinking, fell all around him.

The beast let out a deafening roar as his massive body convulsed in agony. He bellowed in his death throes, a horrible unearthly sound that echoed round the canyon. Then his thrashing began to subside. Like two headlights being switched off, the glowing red eyes dimmed and extinguished. The giant head lolled to one side and thunked on the ground. The monster lay still.

The giant heart continued thumping jerkily underneath Nick.

Gudumph gudumph gudumph.

Then it finally stopped beating for ever.

The three travellers looked at each other in silence for a few moments, scarcely daring to believe that their predator was finally laid to rest.

Then Krista rubbed her hands briskly. 'Well, that got rid of him, ghastly creature! Well done, SB!'

'Well done, all of us,' said Nick, feeling a strange combination of horror and elation. 'We all did it together. Teamwork, I think it's called.'

By the time they left the gorge the monster had reverted to his original state. Before their eyes he crumbled and disintegrated, shrivelling away until he was nothing more than a pile of fossilized remains.

The moon stayed bright, lighting their way, waxing towards its fullness as they travelled. Jarkov, restored to his normal size and healed of his injuries by the Light Fairies, plodded on with even more determination than before.

They finally reached the ruins of the Golden City. Nick glanced anxiously at the stars above, his heartbeat quickening, and Zak followed his gaze.

'Two more days till Solstice Eve,' said Zak, reading his thoughts.

Jarkov swayed to a halt, lifted his trunk and let out a long resounding bellow. Then he pointed his trunk down at the ground, nodded his head and stamped his foot impatiently.

Nick's heart leaped in excitement. 'Looks like we're near the right place!'

'But that doesn't make sense!' gasped Zak. 'We're not over the Pole!'

'Ah, yes,' said Krista knowledgeably. 'But that's the whole point of True North. It moves around as the earth's axis wobbles.'

Jarkov was stamping his foot insistently now, and the Peskies were mithering about, darting at a point in the ground, ready to open it up.

'I think it's time I took my leave, Nicku,' Zak began. 'Not sure if I fancy going under—' He broke off as something caught the corner of his eye. He stared intently at the ruins of Doransk. Everyone followed his gaze: there were definite signs of life. Lights flickered from amongst the broken columns and distant voices carried across the snow.

'I don't believe it!' murmured Nick. 'Someone's living in Doransk again. It can't be *her* come back again! It can't!'

Zak grabbed his arm. 'No. It's not the city coming back to life. It must be Inuit taking refuge before heading south again . . . camping in the shelter of the ruins.' He gazed towards the lights, screwing up his face in concentration. A faint yapping of husky dogs wafted across the cold air. His eyes lit up and his whole body seemed to come alive. 'Yes! Definitely Inuit!'

A husky-drawn sledge broke away from the firelit area around the ruins and raced towards them across the snow. Zak tensed in expectation and Nick put an arm round him, hoping that at last his old friend was going to get his heart's desire. As the dogs sped closer Zak's face broke into a broad grin.

'Zakurak!' called the man on the sledge, waving wildly at Zak.

Zak's face creased up with joy. 'Tanik!'

Tanik drew to a halt and stared in astonishment at the mammoth. He and Zak began chattering away in their Inuit language, waving their arms around excitedly. Zak's face was alight and his black eyes gleamed. He turned back to Nick. 'That's my cousin! My family! I've found them at last – they came up here to look for me and I missed them!'

In moments more Inuit were racing towards them. They gathered round the three adventurers sitting on the mammoth's back and stared in astonishment.

Zak turned to Nick and Krista. 'It's time to say goodbye, Nicku!'

They hugged each other and rubbed noses. Zak looked at them both. 'It's been a great adventure, Nicku. Even better than the last one. But now I must return to my people.' He put his arms round both of them. 'Stick together, you two. You're a good team. And you won't find another girl like this from one end of the earth to the other, Nicku. Good luck with your Mission.'

And, giving Jarkov a pat, he slid off his back, landed on the ground and ran off to join his people.

The Peskies had forged a beautiful sloping shaft wide enough for Jarkov to plod down majestically, in his slow and measured way. They bypassed the Kingdom via a series of far-flung back routes, skirted the Moonstone mines, and finally entered the tropical realms of the NetherWorld. It didn't seem such a terrible place now they knew the monster wasn't lurking somewhere in the darkness. Jarkov swayed along through the tunnels, weaving through the underground forests, the rivers of sludge and the pools of slime. The rocks still heaved around, twisting and turning in new directions, but the Peskies kept everything under control, lighting their path and guiding their way.

Nick had wondered what they were supposed to do once they'd got to the NetherWorld, but Jarkov trudged along with dogged determination towards his goal. Every time he came up against a wall of rock barring his way the glowing Peskies would animate the rocks to open up into a new tunnel.

Nick was acutely aware of his inner compass,

swivelling around like some invisible needle on a dial. But since he'd entered the NetherWorld it had gone haywire. It kept swinging this way and that, every time giving him new hope that at last they were heading in the right direction. Then it would hesitate and waver about uncertainly. It was maddening. He gave up in the end, hoping that Jarkov's sense of direction would be enough.

But after several hours it seemed they were going round in circles.

'Gosh, I'm sure I've seen that rock face before, the one that looks like a dog,' muttered Krista, her brow knitted into a puzzled frown. 'Are you sure he knows where he's going, SB?'

Nick glanced round uneasily. 'Well, the whole point of True North is that it does move around. I think he's sort of chasing it.'

At that moment Jarkov let out a snort of frustration and began swinging his great head around, banging his tusks against the rocks on either side.

'See? He's getting fed up. It keeps eluding him.'

'Perhaps he needs a helping hand, dearie,' came a female voice from nearby. They turned to see Moomsa and Fangle standing in a newly formed opening in the rock. Moomsa's babies were chattering excitedly on her back at the sight of the woolly mammoth. 'After all, you have got a sort of compass inside you. You should use it to help him. You're being lazy, young man!'

'Moomsa! Fangle! It's great to see you again!'

'I see you managed to resurrect the Ancient One then!' warbled Moomsa approvingly. 'Quite a specimen, isn't he?'

Nick and Krista slid off Jarkov's back and rushed over to greet them. After the initial fuss was over, Nick told them the whole story. They patted Jarkov's hairy neck and marvelled at his prehistoric magnificence.

Fangle was staring at him in curious awe, stroking his long curved tusks, then feeling his own curly teeth thoughtfully.

Moomsa's babies were swarming all over Krista and Nick now, babbling and squealing. Two of them were sitting on Krista's shoulders and one of them was cradled in her arms. Petronella had finally crept out of hiding and regarded the whole business with disapproval.

'Well, it's been calmer down here since the monster went,' said Moomsa. 'We could sense it. We knew he'd gone after you. We were worried, dear, but somehow we just knew you would come through. Didn't we, Fangle?'

'Uh?' said Fangle distractedly, staring into Jarkov's eyes. 'Oh, yesh! Knew the boy would do it.'

A strange peacefulness had come over the mammoth; he was making small, affectionate grunting noises at Fangle. They seemed to have struck up an immediate rapport, and now Nick looked more closely he could see that there was a strong resemblance between the two of them.

'Come along now, dearie,' chivvied Moomsa. 'There's work to do. You have to help Jarkov. You can't expect him to find True North all on his own.'

'But my compass keeps going haywire!'

'Patience, boy!' snorted Fangle. 'You have to still your mind, tap into the forces. Heavens above, you've done it before. Now get back on this beast and try again.'

Nick clambered on to Jarkov's back and laid his head against Jarkov's skull. He tried to connect both with the mammoth's inner thoughts and his own built-in compass. He cleared his mind and concentrated hard. Slowly he could feel the two of them drawing together as their minds bonded, then a strong pulling sensation, as though something deep inside both of them had united with the powerful surge of the magnetic forces.

With a sudden jolt Jarkov set off, plodded onwards, and after a few moments halted in front of a rock face. He raised his trunk and let out a long honking sound. The Peskies fluttered over the rocks until they fell away to reveal a large circular cavern. In the middle was a pillar stretching to the ceiling, surrounded by a moat of bubbling slime. The pillar was revolving slowly. And every so often they could see a glittering stone embedded in its face.

'Well, here we are!' cried Moomsa. 'The Cave of the Crystal Chronicle at last! And you'll probably find the original crystal itself inside that pillar. It must contain some sort of chamber. Jarkov will know what to do.'

They stepped into the cavern and immediately felt a magnetic swirling sensation. It was like stepping on to a huge merry-go-round.

'I say, hang on a minute!' said Krista. 'This looks familiar. Isn't this the cave where we landed when we first came down to the NetherWorld? Look at the moat!'

Nick stared round at the cave. She was right; it was the same place! It had been right under their noses and they'd been too disorientated to realize it, or notice the revolving pillar. He eyed the bubbling slime of the moat, and the occasional ghastly glimpses of tentacles breaking above the surface. 'But how am I going to get across?'

'Oh, flibbering fungushrot,' cried Fangle impatiently, breaking off from his adoration of Jarkov. 'Have you learned nothing? What are *they* for?'

He pointed at the Peskies, who were now circling expectantly above Nick's head.

'Oh, yeah.' Nick took a deep breath, clasped the pendant and pointed at the slime.

The fairies flitted over to the moat and darted here and there over its surface. The slimy creatures underneath shrank away and a large reef of rocks rose above the water, creating a natural bridge.

'Off you go then, dear!' said Moomsa cheerfully. 'And keep your head. The forces are very strong at the moment, as we near the Solstice.'

Nick and Jarkov plodded across the bridge, swaying perilously. He glanced nervously down at the moat, where the creatures writhed in the scummy water, but the bridge held fast. When they arrived on the central island he began to feel dizzy. The forces were very powerful here. It was as though he was at the centre of the universe, and all the magnetic forces of the earth were swirling around him. He tried to collect his thoughts, but the vertigo was spinning his head into soup. The glittering stone in the pillar kept passing by, flashing in the gloom like a winking eye.

'What am I supposed to do now?' he called out.

'The Ancient One will know what to do!' called Moomsa from behind him.

Jarkov waited for his moment, then as the stone passed by he lifted his head and struck it forcibly with the tip of his tusk.

The rock slid back to reveal a glittering chamber, studded with precious stones. It was small, but far more magnificent than anything in the palace. In the centre of the chamber was a plinth, also revolving. And on the plinth stood a many-sided cone of pure, shining crystal. A kaleidoscope of moving patterns played across its surface, just like the Crystal Chronicle disc embedded in the wall of Solstice Square.

The original crystal. At last, the magical tool that would enable Nick to make time stand still, rewrite history and achieve the impossible. He *would* be able to deliver gifts to all those children on Midwinter's Eve after all! His heart leaped into flame. Sliding off Jarkov's back he stepped across the threshold into the chamber. The rocks closed behind him.

The cone of crystal winked and glowed at him, beckoning him forward. He strode over to the plinth and went to lift it off.

'Thanks, I'll take that!' came a familiar voice behind him.

The hairs stood up on Nick's neck. It was his own voice.

A bolt of energy shot through him and pinned his feet to the ground.

He whipped round to see his lookalike standing behind him, wearing the red robe. *His* red robe. Smiling nastily he marched over to the plinth and stretched out his hand to take the crystal cone.

The Crystal Chronicle

Nick stared in impotent rage at his hated identical twin. He couldn't move. The bolt of magnetic energy had paralysed him. He was trapped in here with this creature.

The evil twin smirked at him. 'Did you really think I wouldn't catch up with you?'

'You're Magda's demon Light Fairy, aren't you?' Nick whispered faintly. 'You escaped from the Vortex after I defeated her down there!'

The replica sniggered. 'Oh, well spotted!' His voice had a raspy buzz about it now that sent a chill down Nick's spine.

'How did you get in here?'

The lookalike shrugged. 'Well, since you were not obliging enough to allow the monster to destroy you – well done about that, by the way, nice work – and you finally found this place, I decided to take advantage of the situation. Otherwise I would have had a longer wait. You see, only my mistress, Queen Magda, has the key to this cave, and she took it with her. So I hid outside in a crevice and just flew in after you. I'm a Light Fairy, remember, underneath all this.' He indicated his clothes and body. 'We can do anything, travel anywhere. Anyway, it's all turned out for the best. Now I can move things along much more quickly.'

'How?' said Nick in a hoarse whisper, not really wanting to know the answer.

His replica assumed a friendly air. 'Well, I was going to take over the Mission in your place and gather enough energy from the children to resurrect my mistress. But now you have so kindly let me in here, I can just rewrite history. Magda will be back with us very shortly – and your whole Mission will be forgotten, because no one will ever have heard of it!'

'H-how d'you mean?' demanded Nick, dreading the reply.

'Ah, well, dear friend, the Crystal Chronicle has extraordinary powers. Greater than you realized. Not only can it change the order of events, it can wipe them from memory as though they never happened! So all that you've done will be undone!' He shrieked with maniacal laughter. 'Yes! The Golden Era will resume its glorious path! Time will rewind back to that moment in Golden Square, last Winter Solstice Eve, just before you went down into the Vortex with her. And then Queen Magda, the Great and Glorious One, will fly around the world every Winter Solstice Eve in your place, in her magnificent golden sleigh, drawn by your friends the flying reindeer, just as she planned before you went and spoiled it all! She will visit every child's house, bestowing bountiful gifts – and, of course, stay young and beautiful for ever!'

'By preying on their youth, taking their childhood away!' screamed Nick in fury. 'What kind of a present is that?'

'Oh, they won't miss it,' said the lookalike carelessly. 'And Queen Magda, the Great and Glorious One, will reign again!' He began striding around the chamber. 'She will rise once more to rule the world! Her empire will spread across the globe! Her beauty and goodness know no bounds! She will—'

'Oh, give it a rest, will you?' snapped Nick. 'You're boring me. I've heard it all before. It's a load of reindeer poo!'

The lookalike shot him an icy glare and the red lights began to glow in his eyes. 'I'd like to say that you will live to regret that remark, but you won't,' he spat. 'However, you won't die either. Because you won't even have been born in the first place!' He sneered and nodded at the crystal. 'Now I can rewrite history you will never have existed at all!' He laughed, a horrible, high-pitched, inhuman sound that made Nick's spine tingle.

Nick's head began to swim. Numbly he watched as his lookalike reached towards the crystal with a smug smile on his face.

The smile faded immediately as the crystal reacted

violently to his touch, radiating a sharp flash of light. He drew back with a start.

Something was happening to the crystal. Its surface began to swirl with patterns, like the shapes in a kaleidoscope. They shuffled around each other like the pieces of a jigsaw and finally rearranged themselves into a blurred image. The image became sharper till it came into focus, revealing the faces of two elfin boys the same age as them. They stared at Nick and his double as though they were peering at them through a window.

They both looked familiar. One had an air of Krista about him, with the chiselled features of the royal family, reddish hair and piercing, ice-blue eyes. The other was taller, with a mop of unruly blond hair and a rosy-cheeked face. Nick couldn't quite place either of them.

It was most unnerving.

'Crimble!' exclaimed the blond boy. 'Who are those boys in the crystal?'

Nick felt a thrill run through him. These two boys could see them and hear them. But how could they be standing in the cave too? It didn't make sense.

'Ursus knows,' said the other. 'But they're twins, by the look of them.'

'No, we're not!' hissed Nick's double. He was trembling with rage at this unplanned interruption.

Nick leaned forward as far as he could with his feet pinioned to the floor. 'Hello?' he called out to the images in the crystal. 'We can hear you . . .'

The two boys gasped and jumped back in shock.

'Shivering icicles!' cried the blond boy. 'They're talking back to us! What's going on, Vil?'

'Search me, Freddy,' replied the other boy, shaking his head in bewilderment. 'But it's putting the wind up me, I can tell you. Maybe we should get back to the Kingdom, old chum. They'll be missing me.' He held up a small silver coronet. 'I've got a wretched state function in ten minutes.'

Nick felt more prickles run up and down his spine. 'Did you say Vil?' he croaked. 'As in – short for – Vilmar?'

Both boys in the crystal image jerked in amazement and gaped at him.

'I say, steady on, old chap! I'm usually addressed as Your Royal Highness.'

'But – but what's going on?' blurted the blond boy, his eyes round with amazement. 'They seem to know us!'

Vil took control of the situation with a natural air of authority. He leaned closer, speaking loudly and slowly, as though to a foreigner. 'Er, hello? I'm Crown Prince Vilmar, second in line to the throne of the Elfin Kingdom. Or Vil, as I'm known to my closest associates.' He threw an affectionate glance at his companion, who was staring at Nick and his double with bemused wonder. 'And this is my best chum, Frederick Grishkin, mechanical genius. We're not supposed to be friends, strictly forbidden, comes from the wrong side of the ridge. Damned shame, we get on like a crystal on fire. Big plans for the future. And we're not supposed to be here in the Cave of the Crystal Chronicle either. Strictly forbidden too. Get into heaps of trouble if we're found out. So please state your business and we'll be on our way. Who *are* you both, for Ursus' sake? I command you to answer me!'

Nick's head was reeling. This was Vilmar, King of the Elves, ancient patriarch of the Elfin Kingdom. But he was seeing him in the past, as a young man, the same age as him. And the person next to him must be his own grandfather as a young lad. Somehow both of them were here in the same cave, looking into the same crystal, but in another time. Vilmar and Frederick were looking into the future at them and they were looking into the past at Frederick and Vilmar. It was enough to twist your brain into knots.

He shook his head, trying to take it in. Then in a flash, everything fell into place.

Time was just one long continuous ribbon. Like a map which you could look at from above. And events were like places on a map; they could be shuffled around, rearranged into any pattern or outcome, like the moving kaleidoscope pieces in the Crystal Chronicle disc. Nothing was carved in stone. Everything and anything could change at any moment. History could be rewritten. And right now, they were making it up as they went along.

Sudden insight flooded him. This was the true meaning of the Crystal Chronicle.

'I am your grandson, Frederick,' he said thickly, speaking directly to the blond boy. 'My name is Nickolai. I am speaking to you from the future. We are here in the cave too.'

Frederick's rosy cheeks drained of colour. 'But I – I – don't have any plans to get married, ever!' he stammered. 'Girls are stupid!'

Nick laughed in spite of himself. 'You'll change your mind! Girls are OK – some of them are pretty clever.' He thought of Krista, waiting outside in the cavern. 'You'll get married eventually, and have children, and they'll have children too, 'cos I'm here to prove it!'

'Not for much longer!' hissed his double nastily. 'I'll soon put a stop to that.'

Nick ignored him. He wasn't going to let anything spoil this moment. To have grown up without any living male relatives, then to be given a chance to meet one of them at last, was quite something. He had to make the most of it. 'I know it's weird, meeting like this, what with us being the same age and everything, but let's just enjoy it while it lasts! Hello, Grandpa!'

'Oh, please!' spat his lookalike. 'Pass the sick bag!'

Frederick looked as if he were about to faint. Vilmar had to hold him up to stop him from falling to the floor. Nick ignored the waspish comments from beside him and persisted. 'And you, Vilmar. I know you now, as an old man. You're going to live for a very long time. You're my king. Our king.'

Vilmar looked bewildered. 'But my brother . . . he's the direct heir . . .'

'Well, you're king here now. You're a wise ruler. The Kingdom has been through a lot, but you've been a guiding force all along. And you've been a wonderful mentor to me in the short time I've known you, although I've only just realized it. What happens now is really important. To the past, the present, the future, everything!'

'No, it's not,' snapped his lookalike. 'Because none of it counts for anything. None of this will have happened, ever, not even this conversation, when I've finished with that crystal! Now will you all shut up and let me get on with it. And don't listen to him,' he added, jerking his head at Nick. 'He's an impostor.'

Frederick was scratching his head. 'Look, I'm really confused now. Are you two twins?'

'No! We're not!' rasped the lookalike. He pointed a shaking finger at Nick. 'He's a fake! Someone has replicated me! I'm the real Nickolai! The one and only Nickolai!'

Nick groaned heavily. 'Oh, dear! Here we go again!' He turned to his mirror image. 'This whole business is really getting on my nerves now.' It was time to sort this dispute out once and for all. He turned to the boys in the image. 'We're both going to say the same thing, aren't we? So you two will have to decide which of us is the real one.'

'What's all this about deciding?' snapped his fake twin. 'There's no decision to make. I'm going to take the crystal, and that's that!'

Vilmar turned on a charming smile. 'Actually no, old chum, you're wrong there.'

Nick's double froze and his eyes glinted red again. 'What on earth are you talking about?'

'The original crystal holds the power, but so do we. It's just a tool for our use,' said Vilmar smoothly. 'Funny old thing, fate. You have to let it decide, yet at the same time you have to give it a helping hand. Whatever happens now was meant to happen, because it happened. But it hasn't happened yet. So — are you still with me?'

'No!' stormed the lookalike, his eyes burning now. 'It's a load of rubbish! *I* have the power — I just need to take the crystal and that's it! I can rewrite history!'

Vilmar smiled patiently at Nick's double. 'Let me explain. Technically speaking we are in the past, we are what has gone before, whatever you say about erasing it all. Therefore, by dint of historical seniority, we have the power to release the crystal to whoever we feel is the right one, the real Nickolai!'

Nick's double began to vibrate and his eyes glowed fiercely. 'No!' he shrieked. 'You can't stop me!'

'It will only come off the plinth for the real Nickolai,' said Vilmar calmly. 'As each of you tries to remove it, we will have to trust our instinct to know which is the right choice. And if you're the real one, you have nothing to fear. Now one at a time, boys. You first, you in the red robe.'

'Hang on a minute.' Frederick grabbed Vilmar by the arm. 'I'm still really confused. How can we be sure we're making the right choice? How do we tell the difference? They're identical.'

'We'll know,' said Vilmar, suddenly looking wise for his years. 'Here, let's hold my Soulstone pendant together. It'll help us concentrate and divine the truth.' And Vilmar pulled a pendant on a chain out of his front, identical to the one he had given Nick and Krista. It swung on its chain, glowing milkily. Nick glanced at his double. Immediately he pulled the pendant he had stolen from Nick out of his front.

'Look! I've got one too! You gave it to me, Your Majesty!'

'No − you gave it to *me*! He stole it!' cried Nick hotly.

Vilmar glanced back at them. 'Quiet, please, we're trying to concentrate. Do go ahead now, you in the red robe, and see if you can take the crystal off the pedestal.'

The two boys in the image held the pendant together. Nick's double hissed impatiently and lunged forward to grasp the cone of crystal. He tried to lift it but it wouldn't budge. He screamed in anger, and his voice reverted back to the horrible echoey buzzing sound of the demon Light Fairy.

'No!' he rasped. 'Thisss isn't what was meant to happen!'

He pulled and pulled, with all his supernatural strength, but still it wouldn't budge.

There was a long and ghastly pause, during which time seemed to stand still. Everything around Nick seemed to freeze. He felt giddy and unreal. What was happening? Was something going wrong on the other side of time?

Then the action in front of his eyes resumed. His lookalike was still tugging at the crystal, desperately trying to wrench it off its plinth.

'Oh, dear . . . looks like you're not The One after all . . .' Vilmar's disembodied voice floated out. 'Frightful shame for you.'

Nick's double screamed in fury. The crystal began to fizzle ominously, sending out flashes of brilliant Light. There was a violent explosion and a puff of smoke. A terrible, inhuman shriek echoed round the chamber. Nick looked around.

The chamber was empty.

His double had vanished. All that was left was his robe, lying in a heap on the ground, the pendant on top of it. He became aware of a buzzing insect flying round the cave like an angry wasp, glowing a lurid red. It zigzagged back and forth in the air, bouncing off the glittering walls in a frenzy, then it disappeared with a nasty bang.

Nick realized that his feet were no longer pinioned to the floor. He was free to move: the power of the demon fairy had gone and the magnetic bonds were released. He stepped forward, picked up the red robe and put it round himself. It felt wonderful, like coming home. Then he put the Soulstone pendant back round his neck, vowing never to let it out of his sight again.

Stepping up to the revolving plinth he gazed into the swirling, iridescent depths of the crystal. The faces were still there. They were both grinning at him conspiratorially.

'Wha— what happened just then? Everything went sort of frozen in time . . .'

'Never mind. It's sorted now,' said Frederick. 'You just get on with your future.' He seemed more relaxed now, as though he knew something that he hadn't known before.

'Well, that settled that once and for all, didn't it, SB?' said Vilmar heartily, clapping Frederick on the back.

Nick felt a thrill of recognition. 'Hang on a minute – did you say SB?'

'Yes,' replied Vilmar. 'SB. My nickname for him.' He pointed at Frederick. 'Short for Sleigh Boy.'

Nick gasped in amazement. 'But that's what your granddaughter calls me – SB! Only it's short for—' he stopped, feeling self-conscious.

'Short for what?'

'Saviour Boy,' said Nick sheepishly. 'Embarrassing, isn't it?'

'No, it's not,' said Frederick. 'It's really amazing. I'm proud of you. Of what you're going to be . . .' He broke off, and Nick saw that he had tears in his eyes.

'And take care of that red robe. It's the champion's robe, isn't it? For the winners of the Winter Solstice Sleigh Race?'

Nick nodded.

'My idea.' Frederick bit his lip, overcome with emotion. 'It's all just a pipedream at the moment, the sleigh racing. But we're working on it.'

Nick gulped, robbed of words. He suddenly felt the great sweep of history. The two boys continued gazing at each other through the crystal that divided them across the ages.

'I say, I hate to break up this family reunion, but we must get back, old chum. Mater'll kill me if I'm late for the ball,' Vilmar interrupted briskly. He looked at Nick. 'Take the crystal. Now. And do what you have to do with it. Goodbye, SB Junior. Nice to have met you.'

Nick felt a lump rising in his throat. He took one last lingering glance at his grandfather and reached for the crystal cone, reluctantly covering the images on its surface. It felt cool to the touch.

'Goodbye, Prince Vilmar. Goodbye, Grandfather. And thanks.'

He lifted the crystal. It came away easily; it was surprisingly light. He held it up in front of him and it sparkled even more brilliantly than before, but the faces on its surface had gone. He heard two faint voices, fading off into the mists of time.

'Goodbye, Nickolai. And good luck.'

Return to the Kingdom

They were all waiting for Nick on the other side of the moat, peering anxiously into the gloom. As the rocks opened up to let him through, a torrent of Light poured out of the chamber, revealing a breathtaking glimpse of the glittering interior, before it closed up again. Nick strode across the bridge to a rousing chorus of cheers from his friends. Jarkov raised his trunk and let out a long, triumphant bellow. Moomsa's babies squealed with delight and the Peskies set up a shrill squeaking chorus.

As Nick reached the other side of the bridge, the reef that had risen above the surface sank beneath it again. He jumped on to the bank with a flourish and held up the crystal. It sent out a sparkling beam of light, so bright it lit up every corner of the cave.

'You got it then?' said Krista sardonically. 'Well done, SB.'

Nick felt a shudder of familiarity. She was so like her grandfather when he was young.

Everyone clustered round to look at the crystal

cone. It dazzled their eyes and played colours across the craggy walls of the cave, shimmering in the scummy surface of the moat. Nick longed to have a go with it and start tinkering with time, but it didn't seem fair just yet.

'Oh, you are such a clever boy!' warbled Moomsa. 'Look at that pretty thing, children! Isn't it lovely! I just knew you'd do it, didn't we, Fangle?'

'Uhhh?' Fangle glanced over from where he was stroking Jarkov's hairy nose. 'Oh, yesh! Shplendid effort, little elf boy. And well done with the Peshkies.'

'But what *happened* in there?' said Krista. 'We were getting frightfully worried. You were gone ages!'

'Oh – you know, stuff. I had to prove who I was.'

'Well, we'd better get it straight back to the Kingdom,' she said bossily. 'Grampy'll know what to do.'

Nick wondered whether or not to tell her that he'd just met her grandfather as a boy. That would take the wind out of her sails. But then he thought better of it – perhaps some secrets were best left between the people concerned. 'OK, Your Highness.' He did a mock bow.

'Erm – shorry to interrupt, but I have to say goodbye now. I'm off.'

They looked up and realized that Fangle was now sitting astride Jarkov's back. Seeing them both together it was glaringly apparent that Fangle had drawn some of his genetic heritage from the same species as the mammoth. Fangle's curly teeth followed the exact same line as Jarkov's tusks, and his domed forehead, beady eyes and flappy ears spoke of brotherhood and shared ancestry. It was uncanny. Nick and Krista gasped and looked at each other.

'I thought he reminded me of something!'

'But where are you going?' wailed Moomsa.

Fangle chortled and patted Jarkov's shaggy neck. The mammoth grunted and wrapped his trunk lovingly around Fangle's left leg. 'Flibbering fungushes, woman. Haven't you noticed the reshemblance?' He stroked Jarkov's tufty head lovingly. 'I've finally found out where I've come from. What my roots are. We're kindred shpirits, me and Jarkov, from the same shpecies. I always knew I wasn't all goblin. I'm half-elf, a dash of goblin and heapsh of mammoth. We're going off exploring, little trip down memory lane. Bye, all!'

And with that, he urged Jarkov into a slow walk, whistling through his curly teeth, with Torquil flitting around his head. The others watched as the great mammoth swayed majestically towards a tunnel entrance, which had opened up to accommodate his bulk.

'You will come back and visit, won't you, Fangle dear?' Moomsa called after him anxiously. 'I will miss you! And the babies too!' They were now sitting on her back and clinging round her neck, wailing and whimpering in distress.

Fangle turned. 'Of course, Moomsha, mother of

many! I would never leave you for ever, but I have a tashte for travel now! Maybe you can join me on another trip, when those babiesh are a bit older? In the meantime, take care of them. I'll shee you again shoon!'

He waved at them and with a slow and plodding gait Jarkov headed off. As he rounded the corner, Fangle waved one last time. Jarkov lifted his trunk and let out a long resounding bellow in a farewell salute.

Moomsa looked distinctly crestfallen. 'Oh, lordylumps, well there's a to-do now! Fancy that! Drawn his heritage from an Ancient One after all!' She sighed explosively. 'I'll have to learn to live on my own now. I suppose I shouldn't have teased him so much about being a goblin.'

'Oh, come on, Moomsa, I don't think he's going because of that!' said Krista, stroking her rubbery neck.

But Moomsa had begun to blubber. Great big tears rolled out of her button eyes and plopped on to the soggy ground. 'But I'll miss him!'

Krista and Nick tried to comfort her as best they could, but she wove her long neck around and sobbed in strange, jerky reptilian sobs. Her baby dinosaurs continued whimpering and babbling and crawling all over her. Nick and Krista exchanged helpless glances. What on earth do you say to a lady dinosaur whose part-elf, part-goblin and mostly mammoth boyfriend has just gone travelling?

Krista patted her neck and made soothing noises.

'Don't worry, Moomsa. He'll be back soon, quite soon I expect. It's jolly cold up there. And you could always go with him next time, maybe in the summer. He hasn't deserted you.'

Moomsa began to cheer up and sniffed honkily. 'Yes. And I've still got my babies. I've plenty to do looking after them.' She swung her neck round and nuzzled them. They wriggled and cooed and chattered. Then she turned her tiny head round. 'I suppose you'll be going too now, won't you? Back home?'

'Yes, Moomsa. I'm not sure if we'll be able to come back and visit. But we'll always remember you, and what you did for us. You and Fangle will go down in the Elfin Book of Lore. I'll make sure of that,' Nick promised her.

'You knew all along, didn't you, Majesty?' Nick was trying hard to keep the reproach out of his voice. 'About everything?'

Vilmar's ice-blue eyes twinkled. 'Yes, well, I had an inkling, although I wasn't absolutely sure how it was all going to unfold. Anything can happen to sabotage the course of history. But I knew the truth would prevail in the end.'

'Well, it's blimmin' lucky that Krista managed to get me out of the Ice Chamber in time!' said Nick. 'I mean – anything could have gone wrong.'

'Yes, but it didn't,' said Vilmar. 'And you and I both know that it wouldn't, because we met in the cave. So

I already knew that it would all turn out for the best, somehow. How could I admit to a court of law that I, the king of the realm, had broken the rules and gone into forbidden territory when I was a boy? Territory that I had forbidden you and anyone else to go into?'

Nick had to admit Vilmar had a point. 'Yes,' he said slowly, 'of course. Tricky one. I see what you mean, sir. I didn't know at the time that there was a plan.'

'It was a most difficult situation, Nickolai, one that even I had not envisaged.' Vilmar's wizened face took on a haunted look. 'And a most difficult decision too. I suffered agonies of doubt. Didn't sleep a wink after you went down. I still worried that a new and different twist of fate might intervene, even though I'd seen both you and that evil impostor in the cave.'

Once again Nick's mind was reeling with the strange conundrum of it all. Vilmar had known all along, yet he'd had to let things unfold, not interfere in the course of history. Nick struggled to bring the words to his lips. 'But – but if you'd chosen me in the courtroom, instead of that fake, what would have happened then?'

'Who knows, Nickolai? All I knew was that the one in the red robe was the fake, because when I saw you both in the cave when I was a boy he wasn't able to lift the crystal from the plinth. And when your replica appeared in the Kingdom, all those years later, I knew it was all part of the pattern of events. That's why I made the decision I made – and hatched the plan with

307

my granddaughter. So that you would have the freedom to do what you had to do. It was a risk that had to be taken.'

'Ah, yes, Princess Krista,' mumbled Nick, feeling rather embarrassed. 'I have to say, sir, that I seriously misjudged her. She has been my greatest ally, apart from you.'

'Yes, and I hope you will be great friends, just like myself and your grandfather. And do great things for the Kingdom.' He gave a nostalgic sigh. 'Krista so reminds me of my dear departed wife Eva.'

Nick struggled with the idea of Krista being like her grandmother. But then, everyone grows old. Even he would eventually, although he preferred not to think about it. 'You were lucky then, sir, because,' Nick blushed furiously, 'Krista's just about the most amazing girl I've ever met. I couldn't have done what I did without her.'

Vilmar smiled. 'Yes, I expect you'll be friends for life now. Give or take the odd spat.'

'And – I would like to know more about my grandfather. And my father.'

'There is all the time in the world for that,' said Vilmar kindly. 'We will have many talks, and I will tell you everything. I will say, though, that he would have been very proud of you, even though you have been a hot-headed young man who broke the rules. We broke the rules too, and if we hadn't – well, you were in the cave, Nickolai. Sometimes it is necessary to push through the boundaries of law to keep the great cycle of history moving forward. Rebels and revolutionaries are always the ones who bring about great sweeping change. That's what you did in the Golden City to break Magda's evil empire, was it not?'

Nick thought about this. 'Yes, sir.'

'We're both rebels in our way. Although looking at us together you'd never think it.'

Nick shrugged. 'Well, somebody's got to do it, sir.'

A conspiratorial smile passed between them.

Another question popped into Nick's head. 'Hang on a minute. What happened about my replica? What have you told everyone?'

Vilmar sighed. 'He disappeared suddenly, of course. Vanished into thin air. The Kingdom thinks that you and him are the same, that the demon version is down in the ice chamber. And that Krista accompanied you into the Moonstone mines – where the Peskies led you to the crystal.'

He turned and nodded at a greenstone pillar where the crystal sat in splendour, enclosed in an ice case and guarded by the Peskies. Nick had brought them back with him from the NetherWorld. Except they weren't Peskies any more, but glowing Light Fairies with a noble purpose in life – guarding the crystal. They swarmed around it protectively, obviously proud of their new role.

'That's not as exciting as the real truth, sir.'

'No. But it's best people do not know the real truth.

The danger has passed, now that Magda's demon fairy has gone. But elves might panic if they knew you'd been back to the NetherWorld. You are still their greatest hero, and always will be.'

Nick nodded silently, and thought again of the fickleness of the town criers. They wielded so much power over the people, yet they could only report what they were told. As soon as he and Krista had staggered, bedraggled and exhausted, into the entrance cave to the Moonstone mines, they had been whisked into a royal conveyance and escorted through the Kingdom, cheered on by crowds of clamouring, rejoicing elves, before being brought straight here to the palace, where Nick was swiftly ushered into a private consultation with the king.

The town criers had gone into overdrive, rushing round the streets, clanging their bells and shouting the news. The Crystal Chronicle disc in Solstice Square went crazy, constantly changing patterns to keep up with events, revealing endless images of Nick holding the crystal aloft as he swept through the streets.

It had all started again and he had been the centre of attention. But he would just have to get used to it.

'Anyway, not a word to anyone about what passed in the cave, Nickolai, understand?' Vilmar fixed him with his ice-blue gaze. 'Not even Krista. It's our special secret.'

'I haven't said anything to her, sir. You have my word.'

'Good.' Vilmar struggled up from his ice throne. He hobbled over to Nick, leaning on his stick. Through the folds of wrinkles, a youthful fire glowed in his old eyes. 'You have learned your lessons well, Nickolai: to work with others, to know who to trust, to have faith in yourself and the truth, to be patient and considerate, and to communicate with all of those around you. Most importantly, you have learned to command the great forces within you with responsibility and maturity. You have truly proved that you are fit to carry out the Mission.' He laid a bony hand affectionately on Nick's arm. 'And now we all know that you are the one true Nickolai. A noble hero, worthy of the great task of the Solstice Mission. Well done, my lad. I'm very proud of you. And so is your grandfather.'

They stood in silence for a while, gazing at the swirling patterns playing on the surface of the crystal cone.

'And now – to business! Have you worked out how you're going to use the crystal?'

'Yes, Your Majesty,' said Nick, brightening. 'It's really very simple. I will carry it with me on the Mission, of course, stowed away in the folds of my robe. When I leave the Kingdom at midnight, I will tell the crystal to freeze time. Its patterns will stop moving. Then I'll go off round the world, knowing that time is standing still. I've already had a quick practice as we made our way back through the NetherWorld. I froze

311

time, and everything else around me just stopped, but I kept moving. Krista – I mean, the princess – didn't even notice.'

Vilmar clapped his hands. 'Ingenious! Now, everything else is in place. I suggest you go home and rest, dear boy, and prepare yourself for your Mission tomorrow night. Your mother is very anxious to see you.'

Nick heaved a sigh. He was really looking forward to seeing his mother. He had missed her and he couldn't wait to get home.

As the sleigh swept to a halt the front door opened and Ella flew through it. She threw herself into Nick's arms as he climbed out and they hugged each other in silence for a few moments. Nick held her away from him and looked into her face. She seemed to have aged several years since he had last seen her. She was even beginning to look more like a mother, he had put her through so much. But now he was back home, and nothing else mattered.

They went inside. It was warm and cosy, and Nick was delighted to see that the Solstice Cup was sitting on the mantelpiece, in its usual place. He told her everything that had passed since he'd last seen her, skating over what had happened in the Cave of the Crystal Chronicle.

She listened in horror. When he'd finished, she took a deep breath. 'It's happened again,' she said quietly.

'I've missed out on a whole chunk of your life.'

'Well – it was only a short chunk this time. And that's what growing up is all about, Mum. I have to do what I have to do. And you have your life to lead. But we can still be together.'

She thought about this and smiled at him. Then her face suddenly crumpled. 'That day when your horrible fake appeared, and that time afterwards, it was the worst nightmare. I'll never forgive myself for doubting you, even for that short time.' She burst into tears. 'I let you down! I didn't stand up for you! I betrayed you!' Nick tried to comfort her, but she was weeping uncontrollably. 'I turned my back on my own son! And as soon as you went down to the Ice Chamber I knew it was all a mistake!'

Nick squeezed her shoulders awkwardly. 'Yes, but then Vilmar let you in on the plan.'

She sniffed. 'And I would have gone to him anyway, and pleaded for your release.'

'So what was it like when you had to live here with my replica, pretending it was me?'

She shuddered. 'It was a horrible charade. A nightmare, having to pretend that everything was normal. He was so obviously not you, but I had to live this lie, every day.'

He squeezed her shoulders again. 'Well, it's all over now. And – he was so like me. He *was* me, in a way, like another me I didn't know was there. Even I began to have my doubts about who I was. And you were in an impossible situation. If I can forgive you, then so can you.'

She dried her eyes. They sat by the flickering blue-green flames of the fire. 'There's a lot of catching up to do still, isn't there?' she said at last. 'And a lot of making up for things.'

'Yes, Mum,' said Nick. 'But we've plenty of time to do it in. And it's never too late.'

Epilogue
The First Solstice Mission

'Oyez! Oyez!' shouted the town criers, milling about in the crowded streets.

'The time has come at last! Yes, the big night is here! Our glorious saviour, hero of the Kingdom, is to set off at the stroke of midnight on his very first Solstice Mission!'

From lunchtime onwards Solstice Square had been full of stalls selling Solstice goodies and thronging with elves, all dressed in their Solstice best. An atmosphere of excitement had been building up all day. Light Fairies buzzed around like fireflies and elfin children ran amok, hysterical with excitement. They chased each other round the colonnades, and the queue for reindeer rides stretched all the way back to the Equinox Plaza. Only when every child had been given a turn round the square were the reindeer led back to the stables in the Arkfel Caves, where they had been nested in the very best snow wool and fed on the best lavanuts.

The reindeer were sitting in a circle now, with Comet at the centre, giving them a final pep talk. Nick's family sleigh stood waiting in the corner. It was gleaming and magnificent, hung about with millions of tiny silver bells and covered in glittering decorations.

Nick strode into the caves, heaving a large sack full of letters which Joe and Hannah had delivered to the reindeer at the forest edge. Rudolph had brought them all the way up to the Pole, fastened round his back, and a great cheer had gone up in the square as the reindeer team soared through the crack in the roof the night before. Rudolph sprang to his feet, trotted up and nuzzled Nick's neck with his wet nose.

Nick still couldn't believe he'd been reunited with his old friends from the forest. It was like the icing on the cake.

'Pwishtush! It's a bit smart in here! They're making a huge fuss of us. Stable elves scurrying around grooming us, polishing our antlers, petting us and cooing at us, feeding us every five minutes.'

'It's well kushti,' snorted Vixen.

'You're worth it,' said Nick, stroking her nose.

'We've given loads of rides to the elfin children,' said Cupid. 'They had to shoo them all away in the end, said we needed to rest.'

'Quite right too,' said Comet. 'We've a long night ahead of us.'

'I like this celebrity treatment,' said Blitzen. 'We don't get this back at home.'

'Shmoosh! Don't expect it, either,' snorted Comet. 'We all muck in back there.'

Rudolph nudged the sack of letters with his nose. 'Did you manage to read them all?'

Nick smiled, and the circles under his eyes didn't look so dark. 'Yes. Well, I had a team of workshop elves helping me. We've been through the whole lot and the Plaza has been working all night to fill the orders. Mum was furious. Wanted me to rest at home. But I told her this was only going to happen once a year.'

One or two of the stable elves were hanging around curiously, leaning on their brooms, trying to decipher the strange language that Nick and the reindeer were speaking. To them it just sounded like a lot of whistling, spluttering noises.

They were interrupted by a flurry of arrival. It was the princess. Her maidservants scurried along behind her, fussing over her train. Brushing their attentions aside, she strode into the stables. Nick blinked and caught his breath. She was back to her usual radiant self, except now she looked a bit older and wiser. Tonight it was a white velvet cloak with a fur-lined hood, and underneath that a white dress covered in sparkly decorations. She was hardly recognizable as the hardened adventuress he'd travelled with through the NetherWorld and the Arctic Circle. But she wasn't really that overdressed – it was his big night, after all.

'So. All set then, are we?' she enquired, coming into the circle. She began to stroke Rudolph's nose.

'Yes, Your High— Krista. Are you sure you won't come with me?'

She snorted with laughter. 'You must be joking! I'm grounded! Mummy's absolutely furious! But maybe in the future, when I'm older.' She patted her perfectly coiffed hair. 'And anyway, it might mess up my hair!'

They both burst out laughing.

'D'you know, that's the first time I've seen you laugh properly since I've met you,' she said.

He stopped laughing. 'Is it?'

'Yes. You've been so frightfully serious and intense about everything. I know you had to be, to get things done, but it's all sorted now. It's time to lighten up, SB. You've forgotten how to have fun, and that's what you do best really, isn't it?'

Nick frowned. She seemed to know him better than he did. How annoying.

'OK. We'll have a few laughs when I get back, shall we? Do that sightseeing trip you were talking about. I haven't seen it all yet.'

They were interrupted by a stable elf, who coughed politely. He was carrying a set of ornately decorated harnesses, ready to harness the reindeer up to the sleigh. Behind him, Anatole drove in on his delivery sleigh, accompanied by a green sea of workshop elves, bringing the bottomless sack of gifts for the children. He screeched to a halt and the sack wobbled precariously. Grinning in delight, he scratched his wild mop of hair.

'Ready, Nickolai? It's showtime!'

★ ★ ★

At the stroke of midnight, a hush fell over the crowds in Solstice Square. A great ice bell began to chime. Everyone fell silent as a brilliant shaft of Light poured down through the domed ceiling into the cavern. Vilmar stood up and twitched his ancient ears, pointing at the roof. It slid open to reveal the star-studded night sky above, and the Northern Lights poured into the cavern, filling it with swirling patterns of colour.

There was a gasp as the sound of trotting hooves heralded the arrival of Nickolai on his reindeer-drawn sleigh. It glided into the square, laden with its sack of gifts. Cheers rose to the roof and spilled over into the Arctic wastes outside. Nick was wearing his famous red robe, with the fur-lined hood pulled up round his ears. Hidden somewhere in the folds of his robe was the crystal.

He had probably never felt quite this excited in all his life. At last, he was actually doing it, carrying out the Mission he had promised! He was going to bring gifts to all the children in the world on Winter Solstice Eve. And this was the very first time. Nothing would go wrong, now.

He shook the reins and twitched his ears – legally, at last – and made immediate contact with the forces. The sleigh jerked into life and began humming with energy. The reindeer pawed at the ground, nodded their antlered heads and cantered forward, rising

*Cheers rose to the roof and spilled over into the Arctic
wastes outside.*

gracefully into the air. The magnificent craft soared around the cavern, above the tumultuous roaring of the crowds. Nick waved as they did a lap of honour round the square.

'Goodnight, everyone!' he shouted. 'Wish me luck! And Happy Solstice to you all!'

And with an enormous whoop of glee and a peal of laughter the sleigh shot out of the hole in the roof.

This happens every year, of course, and has done ever since that night. If you were outside on the surface of the Pole, here's what you would see: a crack opens in the ground and a sleigh, drawn by nine flying reindeer and driven by a man in red, shoots out and takes off into the sky, leaving a trail of light behind it. Except now the man is quite old and tubby, and he has a long white beard. Sometimes, depending on her availability, there is a very elegant silver-haired lady with him. She likes to accompany her husband on his business trips, when she's not too busy with matters of state. She wears a white velvet cloak, with a fur-lined hood pulled up around her head. Underneath it you can just catch a glimpse of a sparkling silver coronet.

The sleigh soars over the Arctic wastes on its long journey around the globe, heading towards the first settlement south of the Pole, now a town twinkling with many lights. Except there is something strangely frozen about the world, and the twinkling lights of

321

the towns seem blurred and still, as though stopped in time.

The man always visits the same house first, because there are always children in it. He lands his sleigh on the snow-covered roof with a thunk and a clatter of hooves. He heaves his heavy sack out of the sleigh and bundles it over to the chimney. Somehow, despite his expanding girth, he always manages to squeeze down it with his sack.

'You really ought to be more careful what you eat, dear,' says his wife, if she's with him.

'No way!' he guffaws. 'There's mince pies for me and carrots for the reindeer waiting down there. Maybe a drop of brandy too, if I'm lucky. And I'm not wasting any of it!'

When he's filled the children's stockings with gifts, he comes back up, grunting a little with the effort.

'We really ought to be getting on,' chivvies his wife, pulling her robe around her.

'Nonsense!' he says. 'We've got all the time in the world!' And he takes a sparkling crystal cone out of the folds of his robe and holds it aloft.

And they set off again into the sky, his roars of laughter echoing through the cold night air. No one ever sees this extraordinary spectacle streaking across the polar skies, and all these strange events taking place on roofs all over the world, because time is standing still.

The only one who does is maybe a strange-looking man with curly teeth, riding across the snowy wilderness on the back of a woolly mammoth. He seems impervious to this spell.

He chortles with glee and waves at Nickolai as he passes overhead.

ACKNOWLEDGEMENTS

Grateful thanks to my family as always for their support, help and understanding, especially my husband Peter, without whom I would not have been able to do any of this, and my daughter Izzy, who gave me the idea for the books. Also sister Sue Sue, who helps with school visits, Ciara, Georgia and Eleanor, and all my friends for their support and encouragement. Thanks also to the great team up at Hodder – Rachel, Anne, Les, Andrew, Nicola and co., the fantastic kids and teachers at all the schools I've been into, terrific booksellers like Terry Hart and Sonia Benster, the Zoological Museum at the University of Copenhagen, who gave me Jarkov, the Toy Museum in Stockholm, Dee Shulman, children's book illustration tutor at City Lit, whose classes helped me create Moomsa, and finally my bathroom wall, whose steam patterns helped me invent many of the characters in this book and generate much of the story material.

RESEARCH NOTES

To me, research is one of the best things about planning and writing a book. It takes you on a whole world of discovery and adventure! Even fantasy stories need to be rooted in reality, and although the Nickolai books are set in a timeless, mythical past, they do feature real places like the North Pole and real people like the Inuit. Research itself can spark off new ideas and feed the imagination.

Unfortunately I was not able to visit the North Pole! But I was able to visit some museums abroad as well as continue my researches in the UK. You can find full research notes on my website: www.lucydanielraby.com

Arctic Weather and Seasons

There are four high points in the Arctic seasonal cycle – the Winter Solstice (December 22), the Summer Solstice (June 21), the Spring Equinox (March 20) and the Autumn Equinox (September 22). Because the earth tilts on its axis throughout the year, the sun is farthest south at the Winter Solstice, and so there is no daylight. The Arctic winters are one endless night. At the Summer Solstice the sun is farthest north and it shines all day long, circling the Pole once every day. Hence it is called the 'Land of the Midnight Sun'.

Arctic Geography, Geology and the Elfin Kingdom

I was in the very early stages of plotting the first book, trying to decide where Nickolai had originally come from. One morning I opened a newspaper and saw a fantastic picture of a huge cavern that had been discovered under the North Pole. It is part of a huge interconnecting labyrinth of caves and tunnels that had been found inside the Polar ice cap by explorers. I thought, 'That's it! That's the Elfin Kingdom! *Under* the North Pole, not on top of it!'

I wanted the Elfin Kingdom to be a glittering, fairytale wonderland, full of precious natural materials. After some research into Arctic mineral resources I found to my utter delight that there is a mineral called the NIKOLAI GREENSTONE! It runs all the way from somewhere in America up to Alaska. So I decided to make Nickolai's procession sleigh out of Greenstone.

For the overland treks I researched the topography of the Arctic Circle. The ground in the Arctic Circle is so cold that it never really thaws out properly. This is called the *permafrost*. However, the top layer of ground warms up during the Arctic summer. This melted part is called the *tundra* and it sustains life.

During the winter the Arctic Sea is completely icebound, connecting the Polar ice cap to the surrounding land masses, but in the summer the sea melts and the ice turns into huge blocks, like a jigsaw. These are known as *ice floes*.

Prehistoric Creatures

Because the Light Fairies have life-giving powers I decided to use them to resurrect some prehistoric creatures from the fossil remains that abound in the layers beneath the surface of the planet.

I decided that Grimgorr, the monster created by Magda's evil Light Fairy, is derived from the sabre-toothed tiger, mixed in with other more ancient creatures such as dinosaurs. Sabre-toothed tigers were also known as the *Smilodon*. Smilodon first appeared 1.6 million years ago and went extinct about 11,000 years ago. It lived during the last Ice Age, the Pleistocene period, and the pressures of climate change probably caused its extinction.

The other monsters I wanted to feature were woolly rhinos, since they are also very fierce. The Ice Age woolly rhinos had black woolly coats, big square skulls and much longer horns. They were closely related to the modern-day rhino and were probably very aggressive, so I put an army of them in the story.

And finally we come to the star of the show – Jarkov the woolly mammoth. I love elephants, but they live in hot places like Africa and India so I didn't see how I could feature one in a story set in the Arctic Circle. Then I suddenly remembered the woolly mammoth! Imagine my excitement when, after some research, I discovered that in 1997, a fully preserved, mummified carcass of a woolly mammoth called Jarkov, or the Bereskova mammoth, had been discovered by a nine-year-old boy in a silted-up creek in Siberia! He was unearthed (the mammoth not the boy) and has now been transported to an underground cave, where he is being slowly defrosted. Scientists are planning to use his DNA to try and clone him.

I went to a mammoth exhibit in the Zoological Museum at the University in Copenhagen, to see a life-size replica in an Arctic tundra setting, so I could get the feel of what it would be like to encounter one of these beasts. It was definitely worth the trip.

Astronomy

I have made the names of the places in the Elfin Kingdom correspond with the names of constellations of stars in the sky, or the seasons. For example: Orion, Ursus, Equinox, Solstice. Before I started writing *Nickolai's Quest* I drew a map of the Elfin Kingdom and named all the places on it.

Names of Characters

Many of the names are either Russian (like Nickolai, Anatole, Olga, Doblov) or Germanic or Scandinavian (like Helga, Hans, Astrid, Eva). This is because the original myths and legends around Santa Claus and Christmas come from that part of the world, and the stories take place there too.

Elves, Fairies and Goblins

Needless to say, legends and myths about magical beings abound in folklore cultures across the world. The ones we are most familiar with are from Celtic folklore. In most folklore traditions, elves are seen as a very mysterious race of beings, always hidden from human view, dating back to the beginning of time, with magical powers. They are graceful, agile and beautiful, with large expressive eyes, beautiful faces and of course, pointed ears. They are party people – they love music, dancing and celebrations. Their senses are much sharper than humans' and they have long life spans, often living to over a thousand years old. Some even say they are immortal. Most elves are reputed to live in forests but there are underground elves who live in caves.

Light Fairies are the spirit or soul of the elves. Again, fairies abound in world folklore, but I decided to base my Light Fairies on Icelandic folklore, where angelic beings, such as Lovelings, Light Fairies, dwarves and elves are said to live in the forests, lakes and mountains.

Goblins of course represent the dark side. They abound in folklore around the world, and they are usually ugly and villainous. They make trouble for elves and fairies and usually reside in deeper, darker regions.

NICKOLAI OF THE NORTH

Lucy Daniel Raby

One Midwinter's Eve, many centuries ago, a miracle happened at the North Pole . . . the Elfin Kingdom was born.

Years later, the wicked Queen Magda destroys all the elves – except one. Nickolai, the last true elf, is saved by a flying reindeer.

Brought up by human parents in the distant north, Nickolai knows he's different. Teased and bullied because of his pointed ears, he seeks solace with the reindeer in the enchanted forest.

When Magda starts to steal children's youth in order to restore her own, Nick travels north to the Golden City of Doransk to fight her evil – and find his true destiny.